BELOVED ENEMY

Janet Miller

Erotic Futuristic Romance
New Concepts   Georgia

Be sure to check out our website for the very best in fiction at fantastic prices!

When you visit our webpage, you can:
* Read excerpts of currently available books
* View cover art of upcoming books and current releases
* Find out more about the talented artists who capture the magic of the writer's imagination on the covers
* Order books from our backlist
* Find out the latest NCP and author news--including any upcoming book signings by your favorite NCP author
* Read author bios and reviews of our books
* Get NCP submission guidelines
* And so much more!

We offer a 20% discount on all new Trade Paperback releases ordered from our website!

Be sure to visit our webpage to find the best deals in e-books and paperbacks! To find out about our new releases as soon as they are available, please be sure to sign up for our newsletter (http://www.newconceptspublishing.com/newsletter.htm) or join our reader group (http://groups.yahoo.com/group/new_concepts_pub/join)!

The newsletter is available by double opt in only and our customer information is *never* shared!

Visit our webpage at:
www.newconceptspublishing.com

Beloved Enemy is an original publication of NCP. This work has never before appeared in book form. This work is a novel. Any similarity to actual persons or events is purely coincidental.

New Concepts Publishing, Inc.
5202 Humphreys Rd.
Lake Park, GA 31636

ISBN 1-58608-738-X
2005 © Janet Miller
Cover art (c) copyright 2005 Eliza Black

NCP books are available at special quantity discounts for bulk purchases for sales promotions, premiums, fund raising, or educational use. For details, write, email, or phone New Concepts Publishing, Inc., 5202 Humphreys Rd., Lake Park, GA 31636; Ph. 229-257-0367, Fax 229-219-1097; orders@newconceptspublishing.com.

First NCP Trade Paperback Printing: February 2006

Chapter One

In the dark of her bunk Lieutenant Meagan An Flena was startled awake. Among the hushed noises, deep breathing and snores of the hundred sleeping bodies in the Hemingway's pilot's quarters, there'd been a sound unusual enough to disturb her much needed slumber. Opening her eyes, Mea waited for it to repeat.

There it was again. From a nearby sleeping cubicle came a sharp male gasp. Mea tensed, hoping it wouldn't be something she'd need to deal with. As senior pilot she'd have to interfere if there was a problem.

The gasp repeated, then was followed by a woman's moan, the sound mingling with masculine heavy breathing. A bunk began to creak in a rhythmic fashion.

A woman's voice whispered, "Oh, yes."

A man answered her just as quietly, "Yeah."

Mea relaxed back onto her pillow and allowed herself a smile. Just a pair of pilots bunking, and, from the sound of things, the act was consensual. No reason for her to get involved.

Nothing to see here, folks, nothing to hear--pay no *attention to the couple behind the curtains!*

The creaking sound increased, and ruefully Mea stared at the flimsy walls around her. Thin fabric partitions were all that separated the lovers from her quarters. The sounds grew and the bed noises picked up. Must be new recruits she decided, or it was their first time. For a moment she tried to guess who it was.

Anders and Alvenes? No, neither of them bunked close enough for her to hear them.

Shelton and one of her many admirers? Not likely--her bunk was two partitions further down and Shelton had perfected the art of silent passion.

Mea couldn't help her rueful grin. Whoever it was would know better after the ribbing they'd take the next wake period from the rest of the pilots. In Earthforce, with its cramped and communal accommodations, you quickly learned how to share a bunk without making noise--or you stopped bunking, whichever seemed the best solution.

That was one of the reasons she'd quit. To the chagrin of her would-be lovers, Mea couldn't help making noise. After being shushed in the middle of an orgasm one too many times, she'd pushed her last bunk partner onto the floor and told him to take off.

Not that there had been that many partners in the first place. Short and with a tendency for plumpness, Mea just didn't fit the mold of military femme fatale, and she'd lost interest in the few males who'd looked in her direction.

A muffled male cry and the noises stopped. For a moment there was only slightly harder than normal breathing, then a low feminine chuckle. Soft murmurs began, intimate ones. Mea couldn't make out words, but the tone was unmistakable. It had been good for both of them.

Mea couldn't help a small surge of envy. Of all bunking behavior it was the post-sex closeness she missed the most. Unfortunately only a few of her former sex partners had been into cuddling, preferring to say "thanks" and return to their own beds as soon as possible. Another reason for the six months it had been since her last time alone with a man.

Or was it nine months now? She thought about it for a moment. Could it have been a year? Perhaps. It wasn't like she was keeping track. Truth was she had better things to do with her bunk time than have sex.

Stretching out, she tried to go back to sleep. Earthforce motto number one--rest while you can, you never knew when it would get interrupted....

And just then blaring sirens and flashing lights eliminated any possibility of further slumber. With a groan Mea hit the deck, trying to ignore the harsh voice sounding though the speakers in the low ceiling overhead--"Battlestations, battlestations. Pilots to your ships!"

Mea grabbed her clothes from the locker. No need to change the non-regulation skivvies that she'd slept in. These were fresh, donned just before climbing into bed.

Earthforce motto number two--you never knew when you were going to need to dress fast. She quickly pulled on her dark grey uniform pants and lighter grey shirt, and pushed her feet into the nearly-black boots.

Grey, grey, and more grey. Mea stifled a sigh over Earthforce's imposed wardrobe. Growing up in a Traveler enclave, she'd only worn bright colors for the first fifteen years of her life, and she missed them. When she got out of the military, she swore she'd never wear grey again.

In fact only one thing kept her in an Earthforce grey uniform--the small fighter jet she called her own, her sweet little Starbird. A call to action meant she would be flying soon.

Suddenly eager for her ship, Mea grabbed her jacket and the tight-fitting black cap that kept her hair in place under her helmet. She slammed it down over her regulation closely shorn hair. Another thing that she'd do after leaving the service would be to grow her hair back, at least to the point where she needed a comb to take care of it.

Footsteps pounded the deck as she pulled aside her curtain and joined the rush of pilots pouring out of their sleeping quarters and into the short corridor that took them to the Hemingway's launch bays.

Murchenson and Deek ran side-by-side along the hall, and Mea had to smile as she fell behind them. She could swear that Deek was wearing Murchenson's pants and vice-versa. The short length of his pants revealed too much of his boots, while hers pooled around her ankles. An understandable mistake if you happened to jump out of bed and grabbed the first pair of pants you found.

So Murchenson and Deek was the couple making the noise. About time. They'd been sniffing around each other for at least two months. As she watched, their hands found each other for a brief clasp before entering the bay where their ships were docked. Neither spoke, but both seemed to be wishing the other good luck.

Once again Mea couldn't help her pang of envy. That was what hurt the most about her position in Earthforce. She missed wearing bright colors and having her hair long, but most of all she missed being close to someone. It wasn't just her inability to keep from making noise that kept her celibate. If bunking had given her someone to care about she'd still be doing it even if she had to put a bootliner in her mouth to keep herself quiet.

But she cared for no one. Her family was dead except for her brother Jack, and the rest of her people were scattered throughout the galaxy. Once she'd had an entire tribe, but Mea didn't belong to anyone anymore.

Well, except for Earthforce. After the demolition of her people the military had tried to take their place, but even though Earthforce had given her some semblance of freedom, allowed her to fly and gave structure to her life, Mea found she couldn't give them the feelings she'd once held for her tribe. Only the oath she'd taken to serve them kept her loyal ... particularly in a war they clearly had no business fighting.

She pushed past the others and headed for her single-pilot ship with its distinctive wedge shape. The cockpit nose seemed tiny compared to the size of the massive engines at the rear of the ship, but pride filled her at the power of those engines. A Starbird was the most maneuverable of Earthforce fighters, able to turn in the blink of an eye, and fly well in both space and in atmosphere--or so she'd heard. She'd never actually been in atmosphere with her ship, but someday she hoped to be able to remedy that.

As a senior pilot with multiple years in Earthforce, Mea had been able to personalize her ship, adding a set of three overlapping blue-green rings to the tail section. When she passed, she took a moment to give the bottom edge of the lower ring a caress for luck.

Mea climbed the four meters of retractable ladder and jumped into the pilot's seat. She grabbed her helmet and cinched it tight before sliding the cockpit closed. In front of her was a long line of similar small fighters, pilots scrambling inside, hatches closing in readiness for launch.

There was hurry but no panic in their movements. This wasn't a drill, nor the first time they'd done this. After four years of war they'd practiced it a lot. Mea knew that every pilot had followed the same procedure. It was almost routine--even knowing that the Gaians were most likely already out there, waiting for them.

The Gaians, with advanced technology that made them invisible until they wanted to be seen, always seemed to be waiting for them.

Mea tensed as one by one the ships in front of her were caught by the catapult and sent screaming into space. The ship next to her went, and then it was her turn. She resisted a jubilant whoop as the force pushed her against her seat and though the narrow launch tube. No point in amusing the communications officers listening in. A final rush of speed and she was floating in black space, the Hemingway a motionless mass behind her.

In the far distance was the Gaian battlecruiser. At first it was just a dot in the distance, then it seemed to jump much closer. Mea checked her instrument panel. It wasn't quite in firing distance yet.

As soon as she knew she was clear, Mea fired her engines and maneuvered into position between her mother ship and the Gaians. Her job was to keep their battlecruiser from firing its disabling ray until the Hemingway could hit it with its massive p-beam cannons.

The Gaians hardly ever used deadly force and would be reluctant to simply fire on Mea and her fellow pilots to clear them away. Instead they sent small ships after them to harry them out of the way. She'd done this before, run interference by weaving in the space between the ships, engaging the battlecruiser's small ships in an outer space version of a flying dogfight.

The Gaians tried to avoid hitting her ship, but Mea had no such orders and could shoot the enemy. Her hands clenched over the controls for her laser guns. Now all she had to do was wait for an enemy fighter to come close enough.

She didn't have to wait long.

The Gaian fighter seemed to come out of nowhere and streaked over Mea's tiny Starbird fighter like a shooting star. Startled, she stared after it through her clear plastisteel canopy. The Gaian had flown so close she could read the pilot's mark of ownership on the ship's tail.

Grimly Mea stared at the three distinctive green stripes, running parallel to each other and set at an angle across the vertical fin. *Cheeky bastard to fly that close.* He shot away from her, wagging that green striped tail of his as if daring her to follow. Obviously he intended to draw her fire and make her chase him out of the battlefield.

Mea jerked her control stick to one side and slid away from his ship, her movement signaling her squadron mates to spread out. The rest of the tiny ships scattered into a random pattern, intended to hamper the Gaians as much as possible and keep the enemy's battlecruiser and its paralyzing beam away.

Mea turned her ship, first to the left, then the right, using her weapons in short bursts. Her green striped nemesis jerked away, leaving her with a clear view of the enemy's battlecruiser. The powerful ship filled her view, its massive bay releasing another wave of fighters in her direction.

Fortunately smaller ships like Mea's were too small for the Gaians' favorite weapons and so could run interference. Mea had heard one hypothesis that the ray would work but knocked out all life-support, and so in a small ship the pilot would die before rescue. Apparently the life-loving Gaians would rather take hits from the Earth fighters than deliberately kill an enemy pilot.

Mea wasn't so sure she believed that, but as the green-striped fighter returned she didn't have time to think about it. He used his ship to block her path. Unable to use her weapons at such short range, she dodged him by moving into a spiral turn that took her over and around his ship. Through his translucent canopy she could see a wide grin on his face as she swept past him, back to her place in front of her destroyer.

This was a lot like playing space battle games with her brother back on the old mining platform where they'd grown up. They'd used old one-man space scooters armed with tracers, pretending to be fighter pilots. Two years her senior, Jack had been close to the best pilot she'd known. She'd only been able to outfly him by doing something he didn't expect.

Just like she'd do to this adversary. She made her Starbird live up to its name by making a pinpoint turn that took her behind the Gaian again. She got off two shots, barely missing him as he jumped away and led her a merry chase through the battlefield. Mea managed several more shots at him, all of which he avoided, twisting and turning his ship like a weightless dancer. Only at the last minute did she realize he'd led her into a trap, right into the path of two other Gaian fighters, both firing tracers at her.

One beam caught her ship and her displays went crazy. Barely able to control her ship, Mea had to disengage from the fight while they settled down. Just as her controls returned to normal, the Gaian shot by, and she saw his grin.

That Gaian bastard really was enjoying this! Fuming, Mea turned to follow. Somehow she'd make him pay for that grin.

But not today. As she finished her turn, Mea had a perfect view of the battle space, just in time to see the lights on the rest of her squadron blink out. One after another they suddenly went dead in space, Gaian fighters flitting around them unaffected by the paralyzing beam.

Frack it! Either the Gaians were less worried about the risk to Earth pilots or they'd found a way to keep the beam from taking out the life support. She wasn't about to find out which. Jerking her controls, Mea's ship skipped away, avoiding the path of the beam.

Bright arching light scattered across her canopy. The green-striped fighter was back, the pilot deliberately raking her fighter with tracer rays, wreaking havoc with her displays. It was all Mea could to do to turn her ship away. The bastard obviously intended to herd her into the path of the paralyzing beam.

With a muttered growl Mea threw the stick back, causing her ship to perform a perfect loop and come down behind her opponent. For an instant the green-striped rear was in position. She opened fire with her phase guns and the Gaian twisted out of her way, a thin trail of vapor showing it had been hit.

Two new Gaian fighters appeared around her, raking her ship with tracers. She lay down a flood of phasing fire, scoring one of them before she shot by. Once in the clear she began a wide circle, the end of which would bring her back to the battle scene.

As she returned, she realized it was too late. The Earthforce ships lay adrift without lights, only the dim red emergency lights glowing in the ports of her destroyer. As she watched, a Gaian fighter used a tractor beam to push one of the disabled fighters into the docking bay of the Earthforce destroyer.

Just like all the other battles. For months now, Gaian forces had won every time. Once again the familiar sense of dread filled her, for more than the results of this battle. She couldn't help her thought--*Earthforce was going to lose this war!*

It should have been so simple. What had started as a simple attempt to keep a rebellious colony from seceding had turned into a four-year nightmare. With each battle the upstart Gaians whittled away at what had been Earthforce's far superior fleet. Superiority in firepower and numbers didn't mean much when your opponent could disable your equipment at a distance. Only the fact that the Gaians usually avoided destroying their opponents had kept the war from becoming a bloodbath … with Earth taking the bath

Mea knew from experience that Earth wouldn't have been nearly as careful to avoid killing their enemies. The Gaian's self-restraint made her admire them, even as she fought them and she knew her feelings were shared by many in Earthforce … too bad that admiration hadn't made it to the top of Earth's government so this war could have been ended already. Sometimes she believed that only shear stubbornness kept Earthforce fighting.

The Hemingway and its squads of fighters had been one of the few to win their skirmishes, using the fighter cover to attack Gaian ships before they could use their paralyzing beam. With this capture that was over.

The war was over for her, too. She knew the Gaians never released prisoners, and no one knew where those they captured were taken. For a moment Mea drifted above the scene, wondering what to do. It didn't appeal to her to allow herself to be hauled onto a Gaian battle cruiser. They wouldn't kill her, but at the very least they'd take her ship away and ground her indefinitely.

She imagined herself grounded and a lost feeling swept over her. She didn't know what she'd do if she couldn't fly. It would be like the months that she and her brother Jack had spent trapped in cells after her family had been killed. This time she'd be sent to a Gaian prisoner of war camp. Even in her little ship, the walls seemed to close in and panic briefly overcame her.

Bright beams decorated her canopy, washing her face in translucent color and sending sparks through her displays. The green-striped tail of her nemesis streaked over her. The pilot had found her and wanted to force her down with the others.

Mea's hands gripped her controls tighter. No, she would not allow herself to be captured. Her decision born of desperation, she turned away from the battle scene and shot into open space, accelerating away and putting distance between her ship and her enemies.

The range of her ship was limited, but she could make it to a hiding spot. One thing about this area, there were a lot of small sun systems, many with life-bearing planets. She'd even heard rumors that the Gaians were putting their Earth prisoners in prisons built on deserted planets. With so many places to search, Earthforce would never be able to find their people.

On the other hand, that meant that Earthforce regularly sent out patrols looking for the Gaian POW planets and she'd stand a pretty good chance at rescue with a homing beacon. If there was an empty planet, she'd find it for herself. She'd rather wait out the war on her terms rather than as a Gaian prisoner.

Mea used her computer to locate the nearest three star systems and picked one. It wasn't the closest, but it looked like it held the best chance for survival.

After setting her destination she headed there with all speed. She knew her Starbird was fast, probably faster than the Gaian's ship. Even if he followed her, she'd be able to outrun him.

Not that he should. Unlike her, he had a mother ship to return to and there would be little point in risking his life chasing her across the universe.

As she sped away, something relaxed inside her. It felt so good--the freedom of flight, open space around her, beckoning her onward. This was what she'd dreamed of when she'd joined Earthforce. While she'd never admit it to her fellow Earthforce pilots, it had never been her intention to return to the planet she was supposed to call home, or even the asteroid belt where she'd grown up.

No indeed. If she could, she planned to stay out here forever--that was her secret ambition. There was nothing for her back in her home solar system anyway. As soon as she could, she intended to head to the Outer Colonies. She'd heard that they needed good pilots and there were few better than her.

Well, that Gaian who'd fought her hadn't been bad. She had to admit to a grudging respect for whoever flew that green striped fighter.

Her computer beeped, reminding her of how little space she could cover with her limited fuel supply. She couldn't stay in her little fighter long--a Starbird was a short range ship and not intended for extended space flights.

She couldn't go back and couldn't go very far. The fourth planet's signature indicated it might support life, had water, and a breathable atmosphere, her foremost requirements for a place to hide. She set course for the tiny ball ahead.

The planet grew larger and became a globe of blue and green partially hidden by swirling white clouds. She slowed as she approached and went into orbit to look for a place to land.

Her sensors picked up information, and she filtered it through the computer, letting it help her select a likely landing spot. She'd taken the basic Earthforce survival course and knew she'd need water and a source of food to survive long. Fighters weren't equipped with vast supplies of either, so the planet would have to provide them. At least she could already tell that the planet had oxygen.

The computer beeped again, displaying a close up image of the planet's surface. A red dot indicated a place near the edge of one of the large, blue areas. Mea noted the stretch of bright, rich green with a thin wavy line cutting through the vegetation, indicating a stream of fresh water. That looked like a likely spot. She keyed in the location and started a countdown to entry.

The world below filled her canopy. Mea stared at it in awe. Even with five years in Earthforce, she'd rarely visited another planet. Most of her time had been spent on one battleship or another.

It was exciting to visit an actual new world.

The planet had lush plant and animal life and, from the looks of things, was uninhabited by anyone with intelligence. A world of her own, at least for a while.

There was a jolt at the rear of her ship and Mea activated her rear viewer. Aghast, she saw the nose of another ship approaching from behind. Someone had followed from the battlefield.

Another jolt and she realized that the ship behind was actually firing a phase weapon at her, although it was set so low she'd hadn't yet taken any damage. Even so, Mea stilled her engines as if her ship had been hurt. Maybe she could out-fox her persistent enemy yet.

Over her head shot the now familiar green-striped rear of her nemesis from the battle. Deliberately Mea slowed even further to let him run ahead of her. He slowed as well, as if checking to see if she were really hurt.

Firing her engines, Mea quickly turned to put the Gaian in range. Without hesitation, she fired her phase weapons full blast on the back of her enemy's ship. A burst of flame answered her shot, the Gaian ship came to a stop, and its running lights winked out.

Inside Mea exultation mixed with relief. She'd finally disabled him.

She made a slow loop, watching the other ship. Through the transparent canopy she could see the pilot, the lower part of his face visible through his faceplate. He wasn't grinning now.

Her thumbs rested on the firing mechanism of her guns. She could destroy the Gaian ship and kill its pilot. She should--the Gaians were Earth's enemies and thus her enemies. They were at war and letting him go would jeopardize her freedom. After all, he knew what planet she was on and would tell the others if he was found.

Still she hesitated. She had never killed in cold blood, only when threatened. Even then she'd grieved afterward, remembering the bright flash of an exploding ship that signaled another's life had ended. Could she look this man in the face and destroy him now?

For a long moment she wavered, then a shuddering breath escaped her and she pulled her fingers away from the triggers. She was a skilled pilot and would fight if necessary, but she wasn't a killer. Let the Gaian live, for as long as his disabled ship would support life. Maybe he'd be able to call for help and the others would come for him. By then, she'd be on the ground and hard to find, even if they decided to look for her there. It wasn't necessary to kill him. She could elude capture if she needed to.

Mea pulled away from the disabled ship and moved back on course for the planet. She verified that the computer still held the coordinates of the landing spot and started the atmosphere entry procedure. She turned over the descent to her computer and leaned back into the padded seat for the initial drop to the surface. A wild grin spread across her face. She'd never done this kind of landing and in a ship this small, it was bound to be exciting.

As her ship started the descent, she looked into the rear-viewer screen, just in time to see the Gaian ship fire its damaged engines. Vast quantities of smoke bellowed from the rear of the ship, but still it inched towards her, picking up speed as it came.

Mea swore to herself. The Gaian wasn't quite as disabled as she'd expected. Mea watched helplessly as the Gaian ship followed her path into the atmosphere.

* * * *

An hour later and on the ground, Mea unfastened and pulled back the canopy a crack. Warm, moist air wafted into the ship, redolent of the life outside.

Truly redolent. Gagging, she slammed the canopy shut.

Wonderful, she thought. A fine world of her own. Full of living things--and rotting things, apparently. The air stank like the most decayed garbage she'd ever encountered.

Breathing deeply of the air inside her ship, she examined the clearing she had landed in. So this was what they called a jungle. There were certainly a lot of plants around. Big plants that reached to the sky--trees, she remembered they were called, little plants that hugged the ground, and bushes.

Bushes--lots and lots of bushes that lined the edges of the clearing, many with brightly colored flowers. Small things flitted in the air around the flowers. From the tree branches hung ropes covered in leaves and more flowers ... vines, that was the word. They were vines. Some had leaves the size of dinner plates.

Mea leaned back, momentarily overwhelmed by her surroundings. But then she

took several deep breaths and stamped down on her panic. Okay, so it was overwhelming--she wasn't going to let it overwhelm her!

Digging into the compartment behind her seat, she found the emergency kit and pulled out the enclosed portable scanner. It was a handy device. Mea used it to evaluate the life signs in the area, pointing it in various directions through the ship's canopy. The scanner was designed to not only show life forms but also provide information about their chemical content.

Mea knew she could use it to determine what was alive, what wasn't, and with a couple adjustments to the settings, what was edible ... a highly useful aspect to the tool.

As the screen lit up, she gasped at the number of red-marked silhouettes. There had to be over a thousand living creatures just in the area around her ship--three dozen species of insects, alone. So much life surrounded her, she felt seriously outnumbered. Just her luck to land in life-rich environment.

For a moment she considered moving her ship. But she had enough fuel to get into the air maybe once, but probably not twice, not and fly any distance. Using her fighter to explore the planet and look for a less occupied spot would not be prudent.

And she couldn't forget the Gaian ship. He'd hit the ground someplace near here, but he didn't know where she was. If she moved he'd be able to see her fly away, and she didn't need to give him any better ideas as to her location.

Stubborn as the man was, he'd probably find some way to track her. Only an idiot would have followed her to the surface instead of waiting for rescue from his ship. She knew his job was to capture her, but this man had an over-developed sense of duty.

Of course, he might have even been killed in the crash. Mea tried not to feel guilty over that. After all he'd have been fine if he'd stayed in orbit. He hadn't had to follow her down and it would be his fault if he died as a result.

Mea considered her options. Moving was no solution--staying inside the ship wasn't one either. She was stranded so the best thing to do would be to figure out how to survive on this planet. For the moment she would learn how to live with her wild-kingdom neighbors, no matter how many or few legs they had. Maybe they would leave her alone if she didn't disturb them.

Mea reopened the canopy and activated the ship's built-in ladder, which slowly extended the four meters to the ground. She climbed down and took her first steps on the alien soil that was her new home.

At least the ground was fairly solid under its thick bed of leaves. The computer had done a good job of finding a nice, dry place to land. She listened to the jungle around her. All she heard was the wind in the leaves, the chirping of insects on the branches. Since joining Earthforce, she'd been either around people or in the silence of her ship.

An animal's cry nearly sent her back up the ladder before she got hold of herself. The scanner said there was nothing large enough here to hurt her. It was just one of the other animals here ... she'd just have to get used to the sounds of nature.

She took a deep sniff of the air. The smells were another thing to get used to, but those didn't seem so bad anymore. Overwhelming at first, but now she could actually pick up some scents that were almost like perfume. She looked around and caught sight of some colorful flowers ... those were most likely the source. That wasn't so awful. She'd get used to it.

Mea straightened her shoulders and set her jaw. Enough feeling sorry for herself. So she was planted here, but she was free and she wasn't hurt in any way. She even had a working ship and its contents. Landing on a wild planet wasn't optimal, but it sure beat going to a Gaian POW camp.

First things first--water. There was barely enough in her ship for a day. She needed to find the stream, obtain a specimen, and test it. There'd be impurities, there always were, but she had chemicals to purify water and make it safe to drink.

Next was the matter of food. Her scanner told her that the proteins in the indigenous insects would suit her if she could rid their meat of the nasty acids they carried--and if she could learn to deal with the multiple leg issue. In the past her meat had been synthesized and had come from a self-heating bag. It had never come with a head, legs, or wings.

Another screech erupted from the tree cover and she glanced up to see a flash of bright feathers dart out of sight. A bird? Mea's hopes went up. That was at least an animal she'd eaten in the past, at an ultra fancy Earth restaurant with Jack just before they'd shipped out. She still remembered the tender and so very tasty meat.

Perhaps something here would taste like chicken. Of course, that was assuming she could figure out how to catch, kill, and prepare one of the creatures. In her entire life she'd never had to actually kill anything…much less dinner.

Well, she could hold off for a little while with the help of her ship's emergency pack. She had field rations and wouldn't starve for a day or so. By then she'd have come up with a way to deal with the meat problem.

Her scanner still showed no signs of larger animal life at all, including human. All the animals were small and non-venomous and there was no sign of her Gaian neighbor. Still....

Mea climbed up and reached into the compartment next to her seat to pull a long sheathed dagger, her only weapon, and fastened it to her waist. Better to be safe than sorry.

* * * *

The dry, thin, field-ration wafer tasted as flavorless as she remembered from her survival class. Washed down with the "clean" orange-tinged water from the stream, it was a miserable excuse for dinner. Mea leaned against the fallen log she was using as a backrest and unenthusiastically examined the rest of the wafer before wrapping it up and putting it back in its storage box.

Philosophically she considered the extra five pounds that she'd carried since her youth. Unless things improved, she was likely to lose that weight.

Tomorrow she'd have to do something about the food situation. She barely had enough rations for a week, and it might be a month or more before the homing signal she'd set up would bring someone.

She couldn't risk bringing the Gaians to her doorstep, so she'd selected a very narrow band to broadcast on, one only used by Earthforce ships. Free traders and colony ships wouldn't be listening on that channel. She'd have to wait for a long-range patrol to find her.

Whenever that was likely to happen. With the war on, it could be a long time.

Now that the sun had set, the jungle around her had gone from bright, green, and alive, to dark, spooky, and alive. Sitting on the ground beside her ship, Mea watched the encroaching gloom apprehensively. For a moment she wondered if being a Gaian prisoner wouldn't have been a better choice. At least they'd feed her and she'd heard food on a Gaian ship was actually quite good.

A sharp cry from barely a foot away sent her up the ladder again. With darkness, the other living things in the jungle were coming closer.

Light, that's what she needed to scare away the nocturnal inhabitants. Mea fetched a small lamp from the emergency kit and set it on the ground. The cheerful glow illuminated the clearing around the ship and her mood lightened with it.

This might not be so bad. There was an emergency shelter complete with sleeping sack in the hold. She would set that up and make a little camping area next to her ship. The shelter was supposed to protect against insects and other creatures, and she could stretch out in it. It would be much easier to sleep lying down than in the cockpit.

She stood on the ladder and leaned over into the storage compartment behind the seat to look for the shelter.

Her only warning was a soft exhale of breath. Inwardly Mea groaned. *Frack, her luck had run out again ... it had to be the Gaian!*

She reached for her knife, but powerful hands pinned her arms and pulled her off the ladder. Suspended in the air and without access to her weapon, all Mea had was her legs.

Not a problem--she mule-kicked her opponent with one foot. A deep male oof told her she'd connected with something useful and the arms around her loosened. Twisting, Mea broke his hold and jumped away from him, dropping into a roll that left her three meters away, on her feet, knife in hand.

At the sight of the knife, the Gaian stepped back, one hand rubbing his upper thigh. She'd missed the spot she'd aimed for, but not by much. In her roll, her flight cap had fallen off, uncovering her dark hair. She stood with her legs apart, chest heaving in the tightly fitting suit.

Her Gaian opponent's eyes widened in surprise, and he took another step back. "A woman? What the ... you're a woman!" He sounded outraged.

"What's the problem," Mea said, hoisting her knife in readiness. "They don't teach girls to fly where you come from?" Fear lent her a certain bravado, but she was happy her voice didn't shake.

This guy was so big--well over two meters tall and built to match. Most Earth pilots were small, the better to sit in the undersized cockpits, but apparently the opposition tended to fit the planes to their men instead. A man his size might even find her Starbird a tight fit.

And his height wasn't the only thing impressive about him! The Gaian looked like he could break her in half without half trying and he wasn't hard to look at. His finger-length pale blond hair fell in a swooping curve across his forehead, and he had the nicest pair of lips she'd ever seen on a man.

The shock at finding she was a woman must have hit him harder than her foot. A deep shudder ran through him, and he bent at the waist, breathing heavily, eyes on the ground. He was completely ignoring her, his stunner still holstered at his hip while she at least had her knife in hand. She could take him out easily while he tried to catch his breath.

For a moment she hesitated. Blowing away a ship in space was one thing, but to stab a man in hand-to-hand combat was something else. For the same reason she'd been unable to shoot his disabled ship above the planet, she froze at attacking him now.

Mea fought her reluctance. She had to kill him. If she didn't he'd capture her, and that Gaian POW planet would become a reality. At the moment he wasn't paying attention to her so Mea seized what might be her only opportunity.

Stamping down her lack of enthusiasm for the job, she leapt at him, her knife poised to stab him deep in the chest.

At the last moment, he glanced up and grabbed her wrists before she could strike. He dove to the ground, taking her with him and into a long set of rolls. She hit the dirt hard, and the scuffle left her knife in the dirt far from her hand. When they stopped rolling, she was pinned to the ground, his hands stretching her arms high above her head.

Hard male covered her and while his breathing still labored and his heart pounded furiously, it was clear the man was far from incapacitated.

Frack it! Well that was what she got for hesitating so long.

Deep green eyes glared into hers. She could feel the intensity of his fury ... plus, something that wasn't anger.

It was particularly obvious where his pants met her crotch. The Gaian had a hard-on of monumental proportions. Whatever else was going on, he desired her. That was almost as much a surprise as his attack had been. It hadn't been common for a man to want her, much less someone with the kind of sex appeal this man had, and she couldn't help her shock at his reaction.

It seemed a shock to him, too. For a moment he just stared at her, the heat of his breath scorching her cheeks. A struggle showed on his face, then his head dipped and his lips bonded to hers in a soul-searing kiss.

For a moment she just savored him. He tasted good, like man and something else ... like coffee and chocolate mixed together with cinnamon and vanilla. He tasted like--mocha chocolate-chip cookies--her favorite!

Under his spell Mea groaned and went limp. She should be fighting him--knee him in the crotch, perhaps even bite him--but he just felt and tasted so good.

It was the most mind-bending kiss she'd ever received. Forgetting the man was her enemy, Mea couldn't resist reacting to it. She opened her mouth and his tongue took full advantage, engaging hers in a battle nearly as fierce as the one they'd had in their ships. By the time the kiss was over her breath was laboring as hard as his. Where their bodies met she felt the strain of his erection. He moved just a little, and that powerful bulge dragged against her, setting up all sorts of inner whistles and bells. Mea moaned.

Maybe she shouldn't be so quick to try to kill him. If there was one thing she'd learned over the years, there was always more than one way to fight a battle. Maybe she and the Gaian could reach some sort of understanding. After all if the man shared a bunk as good as he kissed.... Without really meaning to, she rubbed him back, dragging her crotch along his erection.

He raised his head and stared at her, his green-eyed gaze scorching hot. He leaned forward and whispered into her ear, "Say no."

Mea wasn't sure if she'd heard him right. "What?"

"No. Say it, as loud as you can. Mean it."

She blinked and took a deep breath. "No!" she shouted.

Another shudder slid through the Gaian, his breath evened out, and she felt his heart beat slow perceptibly. Abruptly he rolled off her and rose to his feet, then darted to the edge of her camp, putting distance between them.

Mea lay where he'd left her, out of breath and wondering what was going on.

Illuminated by her lantern he paused at the side of her camp and pointed a threatening finger at her. "You--stay away from me." Then he stepped out of the light and melted into the jungle. A moment later she heard splashing from the direction of the creek she'd found. His ship must have landed somewhere on the other side.

Mea could still taste his lingering cookie flavor in her mouth and on her lips and the tingle where his crotch had rested on hers. Rising up on one elbow, she stared after him, desire morphing into dismay and fury at his obvious rejection.

"Wait a fracking minute, what do you mean I should stay away from you? You attacked me, you--you--brain-dead space vermin!"

Chapter Two

Once past the stream, Kavath slowed his headlong plunge through the jungle and stopped near a tall tree. He slammed one hand against the rough bark, still fighting for his breath.

Of all the stupid, impetuous, brain-dead ideas ... to run into the Earth pilot's camp and attempt to capture him--that is her--without scouting the situation first!

If he'd bothered to check things and discovered she was a female, he could have taken precautions. He could have hit her with a blast from his stunner and handled her wearing a breather to prevent attachment.

Or thought better of the plan altogether and left her alone.

He'd been too eager, that was the problem, too impulsive in his actions, just as he'd been warned about over and over again. It had been impulsive to chase after her ship when she'd fled the battle and evaded capture, and impulsive to follow her to the surface. He'd have been better off waiting above the planet for his ship to pick him up, and then help his companions find her.

But he'd envisioned an easy capture. He'd planned to secure the pilot and move him to his camp and keep him under guard until his shipmates came to pick him up once mop-up operations on the Earthforce destroyer were complete. Already his fighter was broadcasting his position. It should be no time before they were picked up, at most a day or so.

Going after the pilot alone had been in part a way to ease his wounded pride. If he'd let her get away, he'd never have heard the end of it, particularly after the way she'd flown against him. And that was before anyone even knew she was a woman!

So he'd gone for the glory of capturing the Earth pilot by himself, but instead of an easily manageable prisoner, he had a bruised thigh and a still tingling shaft. What a revolting development. No prisoner, and he was stuck on a primitive planet with a damaged ship that wouldn't fly again without major repairs. A badly damaged ship —he'd barely managed to land his wounded craft and he'd never take off again.

Kavath leaned against the tree. Suppose she'd had a weapon other than that little knife of hers? He might have been forced to really hurt her, or even kill her. Breathing heavily, he closed his eyes. He might have had to kill her. Wouldn't that have been ironic, him responsible for the death of an Earth woman. Even worse, killing a woman he'd attached to. That had to be a unique situation, one for the Gaian record books. Killing his own match--no Gaian man ever harmed or allowed harm to come to his woman.

No, wait a minute.... Kavath shook his head to clear it of that last thought. Sweet Gaia, he still wasn't thinking straight. She wasn't his woman. No way an Earth woman was going to be his wife, much less an Earthforce pilot. It was impossible.

Kavath eyed the tall tree next to him, with branches that spread across the stream. No more being impetuous. Now he'd spy on her and make sure of things before proceeding further.

After climbing the branches of the tree, he carefully moved out onto a long limb until he had a good view of the Earth woman's clearing, lit by the single lantern next to her ship.

At the sight of her Kavath groaned. She looked dazed and angry, and even in his post-attachment haze she was incredibly beautiful. Her brown eyes flashed furiously, and short dark curls, tumbled from their fight, framed her flushed face. The perfect lips that he'd kissed were scowling. She was still grumbling over his abortive attempt at capturing her.

She put her hands on her hips and glared in the direction he had taken from her camp. "What do you mean I should stay away from you? You grabbed and kissed me. It was your fault, you perv!"

He wasn't sure what a perv was, but he knew the tone. The lady was pissed at him.

Kavath chuckled softly. Sweet Gaia, he'd found a match ... and she was from Earth. Kavath hugged the wide branch under him. It was hard, not soft like she had been beneath him on the ground. He wasn't completely unfamiliar with attachment-- after all he'd been through it once, briefly, but then he hadn't so much as touched, much less kissed, the lady he'd attached to. It was much, much nicer to kiss a woman.

The taste of her was still on his lips and tongue, all honey and cream. His body still felt the imprint of hers where they'd touched. When he'd moved against her, she'd reacted, opened her legs wider, even rubbed against him. That had felt amazing, having a woman invite his touch.

He hadn't been the first man she'd touched that way. It was said that Earth women were very experienced with sex and he wasn't sure how he felt about that. Did he want a woman who'd been in bed with some other man? Or several other men?

He had to stop thinking like this. It didn't matter that she was his match. There were women he could attach to. Less deadly women.

This woman was Earthforce, and Earthforce soldiers weren't like Gaians. They were killers and there was no way he could consider someone like that for his mate. She'd even tried to kill him and would have if he hadn't stopped her.

The truth was that she was his enemy. When she'd lunged at him with that knife, she'd meant business. There had been skill in her hand-to-hand combat, much more than he would have expected.

And there were her piloting skills.... Kavath shook his head in rueful admiration. She'd been magnificent. Her aerial acrobatics had reminded him of a hunting lehen, all grace and speed in the air. Why, she'd nearly out-flown him ... okay, he added with a grimace, she had out-flown him a couple of times, particularly that last battle over the planet when she'd wounded his ship. One more shot and she could have destroyed him.

But she hadn't. Kavath stared at the petite woman still pacing passionately around her camp, her dark hair and flashing eyes as wild as she was.

Maybe she wasn't like the others. He'd been taught that the Earthforce would kill without a moment's hesitation and after all, what they'd done at Carras....

Kavath couldn't help his groan at that thought. It was like someone had socked him in the stomach. Even after four years his sister's death was still too fresh in his mind to ignore. Old fury rose and overwrote the aftermath of attachment, and Kavath's body finally settled down. The memory of Carras succeeded where all else had failed to make him see reason.

When Earthforce had attacked Gaia that time, they'd meant to destroy Gaia's future. Destroying a girls' school had been a clear message … *do what we tell you or we will eliminate all you cherish*. It was the only time Gaian forces had been caught sleeping. Since then General Garran had kept Earthforce off his home world. Very few deaths had followed as a result, but that didn't make up for what Earth had done.

This woman was one of those responsible for the death of his sister.

Kavath shook his head. He couldn't allow this Earth woman to be his match. How could he bring such a woman to his home, into his family, when she was one of those responsible for the death of Kaleen?

He wouldn't let himself be seduced by a pretty face, or a woman who spread her legs so willingly. Kavath would simply have to avoid being around her.

He was detached now. If he could keep from attaching to her again, then everything would be fine. Someday he'd meet another woman to attach to. A woman who didn't carry a knife and try to gut him when he was attaching to her.

Of course, he'd still have to keep an eye on the Earth woman. Since he'd followed her this far she was his responsibility, and he'd have to make sure she didn't come to any harm. Not that there was much to do at the moment. So far he hadn't found any serious threats in the jungle, so he could safely leave her alone. When his people found him, he'd send them over to her camp to take her prisoner....

White-hot jealousy ripped through him. Suppose someone else attached to her and claimed her? Kavath clenched his fists. He might not want to want her, but he didn't want anyone else to have her, either. No problem--he'd tell them to wear breathers to avoid his mistake.

In the meantime she was his to keep watch over. Kavath took one last look at his lovely, not-exactly-a-prisoner before slipping back down the tree and heading back to his ship.

The impulse that had made him follow a runaway Earthforce pilot had landed him into far more interesting situation than he'd bargained for.

* * * *

The next afternoon Mea followed her nose to his camp.

After the Gaian's uninvited visit, she felt compelled to return the favor, at least so that she knew where he was. After a night of animal noises waking her every few minutes and the morning cacophony of bird songs as the sun rose, she was anxious for man-made sounds.

She'd never expected to miss the snoring in the pilot quarters, but she did. Perhaps they could talk about his strange behavior the night before. In particular she was curious about the kiss. What kind of custom was that, to kiss a woman, then run away from her?

Mea shook her head. She knew Gaians had strange traditions compared to Earth, but even so … there had to be some sort of explanation.

She followed a narrow trail past the stream and through the brush in the direction he'd gone. Careful as she was, she would have missed the broken branches of the opening into an even narrower trail to his camp if he hadn't been cooking. For a moment she stood and allowed the mouthwatering aroma of roasted meat to tantalize her. Obviously the Gaian must have found something he felt was edible. Whatever it was, it smelled delicious.

Mea followed the scent until she came upon a path of crushed vegetation, clearly the route the Gaian's fighter had taken from the air to its landing spot. The damaged leaves showed evidence of chemical burns from leaking fighter fuel--one of her shots must have hit a fuel canister. The opening in the forest was easy to follow, and she soon spotted the familiar green-striped tail of his fighter.

There didn't seem to be anyone there. Above an unattended fire that was barely more than coals, perched several spits bearing some kind of meat, the source of the appetizing aroma. Mea glanced around the clearing and saw no sign of the Gaian. He must be off somewhere, doing something manly like catching animals. Even so she waited in the clearing's shadows until she was sure he wasn't around before exploring his camp.

For a man he was surprisingly neat. There wasn't the least bit of clutter. A small tent like hers was pitched near a small lantern, and a few other items hung from a tree branch. Rocks surrounded the campfire and a log had been dragged up to serve as a seat, making the area homey. Mea crossed her arms and tried not to feel jealous that the man had a cozier camp than she did. She particularly liked the fire-pit, something she didn't have since she had no idea how to use the fire starter in her emergency kit.

Without access to a sonic stove or micro-oven, her lack of fire building skills was something she'd need to remedy if she wanted to cook anything here. Wistfully Mea eyed his fire. Maybe she could talk him into teaching her how to build one.

Sure she would. Right after she convinced him to stop sneaking around and trying to take her prisoner.

A glance inside the tent showed the same careful organization, including what looked like a much more comfortable sleeping place. The jungle floor under her tent had seemed hard as a rock last night, but his was soft. She poked at the raised space and realized that he'd pitched the tent over a thick bed of soft leaves, making the floor of the tent into a mattress of sorts. A good idea she would copy as soon as she returned.

Mea heard a soft ping, driving her out of the tent. She heard a man's voice and froze in place, afraid she was about to be discovered. Then she realized the voice was coming from inside the ship.

"Pilot Terrell … are you there? Report, Pilot."

Mea's stomach dropped to her feet. Obviously the Gaian's homing beacon had gotten his people's attention and they were coming for him. It was too much to hope that when they got here they wouldn't find her as well.

Mea thought fast. At this point the only chance she had to remain free was to make it harder for the Gaians to find him. Quickly she climbed the ladder into his ship.

The canopy's latch wasn't locked. Leaning in she found the ship's communit and its integrated homing beacon.

"Pilot Terrell. We're having trouble reading your position. Please report your coordinates...." She hit the off-switch on the communit and the voice silenced in mid-phrase. She breathed a sigh of short-lived relief. So they hadn't really found him yet. Turning off the beacon would delay them.

Even so, she needed to make sure the Gaians were never able to find their lost pilot. If Pilot Terrell checked his beacon, he'd just turn it back on. She needed to buy some serious time.

It took less than a minute to remove the most critical parts of the Gaian's equipment and stow them into her jacket pocket. Mea closed the canopy and slid down the ladder.

On her way past the fire, she gave into temptation and snagged a couple of the spits of smoldering meat to take with her. After a night and morning of field rations, they smelled too good to pass up. Maybe the Gaian would think an animal stole them.

* * * *

Somebody had been in *his* camp ... and she'd been hungry. Feeling decidedly like a character in a nursery tale, Kavath stared bemused at what was left of his still cooking meat. He was missing a third of his dinner. He studied the small boot prints near the fire. It might have been an animal but for the prints, whose size seemed to match the bruise he wore on his upper thigh.

He shook his head in dismay. So the Earth woman had managed to track him back to his camp. Obviously he'd underestimated her--something he was going to have to stop doing.

Ruefully, Kavath regarded the four spits remaining. The greens he'd left his camp to find had been intended as a side dish, but now they'd have to make up for his thief's appetite. Good thing she was so small or at least not greedy--she could have taken all his meat.

He followed the tracks around his camp. She'd been in his tent, but hadn't disturbed anything. Then he noticed traces of mud on the ladder of his ship and suddenly concerned, he climbed and checked his communications equipment, flipping the switches every way possible.

Only silence came from the communit.

With a curse Kavath opened the unit's cover and cursed louder when he discovered how thorough she'd been. He didn't have a spare for any of the parts she'd taken, and without his communit and homing beacon the Gaian fleet would never find him.

Frack! Interesting was no longer a good description of his situation. He was totally screwed.

Kavath headed down the ladder and grabbed the respirator from inside his tent, plus a few other supplies, stuffing them into his pocket. Leaving the Earth woman to her own devices had been a mistake, and he was now paying the price for it. One way or another he had to get those parts back. If necessary he'd take them from her ship. If really necessary.... Well, he'd do what it took to get them from her. He checked the charge of his stunner, hoping he wouldn't have to use it.

The last day of camping on this planet had been fun. He'd brushed up on some long dormant survival skills, things he hadn't had an opportunity to practice since leaving Gaia. But fun was fun and this was war.

Gaians didn't leave a man behind if they could help it, but without his communit they had no way of knowing if he was still alive. They wouldn't look for him too long--he had to get back in touch or he might be here forever.

Chapter Three

The Gaian's charge into her camp was so fast that Mea didn't even have time to pull her knife. One instant she was sitting on her new log seat nibbling meat off the spit she'd stolen, the next she'd been hauled to her feet and dragged to the ladder of her ship. Using his big hands and bigger body, the Gaian pressed her hard against the ladder, effectively immobilizing her.

Inwardly Mea groaned. Caught off guard again--this was becoming embarrassing. She tried to knee him in the crotch, but he simply pressed harder against her. The metal of the ladder dug painfully into her back as he used his size and weight against her. Mea didn't have a chance.

She felt every hard muscled inch of him against her … well, hard except for one place. Unlike their last encounter his crotch was soft against her, his erection gone. Instead of lust, pure fury was in his glare over the respirator covering his mouth and nose.

Uh, oh, the Gaian was seriously pissed. He'd seen her with the meat in her hand and would know she'd taken it from his camp. Could he be this worked-up over the loss of a little food, or did he know what else she'd stolen from him?

"I want them back, Earth woman."

She tried for innocence anyway. "The meat? I ate one already. I'm sorry … I know I shouldn't have taken any but it smelled so good." Perhaps flattery would work. "You must have hunted for it. How clever, and you cooked it so well. I thought about trading some rations for it but you weren't around...."

The Gaian took a deep breath, the sound harsh through his respirator. "No, not the meat. The parts. I want the parts you stole."

Double uh-oh. He knew what she'd done to his communit. It had been a mistake to take the food. It might have taken him days to realize she'd been in his camp and find her sabotage. Good thing she'd hidden what she'd taken....

"Are you going to tell me where the parts are?" He pressed her harder against the ladder until her back was near screaming with pain.

"You're hurting me," she whimpered.

To her surprise, he backed off, and looked concerned, although there was still a lot of anger in his face. "Sorry, didn't mean to do that. Forgot you're so ... little."

Enough people had teased her about her height over the years. "I'm not that little."

"I guess not for a woman. When I saw you the first time I thought you were a very small man."

Another thing she'd been teased about. "I am most certainly not a man."

Something that might have been a smile showed up behind the clear mask over his mouth. "As you say, that is most certainly true." The smile disappeared. "You are, however, a problem."

From a pocket he produced a length of cable, which he looped around her wrists and the metal rung above her head, knotting the ends together and securing her to the ladder. Mea twisted and turned, kicking out with her boots, but he avoided her blows, grabbing and securing her ankles to the bottom rung with a second length.

Finished, he stepped back and examined her with an air of annoying satisfaction. "This way you won't be able to kick me," he said.

Mea tested his knots as he stepped away to begin a methodical search of her camp. The cable didn't give an inch and all she managed was to wear some skin off her wrists.

There wasn't much to search, so it didn't take him long to empty her tent and sort through her meager belongings. When he finished, he boosted himself over her on the ladder and did an equally thorough search of her ship, of course checking on her own communit, which she'd relieved of the same parts.

She wasn't worried about missing a call at this point. It wasn't likely her people were around to contact anyway, and she could wait until after he left to replace the parts.

His brow deeply lined and showing his frustration, the Gaian came down the ladder and towered over her. He gave a great sigh. "I guess there is only one place left to check."

"You wouldn't dare...." Mea swallowed her words as with gentle firmness the man searched her pockets, then patted her down. To her surprise, particularly given how aroused he'd been when he'd jumped her the night before, there was no lasciviousness in his touch. His fingers didn't linger anywhere, and if anything he handled her as if she were nothing more than an inanimate object. He didn't find anything but her knife, which he took from her.

Flushed as much from the impersonal nature of his touch as the fact that he'd touched her at all, Mea glared at him. "Are you finished?"

Disgruntled, he nodded and leaned against the ship. "I guess you must have buried them someplace. I hope you remember where."

She sniffed. "I don't know what you are talking about."

"Of course you don't," he said sarcastically. "That's why you took the identical parts from your own communit." He shook his head. "I want them back, woman."

"My name is not woman, or Earth woman. My name is Lieutenant Meagan An Flena and I'm an Earthforce officer." She straightened as best she could. "If you are going to insist on treating me as a prisoner, I expect you to use some respect."

He glared down at her. "Respect? You expect me to respect you for this?" He took a deep breath, the sound rasping in the respirator. "Tell me where the parts are, Meagan."

"My friends call me Mea. You may call me Lieutenant An Flena," she countered keeping her voice low and threatening.

He didn't look impressed. "All, right. *Lieutenant*. Where are the parts?"

"Perhaps you could tell me your name? I feel rather at a disadvantage here."

Since she was the one tied up, that was an understatement. Even so, she could swear she could hear his teeth grinding through the mask.

"Terrell. Kavath. Pilot," he spat out.

"Pilot Kavath Terrell?"

"Yes. Most people call me Kavath. *You* can call me Pilot Terrell. Now that we're properly introduced, where are the fricking parts?" he bellowed at her.

She gave him her most innocent smile. "I'm sure I don't know what you are talking about, Pilot Terrell."

His hands seem to clutch at the air as if they wanted to throttle someone and for an instant Mea wondered how smart it was to bait him. The Gaian code of conduct insisted on treating enemies better than most Earth people treated their friends, but that wouldn't necessarily help her if he really lost his temper. He was so big he could hurt her without even meaning to.

Kavath took several deep breaths and his hands relaxed. "You know that without the homing devices in our ships, no one will be able to locate us. The jungle is too thick here for anyone's sensors to find our ships."

"So?" she countered. "My people aren't around and yours will only dump me on one of your POW planets. What makes you think I want the Gaians to find us?"

"You'd rather stay here?" His eyes widened. "The places we're putting your people are really nice planets. We make sure they have food, water, and everything they need to survive. You'd even be with your shipmates." He glanced around at the jungle that surrounded them. "Here we have only what was in our ships, and that's not enough for a long stay."

"It will have to do." She set her jaw at him. "I'm not giving up."

He leaned over her. "Do you really understand what will happen if we stay here? There are many things in this jungle. Unfriendly things," he emphasized with far too much enthusiasm for Mea. "Things that bite … or worse."

For an instant she wondered what could be worse than being bitten, then wondered if he might mean himself. "You aren't frightening me. I'd rather be here than captured by the Gaians."

"Aren't you forgetting one little thing?" He reached up and tugged at the cable holding her to the ladder, nearly jerking her off her feet. Only the cable around her ankles held her on the ground. "At the moment you have been captured by a Gaian."

She swallowed hard. He did have a point there--she was pretty much at his mercy. For all of the Gaian code of conduct, nothing about this man seemed anything but menacing.

All he seemed to see when he looked at her was an enemy, and one he was holding a grudge against at that. As surreptitiously as possible, Mea tested the knots holding her arms again. She could be in really big trouble.

His hard-on and the way he'd kissed her had made her think he wanted her as a woman. Too bad he wasn't attracted to her now. That could have bought her some leeway with him. Men didn't always think straight when they were hard.

Lifting her chin with his hand, the big man stared down at her, his eyes glaring at her over the mask across his mouth. "Still not going to tell me where the parts are?"

She shook her head and braced herself for his reaction. Angry as he was, anything was possible. He might even hit her with one of those big fists of his. Mea closed her eyes and waited for the first blow.

With a rasping grunt of annoyance, he released her chin and stepped away from her. He strode over to where she'd been sitting and picked up the spit of meat she had been eating. Mystified, Mea watched as he cautiously pulled his mask off, licked his finger and held it in the air for a moment. Apparently satisfied he put the mask to one side, brushed the meat off, and, taking her seat on the fallen log, proceeded to eat the rest of her dinner.

She couldn't believe it. "That's so unsanitary. That was in my mouth!"

He stopped in mid chew. "Interesting point." He took a deep sniff. "I don't see any harm to it, though." His teeth glinted at her as his lips drew back into a full grin. "My tongue was in your mouth last night and I didn't get sick then. I guess you're healthy enough."

Mea gasped her exasperation. "I should have bitten that tongue of yours when I had the chance."

He laughed, the sound feeding her irritation. "You are a fierce little lehen, aren't you? Well, don't worry, I'm not going to give you another chance to bite me. As for the meat, I caught and prepared it and I'm not letting it go to waste. Besides, I'm hungry."

It probably wouldn't do much good to point out that she was hungry, too. The one spit she'd eaten had barely whetted her appetite.

"Why did you do that thing ... with your finger?"

He gave her a cautious look and took another bite. For a moment she wasn't sure that he'd answer her.

"I was testing the breeze to see which way it was coming from. It isn't coming from you, so I could take the mask off."

His explanation simply confused her more. "Why are you wearing the mask? My smell bothering you? I haven't been here that long without a shower."

The question was more a joke than anything else, but he nodded and laughed wryly. "Let's just say that your smell is a problem. I find it distracting." Finishing the meat, he tossed the stick to one side, then found her water bottle. For an instant he examined the reddish contents with obvious distrust, then with a shrug took a deep sip.

He made a face. "Now this could make me ill."

"It's clean enough," she protested. "I used the purifier on it."

"I didn't mean from the germs in it, Earth woman. I meant the taste."

Mea fumed. The nerve of the man. Sitting in her camp, drinking her water, and complaining about it. The water wasn't that bad ... in fact compared to the water on her ship it was almost tasty. As if she'd invited him here to tie her up and take over her camp.

Okay, so maybe she started things by stealing the communit parts. No, wait, he'd started it when he jumped her the first time in her camp. But she'd shot his ship over the planet ... but he'd chased her from the battle scene and had been the first to fire at her, even if it had been with tracer rays.

Of course, that was in the line of duty for both of them. Their people were at war and the Gaians had started it.

Hadn't they? All of a sudden she wasn't so sure and her head hurt trying to figure it out.

What she knew for sure was that she and he were on opposite sides, and at the moment she was completely at the man's mercy.

Even so, she wouldn't beg him to be nice. She tried for bravado instead. "If you don't like the water here, why don't you go back to your own camp and drink yours."

For a long moment he seemed to consider that. "I probably should do just that." He stood up and refitted the mask to his face. "I'll let you think about things while I'm gone. Give me a shout when you're willing to let me have my communit parts back."

"A shout?" Her eyes widened as she saw him head toward the edge of the forest and sudden panic overcame her. She tugged fruitlessly at the cord binding her wrists. "You aren't going to leave me tied up like this, are you?"

"Why not? There is nothing here to hurt you, right?" He opened his arms and indicated the jungle around them. "After all, you want to be here. It is so much better here than on one of our prisoner planets."

"Don't leave me tied up, you … you … obnoxious bastard!"

"Leave my parents out of this, little lehen." She could feel his grin from across the clearing. "Don't worry, I'll be back soon. You let me know if something comes along to bother you. Maybe if you scream real loud, I'll hear you at my camp."

Still tied to her ship's ladder Mea watched in growing horror as the Gaian disappeared into the jungle leaving her to the encroaching darkness.

This was just getting worse and worse.

* * * *

Kavath settled onto his perch in the tree overlooking her camp. He took a deep sip from the water bottle he'd hidden there earlier.

He was determined to keep her safe. She thought he'd gone back to his camp and wouldn't know he was watching out for her, but he was going to stay in this tree until she called. If anything came into her camp that could cause her harm, he'd know about it. In the meantime she might get frightened enough to give him the parts she'd stolen.

At this point he wasn't real hopeful of that. To date she'd shown far more backbone than any female he'd ever known, even more than one of his sisters. It was just a fricking shame she was on the other side. His match, attractive, smart, a good pilot, and gutsy to boot. If this went on much longer, he might try to get her to accept attachment in spite of everything.

It was still early evening, light enough that he could see Mea clearly through the trees. She wasn't moving very much, just shifting her feet back and forth. Perhaps she was trying to dislodge some insect that had crawled up her pants leg from the ground.

Kavath tensed and waited. Maybe she'd call him to help. Hopefully it wasn't anything that bit or that she'd have a bad reaction to.

There was an all-purpose first aid kit back at his camp that he hoped he wouldn't need. He didn't want his little lehen to suffer anything worse than sore wrists and a stiff back. All he wanted was for Mea to give back the parts so they could both get off this planet.

Mea. Kavath mused over her name. An unusual name but he rather liked it. It sounded prickly … very much like her.

It also sounded stubborn, which was also very much like her. As he watched, Mea stopped squirming around and leaned her head back through the steps of the ladder, apparently glaring at the knots holding her hands over her head. She studied them for a moment then seemed to lean forward in resignation.

He perked up. Would she give up now? Kavath waited for her call.

Long minutes passed and she said nothing. He couldn't help a sigh of disappointment.

Leaning back, Kavath tried to relax against the tree trunk behind him. Snagging his pack from an overhead limb, he dug around for the edible roots he'd collected earlier. Nutritious, crunchy, even a little tasty, and he could eat them raw. Too bad he couldn't build a fire under the tree, but he needed to stay up here where he could see her.

Besides the smell of smoke would give him away. He bit the end off one of the roots and chewed it slowly.

Yes, she was stubborn. It didn't look like she was going to give in easily. He might as well make himself comfortable since it looked like she planned on holding out as long as possible. He just hoped she didn't try and hold out all night.

Sleeping in a tree wasn't comfortable.

Even so, he did fall asleep. Several hours later, Kavath had dozed off when an eardrum-shattering scream jerked him awake. He barely had time to note that the planet's twin moons had been hidden by clouds when it sounded again, confirming his first thought that somehow his prisoner had gotten herself into trouble.

From his place in the tree he tried to see into her camp, but it was too dark. Heart pounding, Kavath slid out of the tree and freed his stunner as he tore through the jungle. He splashed across the small stream and through the underbrush. In his rush he barely remembered to secure his respirator to his face before entering her camp.

His gaze swept the area quickly, looking for the most likely cause for her screams. Perhaps she'd encountered one of the larger snakes or rodents he'd seen in the jungle.

But there was nothing … no sign of anything out of the ordinary in the darkness.

Mea was a pale shadow against the ladder, sagging against the rungs with her hands up over her head, her face turned away from him.

"What happened? Are you all right?" Kavath whispered.

She whimpered and he came closer. "Mea, what's wrong?"

Abruptly her hands grabbed the ladder rung over her head, and she swung her feet up and kicked forward, striking him in the chest with the heels of her boots. The sudden attack knocked him onto his ass, dislodging the respirator. It slipped and covered his mouth so he couldn't breathe. Kavath tore it away just as Mea, apparently no longer tied to the ladder, rushed forward to kick him hard in the side of his head. Pain exploded between his ears and Kavath slipped into unconsciousness.

He was barely aware of being dragged along the ground and propped against something hard. When he opened his eyes he was sitting at the base of the ladder. His hands were bound to the rung behind him, and his head hurt like hell.

Mea moved away and there was a flash as her lamp flared to life. The light came towards him, and he saw Mea gloating. His vision blurred and for a moment there seemed to be two of her.

Kavath shook his head, ignoring the pain, until there was only one of her again. A good thing. He didn't think he could handle more than one of her at the moment.

His little lehen nemesis looked triumphant at him. "Gotcha!" she said, with no little satisfaction.

He took a deep breath and instantly regretted it. For a moment he found it hard to breathe, then his manhood swelled to readiness. Heart pounding, he took deep gasping breaths and nearly passed out. It was difficult having both a head injury and a hard-on at the same time.

Kavath shut his eyes. *Sweet Gaia, not again.* Once more he was well and truly attached to his enemy. Why did it have to be this woman? Why not a loving Gaian lady, someone of his own kind? Someone who respected his culture and would be a prize to take home to his parents?

Why did he have to keep attaching to this little Earth-born hellion who flew like a lehen and kicked like an Earthen mule? Obviously he had the worst luck of any Gaian in history.

* * * *

Thrilled at her success, Mea examined her prize. *She'd done it!* She'd planned her escape and executed it, even capturing her enemy in the process. Score one for her, none for the Gaian.

At first she'd been frightened after he'd tied her up and left her for the jungle to eat. But then she realized his Gaian sense of fair play wouldn't have let him abandon her, and so she decided the man hadn't gone far and would be well within earshot.

Just in case he could see her, she'd waited until dark to free herself then let more time pass until she was relatively sure he'd be off guard before screaming. As she'd expected he'd charged in, and she'd taken him completely by surprise.

Now he was tied up in her place and she was the one holding him prisoner. Mea took a moment to bask in celebration. The worm had turned and he was at her mercy.

Her mercy. She had control over him. Over his food, his water. His protection.

He was no longer in charge, she was! She was responsible....

Some of Mea's euphoria died. *He was her responsibility.* The Gaian was now hers to deal with, whether or not she wanted to … and if he was hurt that was her responsibility too. And she'd kicked him hard and in the head with her boots. He could really be injured.

She better make sure he was all right. Suddenly feeling the weight of the world on her shoulders, Mea peered closer at her prisoner.

He was breathing funny again and looked like he was going to pass out. Cautiously she looked behind the ladder and verified that his hands were still bound before coming close enough to examine him. There was a nasty-looking knot on his head where her metal-soled boot had hit him, and a scrape on his cheek where the respirator had been. A wave of concern hit her as she checked his eyes with her lantern. He stared at her with even-sized pupils so she ruled out a concussion.

He was silent as she examined him, but once more she saw the glint of masculine interest in his eyes when her breasts brushed against his arm. She could feel the tension in him at her presence.

Now he was attracted to her, after she'd kicked him in the head and tied him up? She'd heard rumors that Gaians had strange sexual habits, but this was ridiculous. What kind of man was he anyway?

Satisfied he wasn't too badly wounded, Mea moved back to her seat, taking the lantern with her. His steady gaze seemed to follow her as she went.

What was she going to do with him now? She couldn't let him free. He'd simply overpower her again and tie her up, and this time he might even think to remove her boots whose metal-edged soles she'd used to cut her ankle bonds. Having her feet free had allowed her to climb the ladder when it had gotten dark enough and untie the cable around her wrists with her teeth.

Her wrists hurt and her jaw still ached from the effort to free herself. She didn't think she'd ever get rid of the taste of the cable in her mouth. She took a deep sip of the remainder of her purified water and spat it out.

From her prisoner came a rumbling laugh. "Even you don't like your water?"

"It isn't the water. It's the cable you used. I had to untie it with my teeth." Mea took another sip, swallowing this time to soothe her aching throat. Going so long without anything to drink and then screaming loud had been hard on her throat.

"I'm sorry. Next time I'll use a better tasting rope."

Mea couldn't help but stare at him. How could the man joke at a time like this? She'd bested him, disabled his communit and now him, and yet he acted like it was some kind of game. No Earth man she'd ever known would have taken defeat at her hands so well.

Searching the leaf clutter on the ground, Mea found his dropped stunner and examined it. The maximum setting would knock someone out, but like most Gaian weapons it wasn't designed to kill.

Still, it was better than having no weapon other than a knife and at least it was fully charged. If her prisoner got out of hand she could always stun him. That gave her an edge she hadn't had before.

She didn't know why Earthforce didn't routinely equip their pilots with guns, but small arms were only issued to troops assigned to board ships. She supposed it was considered pointless given how rarely they fought outside of their spacecraft. Knowing Earthforce, it was probably a cost-saving measure. The only way a pilot had a weapon was if they privately owned one.

Mea had to admit that a good particle beam emitter or a molecular disruptor could sure come in handy when stuck on a planet with an enemy pilot. Unfortunately she'd never seen the need for owning a peabee or emdee so she was out of luck. Truth was she wasn't that good a shot with a hand weapon.

She doubted that her enemy wasn't proficient with a stunner, particularly after eating the meat he'd prepared. Obviously he was much better at living in the wild than she was. Too bad she couldn't work with the Gaian instead of fighting with him.

"So, now that you have me, what are you going to do with me?" His voice broke in on her thoughts. The Gaian sounded almost calm. With his face just outside of the throw of her lamp, it was hard to read his expression, but his eyes glittered from the reflected light.

He had nice eyes, too, she remembered.

Mea slipped the stunner into a pocket of her flight suit. "I don't know yet. I hadn't gotten that far. I can't let you go, at least not at the moment."

He crossed his long legs in front of him, reminding her of just how tall he was. She tried not to think about how impressively built her prisoner was...or how he'd feel lying on top of her again.

"I suppose that wouldn't be such a good idea," he said. "I'd only have to try something else to force you to give me the communit parts."

Mea pulled her mind away from his long legs and hard body. "You can't force me to give them to you," she said flatly. "Surely even someone as hard-headed as you can see that now."

He chuckled but the sound reeked of embarrassment. "My head isn't all that hard. You put quite a dent in it. What did you have in your boots?"

"My foot--and some steel plating."

There was that rueful laugh. "Ah ... that explains it." His sharp gaze drove through her. "I suppose that's how you got free, with your metal-edged sole."

She shrugged.

He chuckled. "You are most formidable, Earth woman. So what do we do now?"

"Now we wait until I'm sure your people aren't likely to still be looking for you."

"And then?"

"And then I'll set you free."

He leaned back against the ladder. "Just like that? You'll free me?"

"I have no desire to keep you a prisoner long. All I want to do is avoid capture myself. You forced me into this," she told him. "Besides how could I realistically hold onto you? Unlike you, I can't keep you tied up forever."

Kavath sighed. "I hadn't planned to keep you tied up long, just until you told me where the parts were. You just turned out to be more resourceful than I expected," he added with a hint of respect she found almost gratifying.

Walking over to him, she held out her water bottle. "Would you like some?"

"Not now." He shook his head and winced with what looked like pain. He hesitated. "I wonder if you could do something about my headache."

Mentally Mea listed the contents of her meager medical kit. It held a small selection of medicines for various ills, including those for pain. For a moment she wondered how long those pills would have to last her. But she looked at him and the still darkening bruise on his forehead. His eyes were bright and some of that was from the way he hurt. No matter that she was his enemy, she couldn't leave him in pain.

Cautiously Mea slid behind him to the outside hatch to the storage compartment of her ship. She keyed in the code to open it, and pulled out her medical kit.

The Gaian took the pill and a sip from her bottle with easy grace, not even complaining this time about the taste of the water. She could feel his green eyes watch her as she closed the case up and put it away. There was something in that gaze. Approval? She felt like she'd been through some sort of test--and passed.

Uneasily Mea retook her seat on the log. Why was it she wanted the Gaian's good opinion? He didn't mean anything to her. She hadn't even allowed the opinions of her former shipmates to matter that much to her, so why should she care what this strange man thought of her?

It was late and she was tired, but she didn't want to leave the Gaian out of her sight. She couldn't use her tent, but she could use her sleeping sack to curl up in. The jungle air wasn't cold, but the humidity and dark made her want something warm and dry around her.

Mea dragged her sack out of the tent and placed it a few yards from her prisoner. Keeping her clothes on, she slid into it by the light of her lantern. After a moment's hesitation she turned the lamp out. She didn't like the dark, but she couldn't afford to waste the lantern's battery more than necessary.

The memory of the Gaian's camp and its fire-pit came to her. That would be nice, to have a little fire to keep her warm and her camp lit at night. It would probably scare off the wildlife as well. Too bad her survival course hadn't included anything as basic as making fire.

Maybe after all this was over she could trade with the Gaian for survival lessons ... that is, trade with Kavath-- that was the man's name after all. She might as well get used to his name. It looked like they were going to be together for some time to come.

Chapter Four

Mea reached out to him and his hands closed on her arms. His palms and fingers felt like fire and ice sliding across her skin--as hot as one, as stimulating as the other. Moaning, Mea leaned into the big man, so he could reach more of her body. He responded as she'd hoped, moving his hands to her shoulders, then down to caress the sides of her chest.

Her breasts ached for his touch, the nipples pebbling in instant awareness. It was all she could do not to thrust them into his hands.

Mea looked up at his face and saw the green eyes and near-white blond hair of her Gaian nemesis. It was Kavath whose hands were stroking her with such talented fingers. Kavath with a sensual smile and no bruise darkening his forehead.

No bruise? Okay, so she was dreaming. She had to be because she knew very well that the Gaian was tied to the ladder of her ship and not sitting next to her and making love to her with his hands. But it was a very nice dream, and she felt no urge to put a halt to it. Instead Mea gave into temptation and reached to move Kavath's dream hands to her breasts.

He kneaded them with gentle care, the fingers sliding across her nipples. In her dream Mea moaned louder and she heard the Gaian whisper softly in her ear, "I love it when you make noise."

After the number of times she'd been shushed while bunking with her shipmates, his words were sweet.

What a great dream.

His hands stroked her, running up and down her body with expert ease. While one hand focused on her breasts, the other found the juncture of her legs and slipped inside to finger her core. Mea felt a surge of moisture where his finger touched, and she groaned aloud.

His lips came down on hers, covering her mouth with a mind-bending kiss. She breathed heavily, enjoying the feel of his tongue and the warmth inside his mouth. His taste flooded her tongue, like hot rich coffee and chocolate-chip cookies.

So very tasty. She wanted more.

She opened her legs to him and he moved his hand inside her. She moaned again when he slid two fingers inside and stroked gently. A bright flash illuminated the scene as a miniature orgasm flew through her. She could feel the rumbling of the earth around her.

He kissed her forehead, leaving a trace of dampness from his lips. "Mea, you are so hot. So hot, so moist, so wet...."

So wet....

A lightning flash and accompanying thunder woke her, the crashing sound breaking just over her head. Mea jerked at the sound, just as another drop of dampness hit her forehead. She opened her eyes and saw heavy drops of rain falling on her sleeping sack with large plops, beading on the moisture-proof covering without penetrating it.

The hard pitter-pat roused her further, breaking her out of the remainder of her dream. Mea raised her head to stare groggily at the rain hitting the ground.

Through the drops she saw the Gaian still tied to the ladder, his head bowed as if he, too, slept. As she watched he stirred, the drops hitting his broad shoulders and the top of his head. Damn that dream of hers, he looked sexy even tied up. She shook her head to clear it of any lingering arousal. Maybe he just looked sexy because he was tied up and couldn't hurt her.

Meanwhile the raindrops fell and soaked into the ground. For a moment Mea wondered what to do. It was just a little rain. No reason to panic, even if she'd spent little time outside in weather before. Surely it would stop soon.

But it didn't stop. The drops came faster, in longer streams that soaked the leaf littered ground around her, giving off a damp sour smell. Some water splashed in her eyes and she sat up, using the bulk of the sack to cover her head, for once pleased about her diminutive size. The sack was huge around her and kept the rain off.

Lightning split the sky followed by thunder so loud she felt the ground quake beneath her. The rain became a steady downpour as if someone had turned a spigot, and torrents fell that turned the ground around her to mush.

It was still dry in her sleep sack cocoon, but Mea felt the ground beneath her soften. Whether or not it was going to stop soon, she couldn't stay here in the open. When she turned to check her tent, she saw the top bending from the weight of the water streaming down from the canopy of trees overhead. The spot had looked good when she'd set it up, but now she wished she'd put it where it had a more solid roof overhead. Not that there were many places like that in the clearing, except possibly under the ship.

Under the ship. That was an idea. Beneath it was the only dry place around, and the broad wings that flanked the tail would provide better shelter than her rain-wracked tent. Quickly she reversed the bag around her to put her feet on the ground and half-walked, half-slid through the mud to the rear of her vehicle, grabbing her lantern as she passed it. She turned it on, using the faint illumination to find her way. Twice she slipped in the mud, but eventually she made it. Once underneath, Mea pulled herself out of the bag entirely and dragged it to where the ground was still blissfully dry.

Not bad. The space was too short to do more than sit up, but at least she was out of the rain. She left the bag on the ground and looked out through the water sheeting off the edges of the wings.

The Gaian was where she'd left him, still secured to the ladder, the rain pouring down on him. His hair was plastered to his forehead and the back of his neck and even his uniform jacket looked soaked through. As she watched, a shiver went through his broad shoulders.

He looked cold, wet, and miserable. Mea watched as he leaned back and let the water pour into his mouth. *Wonderful … the fool was going to drown himself.* Then he leaned forward and she watched him swallow. Not so foolish, she realized. The water coming out of the sky was probably cleaner than what was in the stream.

She found her water bottle and opened it to catch some of the rain, tasting it after she'd collected some. It tasted wonderful so she set the bottle out to fill completely.

Mea stared in apprehension at the pouring rain and the sopping wet man she'd left tied out in the middle of it. Could this get any worse?

The wind picked up and the rain started coming down at an angle, and even harder than before. Okay, it could get worse. The weather didn't have to prove itself to her--she believed it.

What was she going to do about her prisoner? It was her responsibility to take care of him. She couldn't leave him out in the weather.

Just then a strong breeze blew under the ship. The wind seemed to pierce through her wet clothes to the skin, and she shivered hard. That settled the question of what to do. If it was that bad for her, how much worse was it for him, still out in the rain? Suppose being left out there caused him to get seriously ill? Neither of them could afford to get sick, not with their limited medical supplies.

Would it be possible to release him from the ladder yet keep his hands tied? Maybe if she added another layer of bindings before releasing him--that might work. But then she considered his size and strength. Even with his hands tied, he'd undoubtedly be able to overpower her if he wanted to.

So she couldn't leave him out there and keeping him a prisoner wasn't practical. What else was there?

It was said that Gaians were so trustworthy that they always kept a promise. Okay, that was a possibility. It was doubtful he wanted to stay out in the rain. Maybe she could get him to declare a truce, until after the storm.

Carrying the lamp, she pulled his stunner and crept forward. She shined the light at him, and he lifted his head. Through the damp hair partially covering his eyes she could see his steady gaze.

"Would you like to come in out of the rain?"

He raised his face to the water cascading around him, then returned to stare at her. His lips twitched up into a soggy smile. "I can't say I'm enjoying this much."

She hesitated. "I want your promise."

His head went up and his whole body went on alert. "Promise for what?"

"If I release you from the ladder, you won't attack me. We'll have a truce until morning at least."

He seemed to ponder that. "You'll let me take cover under the ship with you?"

She nodded. "Yes."

A hard blast of wind whipped through the trees, blowing leaves and other litter from the jungle floor into his face. When it receded, he lifted his head and let the water wash his face free of bits of leaves and dirt before turning to look at her.

"All right--a truce. Until morning. Maybe the weather will be better then." Something that could have been a grin took over his face. "And maybe by then I'll be able to make you see reason about the communit parts."

Unlikely, but no point in saying it. She didn't need to get into a debate with him. Mea returned his stunner to her pocket, and crept into the mud behind the ladder. As soon as she was beyond the edge of the ship, water poured onto her back, soaking her uniform through. It was too late to worry about getting wet, so she focused on undoing his bonds instead. The cable was stretched tight, but she finally was able to untie the knots and free his hands.

Just as the cable came loose, another blast of wind swept through the clearing, bringing several of the large palm-like fronds with it. Mea crouched to avoid them, but a larger mass was suddenly between her and the wind. She heard a loud grunt and realized it was the Gaian as he wrapped his arms around her. To her surprise he used his body to protect her, the branches hitting his back and not hers.

Then he was moving, half-lifting, half-carrying her to the shelter under her ship, while behind them branches, leaves, and other debris rained down on the spot they'd just vacated. In moments they were between the fighter's massive twin engines where the air was relatively still. After the fury of the storm outside, the sudden respite felt eerie.

The Gaian still had his arms around her. His smell filled her nose, warm and earthy, intensely masculine. She wanted to bury her head in his chest and indulge herself in his smell. He was so much bigger--and she liked that.

Her reaction confused her. It wasn't like she was a blushing first-year Earthforce recruit, still a virgin. Perhaps she was a little more selective than the average female member of Earthforce, but she'd shared a bunk with her share of men, and had had their arms around her. Why should this man be so different?

He shouldn't feel different and yet somehow he was. She turned to face him and the green eyes that stared with such concern into hers made her tremble in a way that had nothing to do with the chill of her damp clothing.

"Are you all right?" he asked.

She nodded. Then somehow she found herself able to breathe and she filled her lungs with air, letting it out slowly, then breathing in again deeply. Each breath brought more of that earthy male scent and each breath made her wish for more. As she breathed, she saw him watching her mouth and for a moment she wondered if he was going to kiss her. Without thinking she inched forward, anticipating the touch of his lips on hers.

He pulled back abruptly, too fast, and hit his head on the bottom of the ship above them. "Ouch!" he said and glared at their low ceiling. "I can't seem to avoid getting hurt around you."

That broke the spell and Mea scuttled away, out of the shelter of his arms. "Maybe it's a sign that you shouldn't have followed me from the battle. If you hadn't you wouldn't be here."

"If I hadn't, you'd be alone in this right now." He gestured to the storm raging around their meager shelter. "Would you want that? I have to be here to keep you safe."

Mea stared at him. "Is that what this is all about, you keeping me safe? That's why you followed me?"

"Some of it. I didn't want you to get away, but mostly we're not supposed to let anyone come to harm if we can help it," he admitted. "A small ship lost in space ... it can take several days for a pilot to die that way. It wasn't likely that you'd be picked up unless I found you."

A large gust of wind blew under the ship, bringing a handful of ground litter with it that peppered Mea and the Gaian equally. One thing for certain, the weather wasn't playing favorites tonight.

She brushed away the damp leaves with her hands. "Yeah, this place is real hospitable." Mea muttered the words under her breath.

He didn't answer her, but crawled back to the ladder and returned, dragging some of the large fronds that had nearly hit them earlier. As Mea watched, he wedged them under the large engine on that side, propping them against the landing supports of her ship.

"What are you doing?"

"Building a wind-break. The wind seems to be strongest in this direction. If I can block it, we'll be a lot better off." He pulled some long vines off the ground and used them to loosely secure the branches in place. Examining the space left unfilled, he shook his head. "I'll need more though."

Mea crawled back to the ladder and grabbed more of the fronds from the pile, pulling them to him. For a moment Kavath stared as if surprised to find her helping, then he nodded and added them into his makeshift wall while Mea went back for more.

When she'd exhausted the available building materials, she held the lamp as he wove more vines between the stems, reinforcing the windbreak until it barely moved under the wind outside.

It was crude but effective. When it was done the space under the ship was noticeably less drafty, and the wall caught the debris, keeping it from hitting them. Even so, they were both wet to the skin and chilled to the bone. Mea shivered in her soaked uniform as Kavath looked at her and the sleep sack.

"You and I need to get warm. I'd build a fire but there is a scarcity of dry wood, plus it isn't such a good thing to have flames under a fuel tank." He looked at the ship above him with a wry smile and even Mea had to laugh through her chattering teeth.

She clutched her arms around her. "No, blowing up my ship is probably a bad idea. So what do we do? You're the survival expert."

He hesitated for what seemed like a long time before answering. "Body heat. That's the only thing we have on our side, the fact that there are two of us and we have this to cover us," he said, pointing to the still relatively dry sleep sack, "We can build a good layer of leaves to insulate us from the ground, then open your bag up and lie under it together." He hesitated again. "Lie together without our wet clothes."

Mea's jaw dropped. "You want to get naked with me?

In the faint light of the lantern she could almost swear that he blushed. "Not the way you mean, and we don't have to get completely undressed. We can leave our underclothes on. But we need to get rid of anything holding a lot of water." His voice turned persuasive. "It's just to get warm."

"You want me to take off my clothes and lie down with you?" Mea laughed. "All men are the same I guess, even Gaian men."

Obviously offended, he narrowed his eyes. "I am not like an Earth man. I don't want your body, just your body heat."

Actually the thought of getting undressed and lying with this man made her more than warm. In fact selective parts of her anatomy turned red hot.

But he didn't want her body, he'd said. Mea folded her arms and stared at him. "Not my body, just my body heat," she repeated mockingly. "Just to get warm." She shivered again but this time it wasn't just because of the cold.

Fortunately he didn't know the difference. "Look, I promise. Nothing will happen other than we'll both get through this night intact. Neither one of us wants to get sick."

She didn't say anything more, and apparently taking her silence for permission, Kavath brushed the leaves under the ship into a pile. While he did, she undid the long fasteners along the side and bottom of her sleep sack and opened it up into a blanket that he then spread carefully across the top.

Kavath pulled off his soaked jacket and wrung streams of water out of it. His boots came off, then his shirt, leaving him wearing a sleeveless undershirt. The damp fabric clung to his chest and outlined his stomach. Mea couldn't help but stare. It molded to his body and every muscle seemed to stand out. She'd never seen a man built like him before.

"I'm not so sure this is such a good idea...." Her voice trailed off as his pants came off. His underwear was just this side of modest, but there was no hiding how big he really was. Still dressed in his underwear and undershirt, he carefully laid out each article of clothing flat on the dry ground.

"If you undress and lay them out, they'll be a lot dryer in the morning," he told her. One of his eyebrows rose into a quizzical arch as she continued to stare at him.

"Do I really scare you so much that you'd rather sit in wet clothes all night?" The challenge in his voice drove her to answer.

"You don't scare me," she said without thinking.

His other eyebrow joined its twin in mocking disbelief.

With a grimace, Mea pulled off her dark-grey uniform jacket and laid it next to his, then undid her shirt, boots, and pants. Stripped to her underclothes, a tank top with built-in support and under shorts, she turned to see a grin take over his face.

"Under all that grey you wear pink underwear?"

"It isn't pink," she said quickly, for once embarrassed about her non-regulation choice of undergarments. "The color is actually called bright rose."

He chuckled. "A pink by any other name … is still pink. Either way I'm glad to see something non-Earthforce about you."

Sliding under her sleep sack he stretched out on the pile of leaves and spread the blanket over his body and across his broad shoulders. He leaned up on one elbow and held out his hand to her. "Come on, Earth woman. The big, bad Gaian won't eat you."

Dressed just in her underwear, the cold seemed harsher than before and Mea shivered accordingly. But she couldn't crawl into bed with him while he was watching her. It was as if he dared her to join him, to share the blanket with him.

It was only to keep warm. That's what he'd said, and strangely enough she believed him. After all, a Gaian would rather die than break a promise. She was safe with him.

Mea turned off the lamp and let the sudden darkness give her the courage to move to the makeshift bed and crawl under the blanket. She slid across the crackling leaves until she felt the warmth of his body, then turned her back to him.

One of his arms slid beneath her head and the other fell around her waist, his hand resting lightly on her belly. Along her back grew a delicious warmth as he moved even closer, wrapping himself around her. On the back of her neck his breath was a welcome source of heat. Even the leaves beneath them seemed to warm up from their combined body heat.

Without thinking she snuggled back into him, her legs tangling with his. She felt the hard ridge of his erection briefly but he turned away so she didn't feel it again. For a moment Mea wasn't sure if she was sorry or not.

As her body warmed up something inside her relaxed and Mea let out an appreciative sigh.

"Be careful, woman. Someone might make you think you were enjoying this."

Too comfortable to argue, particularly when he was right, Mea decided to ignore the smug satisfaction in his voice. "If we're going to share a blanket, I think we might use each other's real names."

"I suppose you have a point. Please call me Kavath."

"And I'm Mea."

Outside of their primitive shelter the storm raged, but their simple windbreak kept the worst of the gusts of wind from hitting them. For the first time since leaving her ship the day before, Mea felt safe, from the elements and her enemy. After all, she told herself with no little humor, it wasn't like she didn't know exactly where he was and what he was up to.

"Why did you stay around and keep watch over me?"

Her question must have caught him off guard since he didn't have a ready answer. Finally he said, "I feel responsible for you. I should have captured you and didn't. If I had, you'd be safe now."

"You really care what happens to me? Why would a Gaian care what happens to an Earthforce officer?"

"It doesn't matter what you are. You're a human being and Gaians care for all human life, even those from Earth. It's what we're taught. Maybe that's hard for you to believe, but I don't wish to see you come to harm."

"It isn't just because I'm a woman?"

"Not just that. I would take care of you even if you were a man." He hesitated. "I have to admit, I might not be so ready to sleep with you though."

Mea laughed and Kavath joined her.

"You must understand, Mea. Gaia didn't start this war. All we wanted was to be free of Earth's taxes and interference. Earth's government took exception and began the fighting. We plan to finish it, to win, but we don't intend to lose who we are in the process. That's why we take prisoners and don't kill unless we have to."

The lateness of the hour, the stress of the past day, and the comfort of being warm combined to make her sleepy. Without thinking, Mea yawned.

"This was a good idea you had, Kavath. Goodnight."

From behind her came his voice, soft and low, a sexy tickle on the back of her neck. "Goodnight, Mea."

* * * *

How could he have possibly thought this was going to be a good idea? Warm, soft, and sweet smelling, the woman from Earth snuggled in Kavath's arms, as delightful a bundle to hold as anything he'd ever known. She slept as deeply as a baby, comfortable in his warmth and comforted by his presence.

She slept … he did not.

Kavath rubbed his chin against the back of her neck, only to be greeted by her appreciative sigh. He groaned in response.

Not even his quezzle had felt this good when he'd cuddled the furry little beast when he was a child. Of course holding his pet feline was a far different matter than holding a woman he was attached to. It was distinctly uncomfortable to be aroused the way he was, particularly by a woman he had no intention of ever being intimate with.

He'd managed to control himself earlier, between the pain of his head, the cold and discomfort. But he wasn't cold anymore and the pill she'd given him had cured his headache.

She mumbled something in her sleep and pushed her pink underwear-clad behind further into his already very aware crotch, making it throb. Kavath stifled another groan. No, he wasn't cold anymore, but there was a certain amount of discomfort.

How did married men ever get any sleep while lying with the woman they desired? If he could, he'd certainly be doing more than simply holding her body. He'd run his hands across those nicely shaped breasts of hers, his fingers searching for the peaks that poked through the thin fabric so alluringly. He'd reach down to pull off her shorts and use his fingers to explore that intriguing cleft between her thighs and finger her gently until she was panting and as aroused as he was.

He'd use his mouth on her--all parts of her. Her lips were so sweet. What would other portions of her anatomy taste like? All those educational holo-vids he'd viewed when preparing for marriage came back to haunt him. Many of them had left little to the imagination. His imagination was working overtime on what it would be like to make love to Mea.

There was a lot you could do with a woman during sex.

Kavath broke into a sweat, his body overheating at the thought of all he'd do with her if she was his woman. And he could after all--he was attached to her. If she were Gaian...

It was pitch black in their shelter, the planet's moons hidden by the storm clouds above. The darkness around him reminded him of the unlit rooms a couple used during the attachment ceremonies. When a man attached to a woman and she accepted him, they would lie together in a room without any light and explore each other's body without sight. It was said that the eyes could fool, but the rest of your senses never did.

During the one marriage meet he'd been to, he'd been shown the dark rooms but hadn't gotten the opportunity to use one. The marriage meet hadn't gone well for him. He'd attached to a woman, but so had another man and she'd chosen him and not Kavath. He'd left the meet after her rejection, still in pain from the aftermath of attachment, knowing that he'd never see that woman again and if he did, she'd be wearing a wedding band and belong to someone else.

In fact, he knew he'd probably never even know what she looked like.

At least he knew what Mea looked like, every pink-underwear-clad inch of her. And he liked what he'd seen of her a lot. Maybe more than a lot.

If he tried he could imagine the pair of them were in a dark room right now and this was part of their marriage meet. He could imagine that he'd attached to her in the appropriate way, wearing robes and masks, and that he didn't know her face or name.

He could imagine that she was destined to be his wife. His mate, the one woman he could live a long happy life with.

Someone to love, to make love to, and to have his children. *His sweetheart, his lover … his wife.*

Kavath shook his head, took several deep breaths and tried to relax. Mea wasn't his wife, nor could she ever be. She lay in his arms because she needed his warmth, not because she wanted him, and he shouldn't want her.

What made it worse was that he knew he needed to break the bond with her, or he might not be able to attach to anyone else. If that happened he'd be alone forever. No family, no children. No wife. No love.

A blast of wind shook the barrier she'd helped him build, but as Kavath leaned up to check on it, it held firm. He put his head back down and pulled the blanket up to cover her shoulders. They were safe for now, warm and dry and likely to stay that way for the rest of the night.

Mea whimpered in her sleep. She had bad dreams, this little Earth woman. He wondered what disturbed her slumber and he whispered reassurances into the back of her neck until she quieted.

As he continued to hold her he finally began to feel sleepy himself. Closing his eyes, Kavath let himself drift off, her head a warm weight on his arm. He pulled her closer into him, her body's soft warmth sighing gently against him.

He knew she was his enemy … but in spite of everything he had to admit he wished she wasn't.

Chapter Five

Light woke Mea, a faint filtered light still bright enough to bring her to full wakefulness. For a moment her location confused her. She knew she was under the ship, covered by her sleep sack, and lying on top of a pile of scratchy leaves that kept her off the cold ground.

She turned to face the hard body behind her and caught her breath at the sight of pale finger length hair and a chiseled cheekbone and jaw. The rest of the night fell into place for her.

The Gaian. Kavath. She'd slept with Kavath last night to share body heat. She had to admit, he'd been right about that, sleeping together had kept them both comfortable the entire night. She was comfortably warm and even her undershirt and shorts seemed to be dry. She reached over to touch the shirt stretched tight across his chest. That had dried as well, the fabric silky soft under her fingers.

Mea couldn't resist stroking it further. Nice fabric for soldier wear. The Gaians treated their men well. She'd balked at wearing the scratchy undergarments that Earthforce had provided, instead surreptitiously acquiring her own, accepting without argument the demerits her minor act of defiance had generated.

If they wanted her to wear regulation undergarments, she'd told them, they could stop making them out of sandpaper. It was bad enough every piece of clothing was the same drab shade of grey, she wouldn't wear scratchy grey underpants as well.

By contrast the Gaian's undershirt was very nice. She wouldn't have put up any kind of fuss over wearing something made of fabric like that. Curious, she pulled the blanket back a little, noting the way the white material clung to his body. She liked how solid his chest muscles felt under the shirt. Without thinking she explored his torso, letting her fingers trace the curves and ridges across his stomach. Under her hand he felt like warm stone, inviting further exploration.

Around his neck Kavath wore an unusual pendant. It looked like a mesh strap wound tightly into a narrow tube strung on a chain. She let her fingers rest on it for a moment, turning it to see that one side was flat and held an engraving, a set of three angular thin stripes. Immediately she thought of the matching green stripes on the tail of his ship and wondered what significance the band had and why Kavath wore it around his neck.

Lifting her head off his shoulder, she continued to explore his sleeping body until she reached the waistband of his shorts. A significant and familiar bulge rested just below her fingers.

Mea smiled to herself. One thing about men didn't change. Apparently even a Gaian woke with a hard-on. She couldn't resist touching it and it jerked under her hand.

Her dream from the night before and how she'd moaned as his dream-figure had played with her body returned to her. It had been a long time since she'd bunked with a man and her body was primed for action.

Kavath might be a member of enemy forces, but she was attracted to him. He was the first man to appeal to her that way in months.

She studied his sleeping features, the set of his strong jaw. He'd probably had his beard treated to not grow, but she could still see a hint of blond shadow under the skin, a shade darker than the hair on his head. Just that hint of facial hair gave a rough cast to his features.

Big, strong, and virile ... what would it be like to bunk with a man like this? She had to admit, the Gaian turned her on in ways she hadn't felt in a long time. Besides, he'd been so considerate last night. The memory returned of how he'd thrown himself between her and the branches that would have hit her, as well as the sound he'd made when they'd hit his back. He'd put himself into harm's way to keep her from injury and that was after she'd kicked him in the head.

Kavath had been kind and had taken care of her and hadn't asked anything in return. Maybe she didn't know him that well, but what would be the harm in returning the

favor? She reached to stroke his erection again and was
rewarded by his low moan.

* * * *

*Kavath dreamed. His woman lay with him and she had
her hand on him, touching his cock and making it ache--but
in a good way. It got heavier and thicker with each stroke
of her soft hand, and all he wanted was for her to keep
doing what she was doing. Each caress increased the
pressure in him.*

*His woman, his little lehen. It was good, so good that he
could barely stand it. He moaned his pleasure as she
played with him.*

*He wanted more. Wanted to touch her in return, wanted
to hold her, keep her safe and give her pleasure. This was
so new. He'd heard Earth men dreamed of sex this way, but
Gaians didn't--not before they married and held the woman
they attached to in their arms. Only after attachment was it
possible to feel desire.*

*He wasn't married, nor was the woman he held his wife.
He still wore the band he'd intended to give his woman
around his neck.*

*But still he burned with desire and wanted to pleasure the
woman he held and experience her pleasuring touch.*

*She stoked him again and again, and his erection leapt
into her hand, weeping its joy. In him he felt completion
coming, the need for joining.*

*It became too much. Kavath turned to the woman in his
dream, turned to realize that his dream wasn't really a
dream....*

* * * *

Kavath jerked and his hand grabbed hers in a viselike
grip, pulling it away from his still erect cock. Startled Mea
looked up to see his green eyes glaring in fury at her.

"What are you doing?" he demanded.

"N-n-nothing," she tried to say, but he pulled her hands
up over her head and rolled on top of her, using his body to
crush her into the leaves that formed their mattress. Too
surprised to fight him, Mea stared up at him.

He glared down at her. "What did we say about a truce?
That we wouldn't attack each other? Is this how you keep
your promises?"

Mea shook her head in confusion. "I wasn't attacking you. I wasn't doing anything like that." She felt her cheeks turn to flame. "I was just being friendly. By touching you. You know. Touching you *there.*"

She emphasized the word but Kavath continued to glare at her. Finally in frustration Mea blurted out, "You do understand what it means when a woman is friendly with a man."

"Friendly?" Kavath startled and now his face seemed to be aflame with embarrassment. His eyes widened as he realized the position they were in. With his body on top of hers, his still erect cock was poised right between her legs. "Oh, I see. That kind of friendly."

He made a move to get off of her, but Mea trapped his legs by wrapping hers around them. "Where are you going? You have me under your control. You can do anything you want to me," she said, trying for her most seductive voice.

Her ploy didn't work, at least not as far as seducing Kavath was concerned. He blushed harder and seemed to swallow hard. "I have *you* under *my* control?" He laughed but the sound was forced. "That's not how I see things."

"Who says anyone needs to be in control? It's just the two of us here, Kavath. No one to judge us or tell us what to do. Or not to do. I want you … I know you want me." She rubbed his erection with her crotch, suppressing her whimper at how good it felt.

She grinned. "Don't worry … the big bad Earth woman won't eat you--unless you want her to."

Kavath's breath was coming hard and fast. He closed his eyes for a moment and when he opened, raw emotion was in his face, partially desire, but something else as well. Something that made her uneasy.

He leaned closer, his breath hot in her face. "This is what you want? You want me to have sex with you?" He rubbed himself against her for emphasis. It felt too good and this time Mea couldn't help a little moan.

"What would you give me in exchange, Earth woman? If I give you sex, what will you give me?"

This was the oddest conversation she'd ever had before bunking. "What are you talking about? Why do I have to give you anything? We both want to have sex." She stared at him in suspicion. "Is this about the communit parts?"

"No it isn't." Kavath took a deep breath. "Yes, we want each other. I want you. But I can't unless...."

He stared down at her, his face cautious but resolute. "Are you willing to be my wife?"

Mea's jaw dropped. This was *definitely* the oddest conversation she'd ever had with a man she wanted to bunk with. "What are you talking about?"

His green gaze bored into her. "Marriage, I'm talking about marriage, Mea. A man and a wife, bound together for life. Even on Earth I've heard that people marry at least some of the time." He took a deep breath. "That's the price of your suggestion. Are you willing to be my wife? Willing to commit to me forever?"

In her stunned silence his words seemed to come faster. "You and I are matched ... I attached to you so I can mate with you. But you must understand if we do this--" He broke off apparently searching for words. "You must understand, Mea. Gaians mate for life. The woman I make love to and I will be together for the rest of our lives. She'll be my wife, the mother of my children. Can you make a commitment like that?"

Mea looked for some sign he wasn't serious. He honestly expected her to marry him just because she wanted to bunk? Her parents hadn't even been married. She knew Gaian culture was different, but even so, the last thing she expected was a marriage proposal when all she wanted....

She stared into his green eyes. What did she want?

His stare didn't stop. "Yes or no, Mea. Are you willing to be my wife?"

She blurted out the first words that came to mind. "No. I can't...."

Kavath stared at her a while longer, then closed his eyes. He shuddered, his breathing slowed, and the hardness between her legs grew less noticeable. Releasing her hands he rolled off her, then crawled from their makeshift bed to where his clothes were spread out.

Mea watched him dress in silence. He did it quickly, keeping his back to her. She sat up and pulled her open sleep sack around her, trying to make up for the sudden chill of his departure.

When he'd finished dressing, Kavath moved to the higher end of the ship and stood there, a dark mass blocking the light. She thought he looked tense but his voice was matter of fact, almost conversational.

"I know you don't really understand, so I'll try and explain. It's like this for Gaian men, Mea. We don't react to a woman unless she's a match and that happens through our sense of smell. A woman gives off chemicals called pheromones that arouse us … but only a specific woman's pheromones will work for each man."

He breathed deeply of the air coming from the clearing, and Mea realized he was upwind of her and couldn't catch her scent any longer.

"That's why I wore a mask last night. You happen to be my match."

His match? "So we could...." she started to say.

"Yes, we could. But then it becomes permanent. My wife … she'll be the only one I will want, ever. Until I find her, I can't...."

Kavath's voice broke off and he turned to face her. "I can't simply take a lover the way you can."

Mea stung under his words. "I've not had that many lovers...."

He held up his hand. "I'm sure by your standards you haven't. But for me sex means marriage, and you aren't ready to commit to that. You don't want to be my wife and that makes this impossible."

He shook his head. "You are my match and whenever we get too close I attach to you. You reject me, and I detach, but I don't know how many times we can do that before something goes wrong. I could be left unable to ever take a wife, and I can't let that happen."

Kavath raised his hand and Mea saw that he held his stunner again. He must have taken it from her jacket pocket when picking up his clothes. "This will give you a terrible headache, but I will shoot you if you fight me any longer on this. I want the parts for my communit and I want them now."

Somehow Mea couldn't tell him no again. She pointed to the forward landing strut a few centimeters from his feet. "I buried them there, just to the left."

With the ground loosened from the rain it only took him a few moments to unearth the waterproof bag. Kavath removed his parts and tossed the bag to her. She caught it awkwardly.

"Go ahead and put yours back in, too. I won't interfere with your signal--you don't interfere with mine. One side or the other will rescue us. I can avoid your people if they come for you. I can melt into the jungle for a long time. If mine come first, then you'll probably end up in an internment camp, but I promise it will be better than here."

He started to leave, but stopped when she spoke. "Kavath...." Mea began. With a frown, he turned back to her. She hesitated then finished. "I just wanted to say ... thank you."

His frown deepened. "For what?"

She gestured around the shelter they'd shared. "For taking care of me last night. For protecting me and making sure I didn't come to harm. I'm not sure what I would have done without you. You could have ... well, it could have been different."

She felt his hard stare. "Gaians keep their promises," Kavath said.

Without another word he collected his mask off the ground where it had landed during their fight, and then he was gone, from under the ship and the clearing.

For some time Mea sat under the blanket they had shared, trying to put her mind in order. He'd asked her to be his wife as the price of making love. Imagine that.

Of course it was impossible. She doubted she could be the wife of a Gaian pilot and still fly for Earthforce, and she was pretty sure that would invalidate the deal she'd made with Earthforce that had gotten her out of prison.

Even so, she pulled the sleep sack closer around her and breathed deeply of his smell that still clung to the fabric, woodsy, warm, and male.

What would have happened if she had said yes?

* * * *

Back at his ship, Kavath plugged in the communit parts and re-activated the system. For a moment there was static, then quiet, and he tensed in the cockpit, waiting for the unit to connect.

Between the storm and Mea stealing the parts, his communit had been down for a long time. Would anyone still be looking for him? Gaians didn't leave a man unless they knew he was dead, but they had no reason to believe him alive at this point. Before he'd left the battle scene, he'd sent a quick message to say he was in pursuit of a runaway Earthforce vessel. When he hadn't returned to his ship, what were they most likely to think? That he'd been destroyed by the enemy, or would they have picked up his earlier transmissions and realize he was somewhere on the planet?

With an Earthforce destroyer to transport and plant, they wouldn't be able to hang around and look for him. Securing their prisoners would be the paramount concern--his whereabouts and safety secondary considerations.

The static picked up again, but then he heard a pattern in it that he recognized. Kavath pulled a small electronic tablet out of a secret storage compartment in his cockpit and used it to decode the message.

It was an automated message from a small emergency-jump beacon left in space high over the planet. His people had traced him that far, but they'd been unable to locate him further. They'd left the beacon for him to use to get back to them and as a placeholder to start looking for him when they returned.

When they returned. Which wouldn't be for far more than a few days. The message hadn't given details, but clearly the ship was being forced to move out of the area and it would be several weeks or possibly even longer before it returned.

Kavath sat back in the cockpit of his fighter. His ship had sustained serious damage in his fight with Mea, and while he'd managed a controlled landing he wouldn't be able to take off again until he'd repaired it. That was assuming he could repair it. It wasn't like the planet came equipped with a fully stocked repair bay.

Even then he'd lost too much fuel to do more than achieve orbit. He couldn't even reach the emergency beacon they'd left. It held a limited-use jump device he could operate to send him to his people, but he needed to be there to activate it.

Mea's ship seemed undamaged, and he bet she had enough fuel to go some distance. But her people had lost this last battle and were out of commission for the rest of the war. As far as he knew, no one would be looking for her.

He couldn't go anywhere and she had no place to go. They could go no place together ... neither of their ships could take more than one person.

With a heavy sigh, Kavath considered his options. Apparently he and Mea were abandoned here and they would have to make the best of things on the planet's surface until one side or the other found them.

He knew he could survive here indefinitely. What she could do remained to be seen. Sure, she'd turned out to be more of a survivor than he'd expected, but even so she seemed to lack the basic knowledge that would make life on this planet even remotely possible. She didn't have fire and other than the food she'd stolen from him, she was eating emergency rations.

She needed to learn how to find food and how to prepare it. From what he'd seen the only weapon she had was a knife.

With a sigh Kavath remembered the Gaian rules of engagement. One--do not use deadly force unless completely necessary. Two--treat the enemy as if he were your brother--or sister, he amended in the case of Mea.

Three--take care of prisoners and see to it they come to no harm.

Mea wouldn't agree to be his prisoner, but he couldn't stand by and see her come to harm. He felt something towards her he'd never felt for anyone outside his family.

He had to admit she had him baffled. She could be so combative, like when she'd kicked him in the head last night, but then she'd given him some of her scant supply of medicine to ease his pain. Later she'd been unable to leave him in the rain.

Then there was this morning. She'd been so sweet in his arms, and he'd come so close this morning to making love to her ... not something he'd ever expected to happen. In fact, if she'd said yes....

Kavath closed his eyes for a moment remembering how she'd felt in his arms. He'd been consumed by wanting her, enough to ask her to marry him, and even hope for her agreement. If she'd said yes he'd have made her his wife no matter what the consequences would have been.

Most likely he'd have had to leave the Gaian military--
very certainly his family would have been hurt and angry.
Everything he cared about would have been in jeopardy.

Fortunately she had told him no, and again he'd detached.
He should be happy that his suspicion about her
unwillingness to be a wife had proven to be true. She
wasn't at all what he wanted.

Even so there was part of him that wasn't at all happy she
had said no.

Kavath shook his head. This wasn't solving his current
problem. It didn't matter that she was someone he didn't
want to attach to and yet was his match. It didn't matter
that part of him wanted her and couldn't have her. It didn't
matter that while she professed to want to make love with
him, she couldn't commit to marriage.

None of that mattered, because he was Gaian and Gaians
had rules they lived by. She was as abandoned here as he
was. She needed protection. She needed help to survive.

Since she wasn't his wife, he couldn't take her to live
with him, but that didn't make him any less responsible for
her. She needed to be taught how to find food in this jungle
and how to prepare it.

If nothing else, she needed someone to teach her how to
make a fire and whether or not he was the best man for the
job, he was the Gaian to do it. Not because it was his duty,
or because she was someone he cared about.

He had to do it because there was no one else.

Leaving his beacon on, Kavath climbed from the cockpit
and examined the storm damaged remains of his camp.
He'd better get to work repairing things and then come up
with a plan to help Mea … and himself.

Chapter Six

Later that morning when Mea returned from a brief and unsuccessful trip into the jungle to hunt for food, she found a note pinned by a sharpened twig to the ground outside her shelter. It was a politely worded invitation to lunch that afternoon.

Mea read it twice. Kavath had made it clear he wanted to stay clear of her. Why invite her to dine with him? It made very little sense.

However, since purloining part of Kavath's dinner last night, she'd had almost nothing but emergency rations to eat and those were growing very tiresome, not to mention that their number was limited.

She'd tried some of the fruit on the trees near her camp, ones the scanner had said wouldn't poison her, but they were so bitter she'd spat them out. Kavath promised to feed her, so if she took him up on his invitation at the very least she'd get a good meal from the trip.

Even so, it was with severe misgivings that Mea followed the Gaian's trail back to his camp.

Instead of coals, a small fire crackled cheerfully in the clearing. Kavath sat beside it, carefully turning a pair of small brown carcasses on a spit over the flames. She hadn't been able to identify the meat last night, but from the size and shape of the plump bodies now cooking, Mea realized he must have caught some of the bird-like creatures she'd spotted fluttering through the trees.

Apprehensive of her welcome, Mea watched for a moment, waiting in the shadows. She'd hope to avoid his notice, but some movement must have given her away.

Kavath stood and held up his hand. "Just stay over there until I get my mask on."

Mea eased into the clearing, hands open and empty. "Don't worry, I'm not going to get close to you."

His lips twisted in a sardonic smile, even as he placed the clear plastic mask over his mouth. "I just wanted to remind you."

A respirator was normally used to create a breathable atmosphere where there wasn't one, or it could be used to filter out impurities such as noxious smells. Like hers apparently were for him.

She pointed to the mask. "You planning to wear that from now on?"

"Only when I'm around you." His voice was tinny through the mask.

Mea shrugged away an unexpected dismay. She'd enjoyed his dark, deep voice. "It's probably a good idea. You going mad with desire for me every ten minutes was getting a bit old."

His answer was a disgruntled grunt. "Attachment isn't a joking matter. If I can't smell you, it won't happen."

Now that he was wearing the mask, she came forward and took a seat near the fire. The day wasn't chilly, but still she held her hands near the fire and its friendly heat. "How could I forget? You made it abundantly clear the last time we were together how little you wanted to have to do with me."

"Mea...." His voice broke off, muffled through the mask. "I'm sorry if I offended you. You probably aren't used to being rejected."

She shook her head. "You might be surprised. I didn't get around all that often."

"You didn't?" Oddly enough he almost sounded pleased.

She shook her head again. "I'm not here to discuss my sex life with you. I'm not Gaian and I'm not about to become your wife. Enough said. So why did you invite me here?"

"There is more to life than sex and marriage. We need to discuss how we're going to survive together on this planet. We can't ignore each other."

"Oh, I don't know. I could ignore you if I tried."

"Perhaps … but I can't ignore you. I'm responsible for your well-being, and I need to be certain you're okay."

She stood and wiped her hands on her dark grey pants. "I'll be fine, Kavath. You needn't worry about me."

"You know how to make a fire?"

She stopped at the simple question. She'd planned on trying to build one, but hadn't gotten around to it--yet. Okay, she was afraid to try.

"No, I don't know how to make a fire," she admitted softly.

"So, I'll show you how to do it. That way you won't burn yourself."

That pricked her pride. "I wouldn't...."

"Everyone burns themselves once in a while, Mea. Fire is something you have to be careful of and that's why I want to show you how to do it right."

He took a large flat leaf from a pile sitting on a rock next to his fire-pit and used it to pull one of the small bird carcasses off the spit. The meat smelled wonderful and Mea's mouth watered.

Kavath carried it to her, holding it out as if an offering. "Sit down and eat, Mea. We'll begin fire making lessons after lunch."

Was there something warm in the look of his eyes? Did he actually care about her? "Why are you doing this?"

"Because I want to." Over the mask his eyes seemed to laugh. "Perhaps I just want to be sure of your company for a while, even if it isn't in bed. It's a small planet and it's good not to be the only one here."

Thinking that over, she took the leaf from his hands and sat down. Once she got a good whiff of the meat all her resistance to taking his help dissipated. The smell was too intoxicating. Pulling off one of the small leg bones, she nibbled it gently. It tasted even better than it smelled, very much like chicken, but with a hint of something wilder in its make-up.

Juices dripped down her chin and she smiled at him. "It's delicious. Thank you." It was an awkward way to begin, but then the whole business was pretty awkward. She didn't want to be dependent on Kavath.

On the far side of the fire he removed his mask. "It could use salt. The sea is that way...." He pointed to where she remembered the shoreline had been when she landed. "If it's salty maybe we can get some."

"It is," she said around another mouthful of meat. "Salty that is."

Kavath stopped eating and stared at her. "How do you know?"

"My ship's scanners. When I flew in I did a scan of the area and recorded as much detail as I could. Animal, plants, and the local minerals."

He smiled and looked like he might applaud. "Smart! I had my hands full just getting my ship on the ground in one piece." A speculative look crossed his face and he pointed between them. "I wonder if we could trade information. You show me what you have in your computer about the area, and I'll show you how to make use of it."

That made it sound less like he was doing her a favor, but that they were trading information, and it made the whole business of taking his help more palatable. "I like that plan."

He nodded and put another piece of meat into his mouth.

"How did you catch the bird?" she asked. "With your stunner?"

"A stunner!" He looked incensed. "Using a stunner to catch a bird isn't at all sporting."

Mea chuckled of the notion of sportsmanship while collecting dinner. She certainly wouldn't let that concern stop her from eating. "What did you use?"

"A snare, of course. Only way to do it." He licked his fingers appreciatively. "I used to go camping with my school mates. We'd live off the land while we were out in the bush." A happy smile flitted across his face. "Some of Gaia's forests are a little like this."

Great. Stranded on a deserted planet with Kavath, Lord of the Jungle. She remembered an old holo-vid from the classical entertainment channel and mentally replaced the hero of the piece with Kavath. *Wonder if he knows how to swing from a vine?*

Mea eyed the size of his arms, bare since he'd stripped to his sleeveless undershirt. He was probably strong enough to hang onto a vine and swing through the forest. He looked like he could bench-press a small tree, or maybe a not so small one.

She also remembered how those arms had felt holding her close.

His eyes were nice, too. Not too big or small, and the nicest shade of green. A restful color.

His suddenly non-restful eyes stared at her. "What are you looking at?"

She returned her focus to her meal. "Nothing."

They settled into an uneasy silence. With what she hoped was a nonchalant gesture she indicated the ship. "I assume you repaired your communit."

"I did. But it was too late. My people are gone for now."

Mea tried to ignore the sudden guilt she felt. "I'm sorry. I didn't mean to maroon you here."

He stopped chewing and stared at her. "They'll return, but it could be some time before they do."

"Yes. Some time."

Kavath leaned forward. "Mea, I don't want to fight you any more. Last night we had a truce and I think it would be best for both of us to continue that. The war is over for us, at least for the moment. I see no point in harming you and would rather not have you trying to hurt me."

She could still see the darkened bruise on his forehead. So far he'd taken the brunt of their battles. "I get your point. So what do we do?"

"To start, we stop fighting each other. Stay out of each other's camps and particularly our ships unless invited. All right?"

It made sense. Sure, one of them could get the drop on the other, but what good would it do? She wasn't about to kill him, and he wasn't going to kill her. They were equally vulnerable to sabotage. If their emergency signals were disabled again, it could strand both of them forever. Behind her something slithered through the brush and she edged closer to the fire. She did not want to be here forever.

"A truce. Okay, we have a truce." She nibbled more of her meat. "What happens when one of us gets picked up? My people may not honor any agreement I make."

"When that time comes, we'll deal with it. I expect I can elude any Earthforce soldiers sent after me on the ground." His chest puffed out a little in what she suspected was pride. "This is my kind of place. And if it's my people...." He glanced over at her and chuckled knowingly. "I suspect that by the time my people come, you'll be more than happy to go with us, even as a prisoner. Somehow I don't see you lasting out here by yourself."

She frowned and took her last bite. Arrogant man! She could last here as long as he could, and longer if his people came for him.

Not that she really wanted that situation. She didn't like the idea of being left alone. There was another slither from the bushes, and she moved closer to the fire, only stopping when she realized Kavath didn't have his mask on. She didn't want to cause him any more trouble. They'd have to be more careful from now on.

* * * *

"And that's why you need a stone fire-pit, to keep from burning the forest down." Kavath finished his lecture, wishing that his pupil was paying better attention. Instead of staying focused she kept looking at him in a way he found distinctly uncomfortable.

Probably she was still thinking about this morning and how they'd nearly made love. He had to admit it had crossed his mind more than once or twice. Part of him wanted to leave so he could get her off his mind, but he fully intended to stay around until he knew she had a proper education in fire-maintenance.

After they'd finished lunch he'd brought her back to her camp and helped her to select and clear a space for her fire-pit, digging down well past the leaves littering the forest floor for safety. They'd collected dry rocks from the nearby streambed to edge the pit. For some reason Mea had enjoyed this part the most, carefully selecting stones of different colors and widths then making a pattern out of them along the edge and floor of her pit.

A waste of time Kavath had thought until he realized her careful selection of stones had given her a stone pit with a floor more even than his. Besides, her concentration on the stones had taken some of her attention off him.

Of course, it would be wonderful if he could stay focused himself. Somehow his gaze seemed to keep wandering over to her lips.

It was ridiculous. He was detached from her. He didn't want her anymore. She wasn't the right woman for him, nor did she really want him, at least not permanently.

So why did he still want her? Or at least want to want her? It made no sense.

Ruthlessly he forced himself back to his lesson. "You will need tinder and small dry bits of twigs and leaves to start the fire. Go find some and bring it back here. I'll get some larger wood."

Mea moved into the brush and returned as quickly as she could, carrying a large handful of leaves and twigs. She piled it beside her new fire-pit. Kavath dumped his finds next to them.

"Make a small pile in the middle of the pit," he instructed. "Then use your torch to make it flame."

Tentatively, Mea pushed the button on the slender wand, which produced a small flame. The fire-starter had been in her emergency kit, but apparently she hadn't had the nerve to use it until now. Directing the flame at the dried leaves, she gasped as they blazed up.

"I made a fire!" she said with obvious delight and it was all Kavath could do not to laugh. It burned quickly, consuming the available materials and began to dwindle.

"You need to add more...." he started to say, but she anticipated him by grabbing a large chuck of wood and dropping it on top of her dying flames. Robbed of oxygen the fire immediately died, leaving nothing but smoldering ashes.

Mea looked so disappointed he wondered if she was going to burst into tears, which was all that kept him from laughing out loud. "What did I do wrong?"

Holding onto his merriment, Kavath lectured her instead. "A fire needs three things to live--fuel, heat, and air. By dropping too much fuel on it, you eliminated the air and smothered it. Try it again, only this time only add small stuff and blow on it until you get it going."

Mea again built a small stack of twigs and used the starter to set it aflame. Then she carefully followed his instructions.

Minutes later she had a bright little fire and a smile even brighter. Such a simple accomplishment, but apparently something she'd never done before. Kavath grinned at her pleasure.

She held her hands out to the flames to enjoy the heat, but he grabbed her when they strayed too close.

"Careful, Mea. You don't want to get burned." Some of her brightness dimmed. "Burns will happen, such as when a piece of wood sparks, or if you forget and pick up something without realizing it is hot. If that happens, put cold water on it."

"Cold water," she repeated. "Like from the stream?"

"That will work." He patted her shoulder. "The best thing is to avoid getting burned in the first place."

"I'll remember. Thank you."

He gave her a curious glance. "Why is it you've never built a fire before? Is there no wood on Earth at all?"

"I don't think Earth people build many fires these days. Not much wood left to burn."

Kavath couldn't resist teasing her a little. "Earth people? Aren't you an Earth person?"

"I wasn't raised there...." she started to say, but suddenly Mea clamped shut her mouth.

Mea wasn't from Earth? "Where were you raised, then?"

Her eyes flashed at him. "It doesn't matter where I come from. I'm with Earthforce now and one of their pilots. One of their best.". She looked back at the flames in her little fire-pit and her smile turned genuine. "And now I know how to build a fire."

Kavath knew he'd get nothing more from her now. He stood up. "It's time to check my snares. With any luck I'll be back later with some meat, and I'll show you how to cook it."

"I've cooked before."

He grinned at her tone. Mea didn't like being told that she didn't know how to do something. "I didn't say you hadn't, but I doubt that you've prepared anything over an open fire before."

She didn't say anything, but he could see her stubborn streak firing. Time to head back to his camp. "Let the fire die down for now. We can always start it again later on."

* * * *

After Kavath left, Mea sat next to her fire feeling tired, dirty, and beyond irritable. *The arrogant bastard, how dare he grin at her that way?* So she hadn't spent her childhood coping with the wilderness, she bet he'd be pretty surprised at the kinds of things she had done. There were plenty of ways she could make herself useful, and if she had to use every trick she knew, she'd prove it to him.

First of all she needed to be able to find edible food even if it wasn't meat. She didn't have a stunner and most of the animals moved too fast for her knife. She could use her ASP to determine what parts of the vegetation was edible but unfortunately everything she'd tried so far had been too bitter.

A chirp sounded and she looked around to see a tiny bird flit past her to a bush loaded with clusters of berries. She'd tried them earlier and found them inedible. The creature landed on a branch and picked greedily at several berries of the cluster. But the bird didn't eat the bright red berries she'd tried, but the dull looking yellow ones instead. Curious, Mea walked over, scaring the small creature away and tried the yellow fruit. It was sweet and juicy and as she ate several more, she smiled.

So, that was the secret. The birds knew which fruit to eat and all she had to do was watch them and do the same. She'd use the scanner on a plant to verify what her body would tolerate then see what parts of it the animals ate. Maybe by the time Kavath returned she'd have something to add to their diet.

The decision perked her up. Cheerfully she climbed into the cockpit, and fetched the scanner from its spot in the console. While at the top of the ladder, she took the opportunity to study her camp. Kavath's had been bigger, the vegetation cleared away to open it up and make it more difficult for the local wildlife to invade. He'd created areas for cooking, for sleeping, and a fire-pit to sit around.

She had her own fire-pit now, but her tent was still a soggy mess, sitting under the tree that had dumped gallons of water on it during the storm last night. She should move it to a more secure location, possibly under the high end of the ship where it would be protected. She could even move the improvised windbreak Kavath and she'd created during the storm to shelter the unprotected side.

Mea started making mental notes of things to do. It was time to make the place presentable. After all, she had a neighbor to impress.

Chapter Seven

By late afternoon several bright orange and yellow pieces of fruit sat on Mea's makeshift cutting block--a hunk of dead tree turned on its side and scraped smooth with a rock. She used her knife to take a slice from one, ran the scanner over it and took an experimental nibble.

Juice dribbled down her chin and she smiled. Not bad. A little messy, but flavorful and sweet. Overall, rather tasty.

Nearby was a larger gray-green orb with big bumps and a flaky skin that she'd noticed a lizard-like creature nibbling. The lizard had run off when she'd tried to catch it, so she'd grabbed its dinner instead.

She cut a large slice from the side and removed it to sizzle on a thin piece of metal supported by rocks over her fire. It had taken her over an hour to create her stove top, using a steel panel unbolted from inside the storage area of her ship and building up rock walls even enough to keep it flat over the flames.

Remembering Kavath's instructions had made it easy to rebuild her fire, but she'd nearly melted the metal panel before realizing she needed to keep the fire small and burn the wood down to coals before putting it into place.

The result was worth it. On the metal she could cook without losing any drippings into the flames and the smell of the cooking "potato ball" as she'd dubbed the starchy vegetable made her mouth water. She used a forked stick to pull it from the rack and onto a leaf, letting it cool before taking a bite. Yummy. It even tasted like potato, with a hint of onion in the mix. Mea grinned in anticipation. Wouldn't Kavath be surprised when he tasted it?

She still didn't have her own protein source, but the rest of her diet was coming along. A bottle of water sat near the fire, now crystal-clear. After she'd finished drinking the delicious rainwater, she'd decided to improve the taste of what she could get from the stream.

The purifying tablets made the water safe, but running it through a tube filled with sand removed the impurities that gave it the red tinge and improved the flavor a hundred fold. The tube had come from an unneeded part of the ship's life support system. It had been attached to a set of now empty gas canisters, the latter she was eyeing for possible reworking into a set of pots.

She needed something to use for boiling water and cooking food she couldn't prepare on a metal plate. Maybe she could make some potato-ball soup.

Busy with improving her culinary skills, she heard Kavath before she saw him. The wheezing sound from his respirator overcame the constant forest noise around her. He entered her camp and for a moment they stared at each other.

She thought he looked glad to see her … she certainly was happy to see him.

He'd been right about one thing. It was just too alone being alone on this planet. Even in the short time he'd been hunting she'd found herself missing his presence.

That was unusual. She'd been something of a loner from the time she was a child and being in Earthforce hadn't changed that. She'd always been content with her own company. Something else was going on between them, and she wasn't sure she understood or even liked it.

He broke the gaze first, glanced around and noted the gathered fruit then eyed her new stove. His mouth grinned behind the mask. "You're settling in."

Pleased, she shrugged. "As you say, we may be here a while."

"Yes. A while." He held out a bag. "Great job on the stove and just in time. I brought you some game to cook. I bet it would be great fried on a grill."

She took the bag. Inside was another of the small birds and an animal resembling the lizard she'd seen. Suppressing her squeamishness over handling a dead animal she pulled it out of the bag to examine it. A narrow hole in the side indicated it hadn't been killed with a snare.

"I was practicing a new technique," Kavath said and held up a small set of sharpened sticks and a bigger, flatter piece of wood with a knob on one end. "It's a spear-thrower, just like primitive men on Earth used. I read about it in a book when I was a kid. It works really well!" Kavath's enthusiasm was infectious and she found herself smiling at him.

Kavath really was lord of the jungle here, using his knowledge to catch food. Good thing he was on her side for once and planned on sharing with her.

She returned her attention to the bag and examined the carcasses with a mounting sense of dismay.

He expected her to make food out of the bodies, covered in feathers and scaly skin? Plants were one thing, animals another. She hadn't the slightest idea what to do with them. She offered the bag back to him. "Maybe you'd better keep these."

Understanding dawned in his eyes. "I bet you never prepared meat for cooking before, have you? That's okay, I can teach you what to do." He pulled the lizard from the bag and a knife from his belt. "Here, I'll show you how to dress them."

Mea watched as he made a deep cut along the belly, exposing what was inside, and suddenly the fruit she'd eaten no longer rested well on her stomach. She dashed for the edge of camp and moments later expelled the last of her late afternoon snack into the privy hole she'd dug.

Wiping her mouth with the back of her hand she turned to find Kavath trying desperately to suppress his laughter.

"The big, bad Earthforce pilot. A little blood and guts too much for you?"

Shakily she reassembled her tattered dignity and grabbed her water bottle to rinse out her mouth. "I bet you did the same thing your first time."

He shook his head and chuckled, but managed to look sympathetic. "Maybe--I would've been about five years old. This is how it is, Mea. Meat comes from animals and we have to kill them to get it. Once they're dead, we have to butcher them. It isn't pretty, or clean. You'll get used to it, I'm sure." He said the last with an irony she wondered about.

She shook her head. "I'm not sure I could. Maybe I could just eat fruit and potato balls."

"Those are good," he admitted. "But they won't be enough to sustain your health for long. You need fats and protein and the best source of those will be from animals."

He thought for a moment. "I tell you what, we'll work out a trade. I hunt and dress the meat, and you supply the rest. Once a day we'll meet to exchange and prepare food." He eyed her stove again with appreciation. "Your setup is better for cooking than mine, so we can do it here. That way we will both get what we need. Deal?" He reached out his un-bloodied hand.

It was a good plan and meant that she'd get to see him every day. She shook his hand and tried to ignore the thrill it gave her. "Deal."

Within a week the food-exchange near noon had become the high point of her day. Kavath would show up with meat already prepared for cooking, and she'd have a selection of accompanying fruits, prepared slices of potato balls, or similar foods.

Setting up her camp was a way to occupy Mea's mind, and her imagination worked overtime to improve their situation. She used a medical cutter from her emergency kit to make wooden plates, bowls and cups, and as she'd planned reworked the empty gas canisters into pots with lids and a pitcher.

Leaves worked for a while as potholders, but then Mea thought about the animal skins that Kavath wasn't using and decided that dried lizard skin would be better. She asked for and got him to bring the skins from the animals he killed. After a little experimentation she found the best way to make primitive leather from them.

Kavath's look of astonishment when he came by for his share of the food each day made her efforts all the more worth while, particularly when she was able to offer him a hot tea made by steeping a caffeine bearing leaf she'd found.

At first he'd simply collect his half of the bounty and disappear back into the forest towards his camp. But after a while the lack of companionship wore on both of them, and he stayed longer every day as they spent their mid-day meal together and sometimes part of the afternoon.

With her permission he set up an area at the far end of her clearing where he could remove his mask and relax. When he had it off, she kept to her side of the camp until he replaced it. He'd eat his meals and work on small projects, as did she, and they'd talk, normally about inconsequential things.

When there was meat left over from their lunch he'd dangle it over her smoldering fire during the afternoon to cure it for storage, some of which he left with her, taking some of her extra fruit in exchange.

Every week there was at least one day where it rained as hard it had that first night and the dried meat came in handy when a storm kept them in their individual camps for the day.

When it rained too heavily for either of them to leave their camps, they spent the day in their tents. Mea often wondered what Kavath was up to and if he missed her company as well.

He never admitted it, but when the next clear day came and they were able to have their daily food exchange, she could see he was also glad that they could sit on opposite sides of Mea's camp, drink tea and share a meal.

They didn't speak much about when they were likely to be rescued. For the moment the war was on hold, and there was no point in talking about it. Nor did they talk about their relationship .

Over time the hostility between them disappeared completely. If Mea had needed to pick a name for their relationship, she would have said they were friends and nothing more. Two weeks passed, then three, and they had settled into a solid routine. Things went on that way for over six weeks without change.

But then there came the day the pink-zinger went bad.

Chapter Eight

Every day Mea went further out into the jungle, using her scanner to test the various plants growing in the area to check them for nutritional value. With Kavath providing the meat for their diet, she concentrated on contributing vegetables and fruits.

Little of the vegetation was poisonous, although she found the taste of many of the fruits too bitter to be edible unless picked at the height of ripeness. She'd learned her lesson about using the local inhabitants to verify when something was ready to eat.

Sometimes she would lie quiet and watch a likely plant to see what parts the animals would eat and then do the same. Most of the time the plan worked well, and only once did she get severe stomach cramps instead.

Day by day she added variety to their diet--leafy vegetables, fruits and berries. But even so, Mea lost weight, shedding the five pounds that had plagued her from the time of her childhood, plus another five over the six weeks. If this kept up she wouldn't be recognizable by the time she returned to Earthforce.

Sometimes she wondered if some of the men who'd ignored her before wouldn't take more notice now that she was slimmer. It was funny how that didn't excite her. One thing about having as good looking a man as Kavath around was that it did make a woman question why she'd been attracted to someone else.

One of Mea's earlier discoveries was a particularly juicy red berry that could be crushed and the juice collected. While the raw fruit had a rather bitter aftertaste, the juice was delicious and an attractive pink color. It seemed to be at the height of the ripening season for the plant, so the berries were plentiful.

The first day Mea tried the juice, she found herself craving more, and Kavath had a similar reaction. They called it pink-zinger. Stored in a gas-canister turned pitcher, it quickly became their favorite drink.

Mea discovered that the longer the juice sat, the tangier it became. One day she made a point of making it right after breakfast, to give it a couple of hours before Kavath showed up.

After cooking and serving lunch, they retired to their separate sides of the fire. From his side of the camp, Kavath savored his first mouthful of pink-zinger and smacked his lips appreciatively. "Oh, this is the best you've ever made."

"I'm glad you like it." She tried her own cup and enjoyed the sparkling effervescence against her tongue. "It's fizzier than normal, isn't it?"

"It is." He took another deep appreciative sip. "Reminds me of something … but I'm not sure what. You make a tasty pink-zinger...." He hesitated. Sometimes he still didn't seem to want to use her name. Finally he finished his comment. "The pink-zinger is excellent, Mea."

Ignoring the hesitation, she nibbled a piece of meat. "You cook a good bird, Kavath."

Falling into an awkward silence, they concentrated on their food for a while without conversation.

When he wasn't with her, she knew Kavath spent his time either hunting or working on his ship, trying to fix the damage it had taken during their battle. The fact that she had caused the damage wasn't brought up by either of them. Their friendship, if that was what they had, seemed to be based more on silence than on talking.

Some things just didn't need to be said. Such as why he needed to wear a mask around her, and why she avoided letting him touch her. They never talked of the time she'd tried to seduce him and he'd asked her to be his wife.

They didn't talk about it, but late at night when he was back in his camp, and she lay in her tent alone, she missed him and wondered if he missed her as well. Not that it made any difference. She was an Earthforce pilot, temporarily grounded, and he was her enemy. Even if he hadn't been she'd have said no to his proposal.

Probably. Several times over the past month she'd wondered what she'd have done if he had been on the same side of the war. Would she have said no so quickly to marriage with him? She had to admit that even then she'd probably have rejected him.

He'd accused her of not being able to make that kind of commitment and she couldn't argue the point. Could she attach herself to another person the way he wanted, committing to a future spent with another person? She had her own plans--becoming an independent pilot and heading to the Outer Colonies to find the rest of her people. Those plans didn't include a husband with his own agenda.

In the past she'd been helpless to govern her fate. She and her brother Jack had been born on an abandoned mining platform that her mother's people had decided to call home, and Mea had learned in her teens what it meant when you were subject to another's will.

When Earth's government had stepped in to support the rights of the lawful owners of the platform, evicting by force the people living there, and her mother and grandfather had been killed. Mea and her brother had been sent to a facility for wayward youths.

The pair of them had spent months in holding cells before finally being given a choice: an Earth based prison or service in Earthforce. The rest of her people were already gone, scattered to the Outer Colonies and all she'd had left was Jack and her skills as a pilot.

She'd been underage at the time but it had been easy to lie about her age when so few records existed to prove when she'd been born. Besides, Earthforce had wanted her bad enough that they didn't care about her age.

Fortunately, Earthforce hadn't turned out to be so bad, but being locked up and given no choice had taught her a lesson. From now on Mea would keep command over her life. She didn't want to lose control of anything, at any time, under any circumstances. Most importantly she didn't want to lose herself in a relationship with a man, not even with Kavath.

Even so, she did enjoy when he visited her and it was still nice to have him around and to watch him eat the food she'd helped prepare. Keeping company with him was probably as close to marriage as she was likely to get, and she savored it while it was there.

Kavath took a big bite of his meat and washed it down with a big gulp of pink-zinger, having refilled his cup once already. Mea couldn't help noticing his rueful look as he took another bite.

"What's wrong?" she asked.

He shook his head. "I know it is silly given how lucky we are to have any food at all. But the meat tastes a little bland today. I wish we had some kind of seasonings and I miss having salt."

She picked at the rest of her meal. He had a point. Maybe she could find some aromatic herbs that would add flavor, but salt would be welcome.

"We've been talking about walking to the ocean. There might be deposits of salt nearby, or we could collect the water and boil it dry. Maybe we could do that tomorrow."

Kavath perked up. "And we could fish and get a little more variety in our diet. Great idea, Mea. Let's make a day of it and have a real adventure." He lifted a long, thin length of wood he'd been tinkering with in his corner of the camp, using his knife and a thin piece of sharpened metal to make it straighter. "I think if I add some wire prongs to it I'd have a real fishing spear."

"You have wire on your ship?" Mea had looked on hers and found little in the way of wire or thread, which had made her look closely at the vines in the trees around them. One of the longer vines had thin internal threads she'd been able to isolate by banging a rock against long segments. It was good, but burned easily. Wire would be better for anything needed to resist fire.

"Some." He hesitated. "There are these internal supports that I could use." He gave her a teasing grin. "Don't worry. I won't destabilize my ship enough so it can't fly."

"I wasn't worried," she said, although she wondered if that was true. She really didn't like the idea of something bad happening to Kavath.

Funny how a month spent in close proximity to a man changed things. She'd nearly killed him once, but now … now she couldn't imagine her time here without him. She couldn't imagine a universe in which Kavath didn't exist.

Confusion filled her over that. It wasn't just that he was handsome or smart. Earthforce was filled with men like that. But Kavath wasn't just those things. Kavath was … special.

Going on an adventure with him sounded wonderful. She had a couple of useful projects that she'd be able to finish up tonight, in time for their trip. It would be fun to get away from the routine of camp and do something special. "So shall we plan a fishing trip tomorrow?"

Kavath nodded, his mood vastly improved. "Good idea. We'll make a day of it. A day at the beach." He mused with a nostalgic air. "My family lived on an island on Gaia and I grew up next to the ocean. It will be like being home again."

Somehow Mea doubted that a foreign ocean on an undeveloped planet would be that much like a developed planet like Gaia. Certainly having her around wouldn't be the same as his family.

"You know, Mea, you haven't told me much about your home."

Home? Where was that? Certainly not Earth. "There isn't much to tell anymore. Except for my brother my family is gone now, and there is nothing left for me back there."

He flashed her a look of sympathy. "No one to go home to? That's sad. I'm sorry about that."

She shrugged. "I'm sorry too."

Kavath stared moodily into his cup and shook his head. "It isn't good to be alone. People need family." With a single swallow, he drained the contents of his cup. Getting up, he moved to the center of the clearing, where the pitcher of pink-zinger waited.

Mea stared at him. *Kavath had forgotten his respirator.* Fortunately the breeze blew the other way so he didn't attach to her, but she watched, ready to jump out of the way if he got closer. He didn't, just refilled his cup and returned to his space without incident. She kept a close eye on him as he took another deep gulp after settling onto his log seat.

Kavath had never been that careless before. She lifted her own cup, tentatively tasted the sweet nectar, felt the slight buzz at the back of her throat. It was almost like a sparkling wine. She grabbed the scanner off her belt and waved it over the drink. It was close to twenty-five percent alcohol and climbing. As she watched the scanner, the last digit clicked over.

Mea groaned aloud and caught Kavath's attention. "You might want to be a little cautious in drinking the pink-zinger. That taste we've been appreciating is alcohol."

"What?" He squinted blearily into the cup for a moment, obviously already feeling the effects. Then realization seemed to hit him. "Oh, no. How bad?"

She did a quick calculation, hampered by the soft haze beginning to spread across her own brain. He'd had two cups in the last hour, one more than she'd had, and probably a good third of this one. "I'd say you've drunk the equivalent of a quarter-liter of blue-gin." The outer-colony brew was highly concentrated, the better for transportation.

Kavath grimaced and carefully laid aside his cup. "I'm going to be very drunk, very soon and probably for some time. I should probably go back to my camp before I can't make it there." He stood and nearly fell. Grabbing a convenient branch, he eased himself back to the ground. "On the other hand, it may be a bit late for that."

Mea tried to stand and discovered she too had issues remaining vertical. Taking two steps, she found herself on the ground again. When she managed to get back to a sitting position, she looked at Kavath and he looked at her.

Without warning Kavath burst into laughter and Mea found herself joining him.

"Well, we're not going to get a lot of work done this afternoon, that's for certain." He leaned back against a rock. "I guess I'll just hang out here until I can walk straight."

Inwardly, Mea groaned. Getting the pair of them drunk and confined to her camp wasn't at all what she wanted. Sure they were just friends, but in the mood she was in the last thing she needed was to be thrown together with Kavath with her inhibitions compromised.

Mea eyed her guest's tall figure and suppressed another groan. Weeks in the sun had colored his space pallor to a warm bronze and put streaks of platinum through his pale hair. He'd removed his outer shirt, leaving him just in his pants and sleeveless white undershirt. Muscles in his bare arms rippled as he folded them behind his head and her normal hypersensitivity to him went into overdrive.

A very small part of her wanted to have another try at seducing him. Sure he had this fixation on getting married, but the man was simply devastating. Warmth filled her and it wasn't just attraction to a good-looking man. Kavath was more than the sum of his oh-so-appealing parts. He was funny, smart, and honestly good-natured. Sure, at times he was arrogant beyond belief, but she'd gotten used to that. Too bad he was Gaian....

Mea shook her head, trying to clear it of unreal aspirations. She had no business thinking of Kavath that way. Damn that pink-zinger for loosening her libido this way!

"I'm sorry, Kavath. I didn't realize it was fermenting. There must be a natural yeast in the air." She glared at her cup. "Really fast-acting yeast. I should dump the rest of it."

"No, don't. Let it finish. I can use a good strong alcohol for cleaning my ship's engine." He tried to sit up and fell back against the rock, laughing. "Who knows, might be useful as rocket fuel, too."

"Rocket fuel?"

"Yeah. I need some. Lost too much. Somebody punched a hole in my ship and I lost most of my reserves," he said, giving her a playful glare. "I doubt I have enough to get into the atmosphere."

It was the first time he'd told her how bad the damage had been. Without fuel he was stranded here, while she could at least get off planet, although she wouldn't make it very far. He'd said his people had left a beacon for him, but now she knew that he couldn't reach it. Unexpected guilt filled her.

A sudden thought occurred to her. Would her fuel canisters fit into his ship, or vice versa? With the similarities of Gaian/Earth technologies they might and maybe they could get at least one ship off the planet and someplace useful.

Kavath glanced over at her ship. "Speaking of ships, what is that, anyway?" He pointed to the symbol she'd painted on the rear of her fighter, an intricate set of interlocking blue-green rings.

At least this was a safer subject. "That? It's an ancient symbol from Earth, handed down by my ancestors. I have a ring with it as well." She didn't mention where else the symbol existed, tattooed onto the back of her shoulder.

"I like it. It suits you." He shook his head. "Boy, I'm dizzy. This takes me back. I haven't been this drunk since...." He thought for a moment then chuckled ruefully. "Well, since my marriage meet."

Sudden confusion filled her. "Marriage? You're married?"

Kavath blinked at her as if astonished she'd even ask the question. "No, of course not. I wouldn't have attached to you if I were." He continued to shake his head, apparently surprised by her ignorance. "I said I went to a marriage meet, not that I married. A meet is where we meet potential wives. It was two years ago, after I graduated from school. It was one of the larger ones. There were two hundred of us, about a hundred women."

He stopped for a moment then gave her a hesitant look. "We don't talk about our marriage customs much."

The pink-zinger had apparently loosened his tongue as well. Curious, Mea leaned forward. "I won't tell anyone if you don't want me to."

He shrugged. "I don't see any harm in telling you. You've already experienced some of it when I attached to you. You might as well know more.

"As you know, a Gaian man doesn't react to just any woman, but only special ones that we can attach to. We seek our mates at what we call a marriage meet. There are a lot of men and women in the same room, giving the best opportunity to find someone compatible. We dress in dark robes and hide our faces behind masks. The women wear white gowns and veils and we can't see their faces, either. The men line a hallway or the edges of a room and the women walk by in single file. When they come close enough, if we attach, we follow the one we're attached to."

Mea shook her head in confusion. This was the most bizarre marriage ceremony she'd ever heard of. "Wearing masks and robes? Why aren't you allowed to see each other?"

"The eyes can fool you. Attachment is at another level, much deeper. When you attach without sight, you attach forever, at least that's what they say."

She couldn't resist the irony of that. "Hmm, so if you hadn't seen me that first time, you wouldn't have known I was an Earth pilot and you might have wanted to stay attached?"

Kavath leaned up on one arm and even from across the fire she caught a pensive look on his face. "Now that you mention it, I suppose that's true." Then he lay back, shaking his head. "No, it is still up to the woman to accept attachment and you would have rejected me. You said you didn't want to be married."

She wasn't as sure about that as she had been. "So what happened at the marriage meet? You didn't attach?"

"No, I did." He took a deep, painful breath, obviously reliving that moment. "But so did another man, to the same woman." With a grimace he sat up and Mea watched in surprise as Kavath's hands turned to fists and his normally calm demeanor fell away, showing his anger.

He was so easygoing most of the time she hadn't realized what strong passions ran through him. She felt a twinge of regret that his passion wasn't for her.

Kavath continued. "It was such a shock, to feel desire for the first time and then jealousy like that. If I'd lost control I would have fought him, but there are always married people about acting as spotters to prevent trouble. They break anything up before it can get started. It isn't like we can hide the way we feel, so they know to watch when two men attach to the same woman. We are told ahead of time to keep in command of ourselves, and the consequences if we don't. If he and I had fought, then one or both of us could be banned from further meets. We might never meet a woman to marry and no one would want that."

Some of his calm returned as Kavath's hands slowly unclenched. "That's why it is left up to the woman. We both touched her, but she reacted more to him than me. She took his hand in hers, chose him, and as they walked off I detached. They went off to learn more of each other. I went off with the rest of the men, the others who'd failed, and got drunk."

"It upset you that much that she chose another man and so you weren't able to marry her?"

He lay back down on the ground and seemed to watch the branches of the tree overhead. "It's more than that, Mea. I don't expect you to understand, but all of Gaian life is centered around two people forming a couple. It's our basic social unit. In some ways you aren't even an adult unless you are married. Unmarried men and women stay secluded, don't leave the planet much, and can't go places alone, because there is always the chance of attaching to someone unsuitable."

His words felt like a slap across her face and she flushed with anger. "Oh, like me?" she asked, her tone dangerously sweet.

Kavath sat up and held up his hands placating. "I didn't mean that. It isn't that you are unsuitable.... I mean you are, being an Earthforce officer, besides not wanting to get married, but otherwise you're a fine woman. More than fine."

He sighed and shook his head. "I like you, Mea, I really do. What I meant was attaching to someone I couldn't marry at all. Like...." he seemed to struggle to come up with an example. "Like suppose you were someone who was already married," he said, his voice triumphant, obviously thinking this would prove his point. "That would make you unsuitable."

Mea thought of all the cheating spouses she'd known. "A man doesn't attach to a married woman?"

"No, her pheromones will be different. They'll be busy ... or something like that. I don't understand all of the chemistry behind it. Once a man attaches and is matched, then he'd never want another woman, not as long as she lives."

For a moment Mea wondered if the fact that she'd avoided bunking for some time had made Kavath susceptible to her. Wouldn't that be funny, that her pickiness had been involved?

"Mea...." Kavath's voice turned thoughtful. "You don't have anyone special in your life?"

Why was he asking that now? "Only my brother, and I haven't seen him in a couple of years."

His eyebrows beetled together. "I'm sorry for that. I miss my family but I know they are there and will be waiting when I get back home, even though it's been close to four years. The marriage meet was the last time I was on Gaia. That night, I volunteered for duty and shipped out the next morning, still hung-over. Didn't even have a chance to tell my family about my decision. When I finally did they were not pleased."

He laughed shortly. "They won't be happy with me when I get back, but at least I know they will accept me."

"What will you do when you get back?"

"Probably go to work in the family business. We own a transport company and send space freighters into the Outer Colonies. That was one reason I wanted to get married. I'd have been able to get my own ship and take my wife with me. We'd have gone into space and traded. Otherwise I'd have been grounded and I love flying. When I failed to marry, joining the Gaian fleet was the only way I was getting into space."

His story had elements similar to hers even though the circumstances were different. It struck a common chord in her that he joined the military so he could fly their small fighter craft. Also he wanted to go to the Outer Colonies, just as she did.

"I wanted to fly, too. I couldn't stand being cooped up or stuck planetside," she told him. Kavath looked at her with such interest that she immediately felt self-conscious. The pink-zinger was definitely loosening her tongue.

Mea found herself wanting to share secrets she'd barely told anyone. "That's what I want to do when I get out of Earthforce. Go to the Outer Colonies and be a pilot there."

Kavath nodded. "Not a bad plan. You'd do well there." He threw a hand around, indicating the clearing. "You're smart, innovative, just the kind of person that should be out here. You're a good pilot, too."

Coming out of nowhere like that, the compliment flustered her. She was proud of all she'd accomplished, but she hadn't realized he'd noticed. Warmth rose in her cheeks. "I wasn't sure you'd thought that highly of my pilot skills."

Kavath laughed ruefully. "Oh, I noticed them all right. I've never seen anyone fly like you. It's funny--we both joined the military to fly," he mused quietly. "Who would have expected that we had so much in common? Probably one of the reasons we get along so well. Lucky that."

Mea's heart skipped a beat. With Kavath she felt an uncertainty she hadn't felt in years. She wasn't an innocent, but around him she felt like tongue-tied schoolgirl. Some of it was his inexperience. He simply didn't treat her like a desirable woman--at least he hadn't since the last time he'd attached to her. Instead he was friendly, pleasant. Good company, most of the time.

"I feel lucky to have you around." The words caught in her throat. She must be even drunker than she thought, to say something like that.

"Lucky how?"

Oh, well. In for a gram, in for a kilo.... "Well, you're so nice. Good company. Good at catching meat. Handsome." Oh, she was drunk, that's for certain. But still, so was he. Ever since he'd kissed her, she'd thought about how nice it would be to kiss him again. And do more than kissing. With both of them so relaxed … even if they couldn't because he wasn't attached to her and she wouldn't marry him … her emotions swirled along with her thoughts, pink-zinger enhanced.

"Handsome!" Kavath leaned up on one elbow, and grinned mischievously at her. "You think I'm handsome?"

She waved one hand at him. "Oh, you know you are. Hasn't anyone ever told you? A guy like you … you'd break every female heart in Earthforce."

Kavath laughed. "My mother always liked the way I looked, even if my sisters teased me about being skinny." He lay back down, stared at the sky. "Maybe if that woman at the meet had seen me, she would've picked me."

He was still mooning over a woman he hadn't even seen? Irritation made her scowl. "You were in love with her? This woman you never even saw?"

He looked at her, confusion on his face. "Love? Not the way you mean it. I wanted her, wanted her to become my wife. I'd have fought to protect her even at the risk of my own life."

"But you would have bunked … that is, you would have had sex with her, even if you didn't love her?"

"Bunked?" Kavath laughed at her choice of words. "That's a funny way to describe it."

Mea's cheeks burned. "It's not that funny. It's what we call having sex in Earthforce."

He chortled. "Bunk. She bunks, he bunked, we are bunking," he said, playfully trying different conjugations of the verb. "Well, you learn something new every day," he said.

His laughter faded and his voice turned wistful. "To answer your question, yes, once she'd accepted my band and given me hers, we'd probably have made love." He gave her a wry glance. "Perhaps I wouldn't be as proficient as one of your Earth men, but I know what to do. They show us instructional videos to help us understand."

Mea thought she saw a glimpse of a blush on his face, but decided not to tease him about it.

"It would be dark and I wouldn't see her face, but I would know her touch and her smell, the taste of her mouth. The next day we'd meet face to face and know each other, as much by those things as by the bands."

"What do you mean by band? Like a ring?"

"No, a wrist band." He held up the strange pendant he wore around his neck and with a quick jerk, unfastened it from its chain and stretched it into a long narrow strip of flexible metal. She saw that the narrow engraved part of it that she'd noticed before was actually towards the middle of the band when unrolled.

He ran his fingers across the thin lines running diagonally across the metal. "This is my mark and my wife would make one with hers. We'd exchange them during the marriage meet. I made this band for the woman I attached to, but since she didn't accept me, I kept it. A bunch of us decided to wear the bands this way, around our neck. That way we won't ever forget why we're out here, what we have to lose if Gaia doesn't win the war...."

His voice trailed off and it seemed like he was going to say more, but decided not to. She watched as he re-rolled the band and fastened it back to the thin chain around his neck.

He turned the pendant around with his fingers and stared at it. "Maybe when we had sex the first time, I wouldn't have been completely in love with my wife, but I would have been eventually. We love our spouses, Mea. Even if our customs seem strange to you, we promise love forever. That's the way it is on Gaia."

Kavath leaned forward and studied her from across the fire. "Why are you so interested in this? Were you ever in love with any of the men you *bunked* with?"

His tone mocked her and she didn't like the emphasis he gave the word. "No, not really. I liked them, at least before we did it."

That seemed to give him pause. "You didn't like them afterwards?"

"I still liked them … but it was different. Awkward."

"Why would it be awkward? The man was able to hold you, touch you." Was that a trace of jealousy in his voice?

"Awkward because he didn't want to do it again. Once a guy has had you he doesn't always want to do it again."

"What? Why not?" Kavath looked honestly confused.

"Because he wants someone new. Someone he hasn't had before. Men are like that," she said. Apparently this was totally foreign to Kavath because he continued to look confused as she tried to explain.

"It's the thrill of the chase that a man wants, not having the woman."

"Not Gaian men," he said emphatically. "The chase may be fun, and the having something to look forward to, but the thrill is in the keeping. I will never want another woman."

He sounded so pious and after the "unsuitable" crack he'd made before Mea couldn't help her retort. "How would you know you'd be faithful when you haven't ever been with a woman?"

A muscle tightened in his cheek and Kavath's face grew angry. "Does that make me less of a man in your eyes, Mea, that I'm a virgin? I was enough of a man once for you to try and seduce me."

She blushed. Well, she wasn't going to let him make her feel guilty over that. Mea shrugged as if it hadn't meant anything. "I was attracted to you, and you were there. You weren't fighting it that much when you were asleep."

"You wanted to bunk with me that morning."

"And what's so wrong about that?"

"What's wrong?" Kavath said. "You offered yourself to me as if it was nothing. I thought you were different, better than that."

Now she did get angry. "I didn't offer myself to just anyone, the offer was to you. And it was in the past, the distant past and now rescinded, you pompous jackass!"

Kavath looked as angry as she was. "Pompous jackass? Just because I prefer not to dally with someone who thinks of herself as available...."

"*That is enough!*" Furious, Mea stood, ignoring her dizziness. "You think you have all the answers, that the Gaian way is best, no matter what." Searching for stability, she propped herself against the edge of her stove.

"Maybe I'm not "suitable" for you. I know I'm not some cloistered Gaian virgin waiting for you to sniff her out. Earth is different from Gaia, and Earthforce even more so. I joined when I was barely eighteen, and what you'd call my virtue became a moot point soon after. But understand this, I don't 'offer myself' indiscriminately, not now, not ever."

Standing was too much of an effort. She settled to the ground, put her head in her hands. When she raised it, she saw him staring at the ground with a look of profound regret on his face.

"You're right. I don't have all the answers." He took a deep breath. "I care for you, Mea. I think about you. We're so alone here. In my camp at night, sometimes I can't sleep. I think of you, wish you were with me, so we could talk."

She couldn't help her snort of disbelief. "Talk?"

He gave a short laugh. "All right. Some talk, some … other things. I may be impotent at the moment, but I'm not dead." His voice held no sarcasm. "I remember how you felt. What it was like to kiss you. I'd like to do it again. It isn't that you aren't good enough, believe that. But we come from such different backgrounds, I'm not sure how we could ever get past them."

She had to admit he had a point. Their backgrounds were very different and Kavath only knew part of hers.

"We're both waiting for our people to find us. I think we may be friends, but we're still committed to our people, and they're at war." He faltered. "As for the rest, I'm not looking for a 'cloistered Gaian virgin' as you put it. The way things are the chances are good I won't find a Gaian wife."

Kavath's voice turned pensive. "Maybe if we'd met later … there's been talk. Some of our men have found wives amongst the Earth prisoners we've taken. I've heard that after the war, we may invite women from Earth to visit Gaia and I might end up with an Earth wife anyway."

An Earth wife who wasn't her. She didn't like to think about why that bothered her, only it did. Some other woman would have Kavath to love.

He grabbed his respirator and staggered to his feet. "I think I'm better now. I'll be able to make it back to my camp."

He paused before leaving the clearing. "What I said, about your offer that morning--I'm sorry I said that, it was wrong. As you say, we come from different people and putting your hand on me wasn't out of line from your perspective. If things were different, if I were an Earth man, I'd have been happy to have 'bunked' you that day."

The slight smile on his face took away the sting of his teasing. "And the next, and the next--I would not be looking for the chase. Part of me wishes I could accept a simple affair with you. But Mea, I'm Gaian--and I can't be anything else."

She waited until he was nearly to the trees. "Are we still going to the sea tomorrow?"

"If you want to." He paused.

"I do."

He smiled, for once without the respirator hiding his mouth. "Then I do too. See you tomorrow, Mea."

After he was gone, the clearing felt so empty. Mechanically, Mea collected Kavath's discarded plate, chopsticks, and cup and cleaned them before settling into her tent for a good cry.

Chapter Eight

It was a beautiful day to go to the beach. With his new fishing spear in hand, a light heart and lighter step, Kavath set off for Mea's camp early that morning, eager to begin the day. An entire day to be spent playing and gazing over a new planet's ocean, checking out the sea-life for edible items.

A day they'd spend searching for salt to make their meals tastier and to help preserve foods in case of bad weather. A day full of sun and exercise and fishing.

A day to spend with Mea. Even after yesterday's awkwardness, he wanted to see her. He blamed himself for the entire mess, although the fermented pink-zinger had been the reason for his outburst. Even so he'd no business bringing up their past and her attempted seduction of him, and certainly for implying that she wasn't good enough for him. She was more than good enough. She was his match in all ways but one. She wasn't someone who could commit to being married.

Maybe if he apologized again, it would help. Maybe he could explain how it bothered him that she'd brought up how little experience he had with women and that's why he'd said something so stupid.

She'd probably understand that. At the very least it would give him a reason to talk to her.

Kavath sped down the path. Talking to her would be good and after all they'd be together all day. He had the next several hours to spend with his sometimes infuriating but often enjoyable little Earth pilot. Perhaps they could picnic on the beach, build a fire to cook their catch and watch the sunset.

Well, probably not that. Staying that late would mean they'd have to walk back through the jungle after dark, and while he was comfortable in the jungle at night, she wouldn't be. He didn't want her to be frightened going to or from the beach. She might not want to come again and that would be a shame. He liked having her with him.

Of course it took quite a bit to frighten Mea, so maybe they could stay until dark after all--he'd leave that decision up to her. In spite of his words to her yesterday, Mea had a place in his mind that no other woman occupied. In fact, it was getting difficult to imagine not having her around.

Kavath's pace slowed. In fact, it was getting very difficult to imagine Mea not being around. Even without the draw of attachment, just talking to her made his day. They were friends and becoming closer all the time.

So what was wrong with that? He liked her, and she liked him. They might not be suitable mates, but otherwise they had a lot in common. There was no reason they couldn't be friends.

Well, except for the fact that they were on opposite sides of a war. And that she was a woman and his only women friends were all married. He didn't know any men who were friends with an unmarried woman.

Besides, it wasn't really just friendship he felt for her. Even now, the memory of lying next to her made him hot in a way that had nothing to do with the tropical sun beating down through the trees. Not aroused, exactly. But there was a tingle where there shouldn't be anything.

A memory of arousal. That's what it was. An echo of something he'd felt once and that part of him wanted to feel again. A part of him that didn't want to be just friends with Mea.

He wondered what she looked like when wet. How see-through would those pink undergarments of hers be?

Kavath shook his head to clear it of such thoughts. This was dangerous territory. Mea didn't want him the way he wanted her, and to presume otherwise could make it difficult for him to ever find a woman of his own. It didn't matter that she was otherwise just what he wanted.

Kavath stopped and leaned against one of the trees growing along the trail. Maybe this was a bad idea, spending so much time together. There was so much that could go wrong. It wasn't really necessary for them to both go to the shore.

But he wanted to go and so did she. It only made sense for them to go together. And besides, it wasn't like they could avoid each other, not on a planet where their survival might depend on the other being around. A man could go crazy living alone and he wasn't so sure she'd be able to survive without his help.

Well, that wasn't strictly true. Since their initial few days on the planet Mea had learned a lot about living in the wild and she was forever surprising him with new ways to make things better for them. Some of her ideas, particularly the stove and her cooking pots floored him with their inventiveness. Whenever he asked how she'd known how to make something, her answer was evasive and it made him more curious than ever about her background.

Recently she'd talked of learning to hunt and she'd actually shown an interest in the lizards' skin, asking for them instead of letting him bury them with the rest of the garbage from their food. He'd seen her stretching the skins out and drying them to make leather. What she had in mind for them, he didn't know, but it was fun to imagine her running around in a lizard-skin swimming suit like a heroine in a holo-vid.

Kavath smiled. A lizard-skin outfit would look great with her dark hair. That part of him that shouldn't be tingling, tingled again.

Kavath shook his head again. Mea wouldn't much appreciate him fantasizing about her that way. Although sometimes the way she looked at him, the way she acted, it was like she was thinking about him the way he thought about her. She was his match … was she reconsidering marriage? If she did, how would he take that?

Part of him knew the answer to that, the part that still held a phantom ache for her. But he couldn't do anything unless she agreed to respect his wish for marriage and in the meantime he'd just have to be careful not to get too attached to her.

In all possible meanings of the word.

* * * *

She was waiting for him when he got to her camp, wearing her grey uniform shirt and pants. Even her boots were securely fastened to her feet and there was no sign of the lizard-skin outfit he'd imagined. Resisting the urge to sigh, Kavath instead secured his mask in place before coming closer.

"You ready to go?" To his ears his voice sounded tinny through the mask.

Mea nodded and grabbed what looked like a large bag off the ground, made of strips of some kind of leather fastened together with a lacing of bramble vine cord. From the scaly texture, the rest of the bag appeared to be made out of lizard skin.

So that's what she'd done with the skins. Kavath couldn't help his disappointment over that mundane use, even as he recognized its usefulness.

He wondered over the construction of it. "How did you make that?"

Mea almost seemed embarrassed by the question. "It wasn't that hard. I cut the pieces to size and used my knife to make small holes, then laced the pieces together." She shrugged. "My mom taught me to sew when I was a child. I made a lot of our clothes."

Kavath came closer and examined the workmanship. "You can sew? I didn't think that anyone from Earth would actually know how to make clothes."

"It's unusual," she admitted. "My mom, actually my entire family ... we're kind of throwbacks in some ways." Hoisting the bag onto her shoulder, Mea headed for the edge of camp. She called back to him, "I checked our route on my computer's map, and it seems best to follow the stream. That goes directly to the ocean. It's a good three kilometers from here--maybe we should get going."

That was the second time she'd talked about her family only to clam up immediately and it made Kavath curious. Even so, much as he wanted to know more she clearly didn't want to talk so he let it drop.

The hike was harder than he'd expected. The edge of the streambed was rocky and made for tricky travel even if it was, as Mea had pointed out, a lot easier to follow the stream than cut directly through the jungle. Even with the ocean only a few kilometers away, going to and from would be difficult unless they found a better route.

Kavath began planning how to build a better path. They could build up the bank of the streambed in the places it was the most difficult, a little at a time. In no time they'd have easy access, assuming that this trip made the effort worth while.

He was preoccupied with plans when Mea came to a sudden halt in front of him, staring straight ahead in open wonder.

They had reached the ocean. Kavath had a brief glimpse of a broad expanse of white beach and the deep blue ocean beyond before he ran into Mea, still dumbstruck at the sight. Thrown off balance he clutched her shoulders and pulled her backwards. She fell into him and as she did, he put his arm around her chest to steady her. Against his arm her breasts were a soft warmth through her shirt.

The tingle in his cock tingled again, even harder.

"Sorry," he said, helping her back onto her feet and releasing her immediately. To his ears his voice sounded strained and Mea gave him a strange look that as much as said, "What's wrong with you?"

Nothing was wrong with him, nothing at all. Nothing except that he was reacting to a woman he had no business reacting to.

Shaking her head, Mea stepped onto the beach, returning her gaze to the ocean. "It's so big," she said quietly, her voice hushed, drawing his attention to the view.

"It is," he agreed with her. "Very big."

He'd seen beaches and the ocean on Gaia, but this seemed bigger somehow. The water extended well to the horizon, a vast stretch of blue topped with small tips of white.

It wasn't a quiet ocean, but turbulent--wind-whipped into waves that crashed into the beach with a heavy rhythmic sound. Floating on the strong breezes that swept the beach, birds dipped and soared and occasionally dove into the water. As Kavath watched, one big bird repeated the action in front of him, rising with something wriggling in its beak.

Seabirds were catching fish. Kavath smiled and hefted his new fishing spear. The birds weren't diving very deep, which meant the fish were right at the surface. They'd be easy to catch, even with his primitive spear.

The imaginary beach cookout he had envisioned might be possible. They still needed to verify that the fish would be edible, but so far the birds had been and the birds were eating the fish. That was a good sign and Mea's handy little scanner would tell them for certain if they'd suffer any problems.

Eager to explore the moving water, Kavath moved past Mea to where the white sand beckoned and sat on a large rock to unfasten his boots and pull them off. He shoved one foot into the sand and wiggled his toes against the slippery grains.

Immediately he pulled it back, cradling his foot and blowing on it. White sand and a hot tropical sun made for burned toes, even if the wind from the ocean kept the air on the beach from becoming too hot.

"What's wrong?" Mea asked, although he could swear there was amusement in her voice as if she already knew the answer.

"The sand is hot--too hot to go barefoot. Frack it, my feet used to be tougher than that," he said, glaring at his toasted toes. "I've been in space too long and worn shoes much of that time. I guess I'll have to keep them on today as well." He looked mournfully at the ocean beckoning him. "That will make it more difficult, though. Hard to swim in space boots."

Mea sat a few meters away with her bag. Opening it she reached in and pulled out what looked like a couple hunks of lizard-skin loosely attached together with dangling cords. "Perhaps these will help," she said and tossed them to him one at a time.

Kavath caught them in midair and examined them. They were footwear of sorts, in the form of a pair of crude sandals. Two long ellipses of lizard skin were bound together along the edges with bramble vine cord and reinforced with something between the skins to form a sole. Cord was tied across the top in an attractive pattern and then led to a raised portion of skin at the heel from which two long cords dangled the perfect length for tying around his ankle.

He slipped them onto his bare feet and, with a few adjustments to the cords, found that they fit perfectly and securely. Lightweight and comfortable, they felt like they could stand up to more than a few trips to the ocean, and standing on the sand he could barely feel the heat through the double-skinned sole. With the pale cord contrasting nicely with the green-blue scales of the skin, they even looked good.

He turned to see Mea slip a similar pair of sandals onto her feet. Around her delicate ankles the ties looked particularly attractive. Her pair was darker and they appeared molded to her feet.

She raised her heels off the sand and admired her footwear. "I figured we might need something other than our boots and we had all those skins. I decided to make something from them."

"You made these … for me?" It was more than the fact that the sandals were useful in protecting his feet from the sand. She'd *made* them, using raw materials.

As inventive as everything else she did was, this was more than making pots out of gas canisters or cups from a hard nut. Without anyone to instruct her, she'd figured out how to create sandals out of a set of skins and some binding cord. He wasn't sure he could do something like that, much less do it with such skill.

"I made mine first. When you wear them in the water and let them dry, they will stiffen up around your foot and be a perfect fit."

He flexed his feet, enjoying the feel of the sand underneath and the cool air blowing the top of his feet. The raised edges would keep the bulk of the sand out and they'd be a lot better for exploring the coast. But it wasn't their practicality that floored him.

No one outside of his family had ever made him a present like this. He wanted to pick her up and kiss her for it, and he would've if he weren't wearing a mask.

"You even got the size right," he muttered, still overwhelmed.

Mea seemed uncomfortable with the way he stared at her. "I got your size by measuring one of your footprints near the stream. You know, where the mud is thick? I just cut them back a little to account for your boots."

"How did you know how to make something like this?"

"Where I grew up … we got holo-vids in sometimes about the way people used to live on Earth. It isn't so hard to figure out how to tie a piece of skin to your foot once you know it can be done."

Now she was defensive as if he was insulting her. Kavath gave in to temptation, stepped over and pulled her up into a rough and awkward embrace. He might not be able to kiss her, but she certainly deserved a hug.

"Thank you, little lehen. I really appreciate your present."

She stiffened against him, then relaxed and put her arms around his waist, burying her head in his chest. He'd only planned a short hug, a gesture of appreciation, but it felt so good to hold her after all this time that he couldn't seem to stop. He pulled her closer, enjoying the feel of her smaller frame against him. She was soft where he wasn't, small but strong. He felt her muscles but also felt the skin like satin over them.

She felt wonderful, like milk and honey to a man dying of thirst.

It wasn't just that she was a woman and someone he'd attached to in the recent past. She couldn't be what he needed after all. It wasn't sex that made her feel so good. She felt good ... because she was Mea. Because she was his friend and it was good to hold his friend that way.

It was very, very good.

For the first time in a long time he resented having to wear the mask, having to keep his nostrils free of her scent, not being able to simply enjoy her the way any other kind of man could enjoy a woman. Why was it so important that he stay detached from her? Why couldn't he want this woman, if not for forever at least for now? Even without being attached he didn't want to let go of her.

Finally she was the one who broke their embrace and pulled away. Mea took several steps away, toward the beach. She didn't look him in the eye and he could sense confusion in her.

"We should see if there are any fish. Or salt. That's what we came for."

Holding her boots with one hand and her bag across her shoulders, Mea slipped away and if he hadn't known better, he'd have sworn she was as much running from him as heading to the shore.

His gaze followed her to where the breakers hit the beach in a pounding rhythm. The sound was soothing, slower than his rapidly beating heart and Kavath let it wash over him for a moment. He needed to calm himself before he made a complete fool of himself over a simple gift. Perhaps she didn't feel the same towards him, at least not enough to commit. He'd made it clear to her that unless she could agree to marriage, he couldn't want her.

Even if she was everything he'd ever really wanted.

It took a moment, but once he had himself under control, Kavath followed her down the beach.

* * * *

Mea needed a moment to compose herself after leaving Kavath's arms. She'd stayed up late the night before finishing the sandals, amusing herself by imagining his reaction to them, but of all the reactions she'd imagined, having him grab and hug her that way hadn't been one of them. She didn't know what was worse--that he'd hugged her as if he wanted her, or that she'd enjoyed imagining he wanted her.

Shaking her head at how complicated she could make a simple hug, Mea turned to stare at the imposing expanse of water ahead of her, her first glimpse of an actual ocean. It was really big. She'd thought deep space was imposing, but an ocean was a different thing altogether. Water stretched to the horizon, undulating under the open bowl of the sky, forever in motion. She could feel how immense it was, could feel the weight of all that water in front of her.

Waves beat upon the shore at an alarming rate and there seemed to be so much power in them. In her brief time on Earth she'd never been to the shoreline, but now she wished she had. Were all oceans like this, so big, so massive and powerful? The noise of the waves nearly deafened her until she realized that the constancy of its roar made her able to tune it out.

If only it was that easy to ignore Kavath. She wasn't sure what made her more nervous--the ocean in front of her, or the man behind. Both had her baffled, as she had no idea what to do with either of them. A man of her own kind, one from Earth and in Earthforce, you either ignored them or bunked with them. Problem solved.

How did you deal with a man you couldn't ignore or bunk?

Large rocks dotted the sand where the waves hit, worn smooth in spots and covered in still damp dark-brown vegetation that gave off an intense smell, not completely unpleasant. Force of habit had her running her scanner over the large flat leaves to see what was edible. To her delight much of it was, and it included traces of several nutrients they'd been lacking, including salt. Even if they didn't find salt in its pure form, cooking with these leaves would impart some taste to their food.

Pulling out a collapsible gathering bag she'd knotted from binding cord, Mea used her knife to cut free several of the larger leaves and stuffed them into the bag. The task engrossed her so much that she forgot the ocean behind her until a particularly large wave soaked the back of her pants.

The cold water shocked her and Mea scampered out of reach of the waves, only to hear Kavath's laughter. She turned to glare at him, and ended up staring in admiration instead.

While she'd explored the contents of the rock, he'd stripped down to his white underpants and sandals and stowed his clothes on top of a rock high on the beach. Carrying his wire-topped fishing spear, he came toward her, bare-chested but for the marriage band pendant he still wore around his neck. The ocean breeze blew his finger-length fair hair into a halo around his head. Only the mask he still wore kept him from looking like some kind of primitive ocean god.

Mea swallowed at how outrageously sexy he looked. He appealed to her on a primitive level. Too bad the appeal was one-sided. Unless he was attached to her, he didn't want her and even then there were strings. Strings like the metal band he wore around his neck.

His smile dimmed slightly as he came closer, and she saw concern in his eyes. "It is best to avoid turning your back on the ocean, Mea. You never know when a large wave will come and knock you off your feet."

Using his spear he pointed up the beach where the birds dipped and wheeled over the water. "I'm going to try fishing up there. Can you keep from needing me for a while?"

As if she needed him at all! Mea narrowed her eyes at him. "I'll be fine. Go fish."

He grinned at her through the clear mask as he headed up the beach. Grimly, she went to where he'd left his clothes and stripped off her wet pants. If Kavath thought it was safe to leave his clothes there, then it was probably safe enough for hers as well. She laid her pants out where the rock was warm and left her jacket and backpack, after putting the scanner in her shirt pocket.

Unbuttoning her uniform shirt for coolness, Mea returned to the rocks. An hour later she'd found more edible seaweed, plus some kind of small animals that lived in hard shells. Their multitude of legs bothered her as well as their intense purple color, but the scanner said there was no obvious reason they couldn't be eaten.

She used binding cord to tie several large leaves of seaweed into a small container to hold a couple of handfuls of the sea animals. It wasn't very sturdy but she hoped most of them wouldn't escape. If she needed to, she knew where they were and could get more.

Mea decided to look for Kavath. She kept a careful eye on the uneven waves, but even so as she walked along the shore her feet got wet as a particularly large one hit. Now that she was used to it, the water didn't feel cold and she even welcomed it.

She found empty shells along the shore, some very large, some the size of her fist. Mea picked up one of large ones, filled it with water from the ocean, and poured it out. It held a lot of water and was thick. She doubted heat would bleed through it like the nut-cups and at the very least she could use it as a mug for hot beverages. Rinsing it carefully she put it into her bag then looked around for a second one. No point in only having only one mug, not with Kavath around.

That made her pause for a moment. When had she stopped thinking in terms of just herself? She might not want a life partner like a spouse, but in reality with Kavath around, she might as well be his wife the way they were living together. The only difference now was that they weren't having sex.

She could see Kavath in the water now, standing waist deep in the surf several meters away. His arm came up and she saw the spear flash down into the water and come up with a creature the size of her forearm wriggling on the end. He pulled it off the spear and lifted a cord to string it next to several others.

So he was actually catching fish. Mea laughed, anticipating how pleased he'd be. That was Kavath, hunter to her gatherer. Between them they made a pretty good team in the battle for survival. Too bad temporary teammates were all they could ever be.

Mea looked in her bag at the few leaves of sea greens and her little package of shellfish. Today she hadn't really held up her gatherer end of things and Kavath looked well on his way to catching a lot of fish. She needed to do something spectacular to keep even with him.

For a moment she eyed the dark-green edge of the beach where the jungle began. She could explore there and see if there was fruit or other vegetables to gather, but she'd been doing that every day since they'd arrived.

Today she wanted more of a challenge than the jungle offered. They'd come to the beach for fish and salt. Kavath was making good strides on the fish front and she'd found some edibles, but she'd yet to find salt in usable form. Cooking with salt water didn't seem like an alternative once they were back in camp and it would take time to boil dry a pan full of ocean water. If possible she'd like to find dry salt.

So where would dry salt be found near an ocean? Perhaps someplace where seawater had been left and dried, leaving the salt behind? She eyed the columns of rocks around her and began searching their tops for depressions.

The first couple of rocks were too flat, but she found a suspicious crusting around the edge of a pit on the third. Her scanner told her the white granules were salt crystals and in relatively pure form. Exultant, Mea used her knife to scrape as much of it as she could onto a large flat leaf of seaweed.

A few moments later she found another encrustation on a rock closer to the ocean and added that to her collection. A rock just at the water's edge yielded the largest amount yet, nearly half a handful of white crystals. Happily Mea collected it into her leaf, folded and tucked it into her seashell mug for safekeeping.

As she did, a large wave came up and caught her legs, nearly drenching her. Dancing up out of the wave's reach, Mea examined her bag, noting with relief that the seashell was still dry. Even so, this would never do. The salt she'd labored to obtain would melt away if it got too wet.

Mea found a large flat-topped rock high on the beach to store her bag. She took off her shirt, leaving the scanner in the pocket, and tucked it inside.

It seemed like larger salt incrustations would be on the rocks actually in the water. She'd just wade out and collect them, using separate leaves of dry seaweed for each and use the scanner later to confirm they were salt. That way if one of the deposits turned out to be something else, she'd avoid contaminating the rest.

She'd collected three more leaves of salt and stowed them into the seashell in her bag before she decided to try one of the rocks beyond where the water went higher than her knees.

For a moment she hesitated. Born and raised in space, Mea had never been in deep water before and didn't know how to swim. But she watched Kavath splashing around in the water with his ever-growing string of fish, and she wanted to have enough salt to finally impress him.

He'd loved the sandals, enough to forget she wasn't suitable for him and hug her. They were here because he'd gotten tired of bland food. Maybe if she collected enough salt he'd forget she was from Earth altogether.

Mea stowed the last leaf of salt in her bag and turned to study a set of three rocks well out into the water. It was far, but she could wade out there. There was likely to be plenty of salt on their tops. Grabbing several extra large leaves of seaweed, Mea waded out through the inconstant waves into the ocean.

Chapter Nine

His mask hanging from its strap around his neck, Kavath studied a fish floating a mere two meters away, blissfully unaware of its fate. With a slight smile he raised his spear and waited. Patience was a virtue when fishing, and he was practicing

Fishing had been even better than he'd expected. He had a whole string ready for the grill tonight, and to smoke for later use. One more and he'd be done for the day.

Kavath imagined Mea's delight at his catch. She'd smile at him, thank him, and tell him how great it was to have him there. Every day he tried to do a little better as a hunter than the day before, just to see that smile. Mea's smile was the best reward.

The fish drifted leisurely into the reach of his spear. Kavath slowly pulled back his arm and prepared to strike.

The fish drifted closer. He kept as still as one of the nearby rocks. Another flick of its tail and it was within reach.

Kavath threw the spear and the sharpened spikes of wire drove through the body of the fish. It quivered for an instant on the spear and then lay still, only a drift of blood indicating its demise.

Triumphantly, Kavath added his latest acquisition to his string, threading a piece of binding cord through the animal's gills to secure alongside the rest of his catch. Since they'd arrived at the beach he'd caught ten fish in all, more than enough for dinner today. He planned to cook several this afternoon for dinner and smoke the rest of them over a low flame to keep.

Flushed with accomplishment, Kavath swam to shore and began to wade out of the water. He'd looked back once to see Mea on the shore with her bag, gathering something from the rocks. He hoped she'd seen him catch a fish and would be proud of him. Maybe she'd applaud as he came on shore and come to hug him.

Unfortunately when he emerged from the water she was nowhere in sight. He saw her bag lying on top of a rock and placed the string of fish in the sand nearby. He found her shirt inside, which meant she was stripped to her tank top and underpants.

Eagerly Kavath looked around the beach, delighted at the idea of seeing Mea dressed only in her bright pink undergarments again. He had to admit that pink was definitely his favorite color at the moment, although he still had hopes for the blue-green lizard-skin outfit he'd imagined. Since she knew how to sew, maybe if they stayed here long enough he'd finally get her to construct something like that.

But as his gaze searched the shoreline, he saw no sign of her. No flash of pink on the sand or in the shallow water nearby. He looked back towards the jungle, but there was nothing there but solid green, no Mea.

Suddenly uneasy, Kavath looked towards the ocean. She wouldn't have left her bag and shirt behind if she was going into the jungle, but she might if she'd decided to swim. He was competent in the water, but he'd grown up near an ocean and knew its beauty--and its dangers. He had no idea what Mea knew about the sea, but one thing he did know was that she wasn't afraid even when she should be. The memory of her turning her back to the uneven surf came to him and he grew even more concerned as he searched the water for signs of her.

There. Kavath came to attention as a blob of pink topped by wet brown hair bobbed on the surface several meters out from shore, near a large formation of rock. He knew the water there wasn't much more than chest deep … on him. But Mea was a lot shorter than he was and from the way she struggled against the push and pull of the waves, he wasn't certain she could swim the way he could.

A large wave came in and knocked her off her feet and she disappeared under the water. For an instant he froze, willing her head to pop to the surface, but it didn't. He dropped his things and charged to where she'd been.

Quickly Kavath waded out to where he could dive into the water. In spite of his hurry he remembered to fasten his mask across his mouth, then he swam as fast as possible to the three great rocks where he'd seen Mea last.

Water mixed with flecks of sand swirled around him, nearly as clear as it had been where he was fishing, but he saw no sign of her under the surface. Tamping down his fear, he swam to one side. Maybe she'd gotten caught in an undercurrent and swept further down the coast. The seconds stretched as he searched, and it grew harder and harder not to give in to panic.

Inside his chest his heart seemed to seize and stop beating. Mea was gone--really gone-- and he'd never see her again alive, never hold her again....

It was too late. He'd lost his chance with her. Struggling with his fear, Kavath turned his head one more time in a slow pan of the area.

There … a flash of pink!

Out of the corner of his eye he saw it, a brilliant pink that didn't belong in nature and certainly didn't belong in this water--the bright rose color of Mea's underclothes. He turned his head and there it was again, several meters away and deep under the water. Kavath swam as fast as he could. He dove and his seeking fingers found her flesh, limp and cold. He grabbed her hands and pulled her to the surface, turning her head so her mouth was in the air. But her eyes were closed and she didn't suck in any air and the breath caught in his throat. He quickly swam into the shallow water, then lifted and carried her limp body to the shore.

Heart pounding so hard he felt like it would burst from his chest, Kavath laid her onto the sand then fell onto his knees beside her. Her eyes were still closed, mouth open, and her chest didn't move. She wasn't breathing. Head on her chest, he listened to her heart, heard a faint thump, then another. So she was still alive, but not for long.

Long ago training came to his aid. *Rescue breathing.* He had to breathe for her, blow air into her lungs.

He pulled the respirator off and dropped it into the sand. He turned her to one side and let the water pour out of her mouth, then pushed her onto her back, making sure to clear her airway. Covering her mouth with his, he blew air into her, felt the rise of her chest under his hand. Pulling his mouth away, he felt the air blow out of her lungs, past his face and deep into his nostrils.

Attachment was immediate, but he barely registered it when his shaft hardened. That wasn't important but attachment also meant he had to fight for his breath, and that he labored to get under control. There was no time to spare--he needed air to breathe into her. His woman was dying, he couldn't think about anything else but getting his next breath so he could save her. He forced his breathing under control and once more blew air into Mea's mouth, felt her chest rise and let it fall again.

It took six times before she coughed, her body jerking, and then her eyes flew open with a look of panic deep within them. She stared at him with wide eyes and then turned from him to throw up into the sand, coughing and retching the rest of the water out of her lungs and stomach.

He held her shoulders as she emptied herself into the sand and Kavath let go of the fear that had clutched him when he'd first seen her unmoving body under the water, letting it morph into disappointment and fury.

Why hadn't she told him how poor a swimmer she was? And if she couldn't swim, why was she going out that far into the water? He knew how fearless she was, but was the woman completely insane?

His hands clutched at her shoulders and he resisted the urge to shake them. What was he going to do with her?

He didn't trust his voice, could barely trust his hands on her. Instead of scolding or giving her a shake, he continued to hold her shoulders as her body worked to expel the water she'd taken in. It would do very little good to yell at her now. He'd only scare her and no doubt she was frightened enough. Maybe it would be better to pull her into his arms and try to kiss some sense into her. His woman should never endanger herself like this. He'd have to find some way to keep her reckless nature in check in the future. It would be a difficult task, but he needed her with him....

What was he thinking? Mea wasn't his woman! Hands trembling, Kavath released her shoulders and scooted away from her on the sand, fighting the urge to grab her and hold her close again. He shouldn't be thinking thoughts like this about a woman who wasn't his wife. She wasn't his, not that way. The problem was that he had attached to her again, that's all.

He couldn't trust himself to touch her. If he did, he would snatch her up in his arms and either shake her or kiss her. Who knew where that would lead?

Kavath forced his hands to his side. She was frightened enough and needed to be taken care of. She lay trembling on the sand, tears forming in her eyes. Schooling his voice, he spoke softly to her. "You're going to be all right. Just lie here. I'm going to build a fire."

She didn't say a word until he'd collected their belongings and found a place high above the water line near the creek they'd followed from their camps.

It was too late to head back to their camps tonight. Mea wasn't in any shape for the hike back through the woods in the dark. The late afternoon cookout and sunset watching had gone from being a wishful dream to a necessity.

Even more, they'd have to sleep out here tonight. To make camp, they'd need fresh water from the stream. He piled their stuff near a few large logs they could use as a windbreak from the ocean breezes and returned to collect her.

Mea was sitting up and staring at the ocean when he returned. For the first time he saw true fear on her face as the waves came crashing in. At least something had gotten her attention, although it bothered him to see such an emotion on his little lehen's face. It could be for the best, though. Maybe now she'd be more careful.

She was holding his respirator in her hands, turning it over and over. "Don't you need this?" she asked as she handed it to him.

He took it and looped it on his arm. Mea stared at him, then nodded. She knew that he'd attached to her again and no longer needed to wear it.

Mea tried to protest when he lifted her into his arms, but he quelled her argument with a single look as he carried her to their temporary camp. She felt cold, her skin clammy. The chill of the water and wind, and the shock from her near drowning was affecting her.

Kavath knew shock could be as much a threat to her health as the water had been. He needed to get a fire going as soon as possible. Fortunately there was plenty of dry wood on the beach, and his jacket held his fire starter. In the meantime he gently placed her onto the sand behind one of the large logs and wrapped both her jacket and his around her before heading off down the beach to collect wood.

* * * *

The sand was still heated from the sun, but Mea couldn't seem to get warm anyway. She shivered under both jackets while Kavath gathered wood and built a fire nearby. Her throat hurt and her stomach ached and she felt like she'd been hit in the chest. Cold, wet, and miserable, and she hurt--this beach trip hadn't at all turned out the way she'd hoped.

What made it worse was that she knew it was her fault. She'd waded out into the ocean, trying to reach the big rocks to look for salt when she'd suddenly been in water too deep to stand in. A set of big waves had knocked her off her feet and she'd gone under. She tried holding her breath, but there had been nothing but water around her and she couldn't reach the surface. Then all she remembered was the feel and taste of saltwater in her mouth and not being able to catch her breath.

After that, the next thing she'd known she was on the beach and Kavath was holding her as she retched into the sand. That made twice she'd thrown up in front of him. It was getting to be a bad habit.

He'd saved her life--she knew that. He'd pulled her out of the water and breathed air into her after she'd nearly drowned. That's why he wasn't wearing his mask--he'd taken it off to help her and now it was too late to put it back on. No doubt he was attached to her again.

No wonder he was acting so angry. He was probably furious with her for being careless after he'd warned her about the waves. Mea sighed. Here she'd been trying to show how useful she could be, and in the end Kavath had been forced to rescue her even though it had meant attaching again.

She'd intended to show how she could take care of herself and instead she'd only proved the opposite. It was enough to make an independent-minded woman very depressed.

Mea huddled under the combined weight of their clothing, hurt and cold. When he returned Kavath gave her a worried glance and added his shirt to the clothing covering her. It held his scent, which was somehow comforting, and she clutched it around her while he worked to make a fire from gathered driftwood.

Soon it flared up with a cheerful warmth. She crept closer, holding her hands out to it, hoping the heat would dispel the chill she felt deep within. For a long time Mea felt the weight of Kavath's stare, as she struggled to regain some semblance of normalcy. She ran her hand through her hair, for once grateful it was so short. One of her sandals had come loose and dangled from its ties to her ankle. When she re-secured it to her foot, the simple task felt like a momentous accomplishment.

After a moment Kavath got up and handed her a bottle of water, which she used to rinse out her mouth, eliminating the last of the sickness before drinking a little to soothe her sore throat.

"How are you feeling?" he asked finally.

"Better." She couldn't meet his eyes.

"You want to tell me what happened? What were you doing out there?"

He was so serious. She wondered if some levity would help. She tried lifting one eyebrow and glancing sideways at him with a sheepish grin. "Drowning."

His face hardened and Mea's heart plummeted. So much for taking things lightly.

"Why didn't you tell me you couldn't swim?" he asked.

"I didn't know I couldn't. I've never been in deep water before," she added at his disbelieving grunt.

"They don't have water on Earth?"

"I didn't spend that much time on the planet." She shrugged. "You made it look so easy the way you were floating about in the water--I thought I could do the same."

She heard the tension in his voice and she realized it wasn't really anger he was feeling. "I almost lost you, Mea. You could have died."

He'd been afraid for her. The knowledge that he cared warmed her more than the fire. But as soon as that thought came to her, so did the realization that it didn't really matter. No matter how much he cared, she was still from Earth and not someone he could love.

That knowledge hurt and she couldn't help striking back at him with words. "How can you lose what you don't have, Kavath?"

For a moment he froze, then his face darkened as he turned a furious glare on her. "What does that mean?"

"I don't belong to you or anyone else." She didn't know why she was baiting him this way, but she couldn't stand the way he was staring so angrily. Sure she'd been stupid, but it was only her life that had been at stake. Why should he act as if he was the one who'd been hurt?

"Why are you so worked up over this? I had an accident that was my fault and it could have killed me. I admit it and I'm grateful you helped me. I thank you for saving my life, but beyond that, we're still on opposite sides here. Why are you taking this so personally? What does it matter to you if I died?"

"Mea," Kavath's voice broke off and he swallowed convulsively. "I know you don't belong to me, but that doesn't mean … I mean...."

Suddenly he was on his feet and on her side of the fire, lifting her by the shoulders to stand next to him. "Are you saying your life shouldn't matter to me? You're wrong. Do you want me to show you what you mean to me?"

And then his mouth was on hers in a bruising kiss, an angry kiss, but there was more than anger in it. Passion was in it, long-denied passion--want, and desire. His mouth attacked hers but she didn't step away from it. She met him with her own anger and frustration, furiously kissing him back.

If this was how he intended to show what she meant to him, then she'd return the favor. No one had ever accused Mea of stepping away from a fight. Forgetting her pain, she wrapped her arms around his waist, cinching him to her. She heard a satisfyingly surprised grunt from him at her strength and then his arms were around her and he was holding her equally tight.

Between them she felt his erection solidify, prime evidence that Kavath had most certainly attached to her again and wasn't at all immune to her at the moment. She rubbed against him and he groaned aloud.

His kiss gentled, turned less punishing and more seductive and she responded in kind, letting her tongue slide across his. His mocha chocolate flavor overwhelmed her until she couldn't stop wanting more.

With another groan, Kavath lifted her into his arms and knelt in the sand, lips still locked on hers. His breathing was as fast as hers and she could feel his heart pounding through his bare chest. All that he wore was that necklace of his and his shorts.

She was no longer cold, but aflame; her skin felt fevered. The jackets fell off her shoulders, and then Kavath's hands ran along the edges of her tank top and shorts, seeking her skin. He moaned when he found it, caressing it with fingers that trembled. Fumbling, he pulled her tank up, baring her further, her breasts falling into his hands.

He pulled away then, to stare at the softness of her breast in his hand. He seemed dumbstruck, as if he'd never seen or felt the weight of a bare breast before. In some part of her mind Mea realized that most likely he hadn't. With a gentle hand, he lifted the breast to his lips, and hesitated. For a moment his breath blazed against her skin then he carefully closed his mouth over the nipple.

If Mea had been hot before, now she was on fire, moaning under the effect of his near worshipful suckling. Kavath might be new to touching a woman that way, but there was nothing wrong with his technique.

She arched into his hand, raising her back, and Kavath took advantage of that to slide his hand beneath her, lifting her closer to him. Mea moaned as he recaptured her nipple and sucked on it harder.

It had been way, way too long since she'd been in a man's arms and Kavath was no ordinary man. She could no more stop herself from reacting to him than she could breathe underwater and she'd already proved today how lousy she was at that.

Even so, she felt as if she were drowning in the sensual depths of his arms. She clung to him as he switched his focus to her other breast.

He'd said he wanted to show her what she meant to him. She got the idea, oh yes, she did.

Kavath moved her onto his lap, cradling her in his arms, still using his tongue to caress her nipple. He raised his head and laid a line of kisses along her throat, moving up to her ear. In it his voice was a harsh whisper. "Say you want me, Mea. Tell me."

Her answer was obvious. "I want you. I want you so much, we can't stop now."

He turned her face and she saw the depths of emotion in his green eyes. They seemed to bore into her. "You know what I want, Mea. If I make love to you, will you be mine?"

Part of her heard the question but didn't care what he meant by it. All she wanted was for this not to end. Never had she wanted anything more than that right now. She wanted him, needed to feel him inside her and his body on top of hers. Maybe it was the result of being denied for so long…maybe it was the shock of nearly drowning, making each breath she took now seem so sweet.

Whatever it took, she wanted sex with Kavath. She breathed in his scent, reveling in it. "Yours, sure, whatever. Just do it."

Then she was in the sand again, and Kavath was pulling off her clothes, then his shorts, revealing an erection that made her mouth water. Hands down, Kavath was the most beautiful man she'd ever seen. She couldn't help a little moan. All that time they'd spent not being naked together. It was a darn shame.

He must have felt the same way, because now he wasted no time. She barely had a chance to admire his form before he was lying on top of her. He stared into her face with serious intent. "I intend to hold you to that, Mea. You *are* mine."

Before she could react, he was pushing his way inside her, his hardness filling her. His shaft was big and hard and it felt incredibly good.

It was so big he had to work to get it in, and as she moaned, he stopped part way to stare into her face in concern. "Are you all right?"

Impatient, Mea grabbed his ass and pushed on it, raising her hips to impale herself further. "Don't stop now!"

A grimace that could have almost been a smile slid across his face. "I won't, my own, I won't." He heaved and drove forward, sheathing himself entirely within her. Leaning forward onto his elbows he stared down at her, his face flushed with triumph. "Mea...." He spoke her name as if it was a prayer.

Mea wanted no part of his worship. She wanted sex – now--in the sand and with this man. Using her feet as leverage she raised her hips under him. "Kavath, you promised you wouldn't stop."

"Such an impatient woman! That's something I didn't know. I will have to remember that." And then he pulled back and rocked forward and Mea forgot everything including her own name as they made love for the first time.

The instructional films they'd shown him to prepare him for marriage must have been very … instructional. He knew just what he was doing and it wasn't long at all before Mea was crying out beneath him. Kavath demonstrated better sexual skills than the few Earthmen of her acquaintance. Oh, he could bunk with her anytime, anyplace--she wouldn't mind at all!

He didn't seem to be minding either, nor was it apparently much of a problem losing his virginity. Kavath threw himself entirely into making love with her.

Mea's feet dug into the sand as she came close to orgasm, her body tensing as Kavath slowed, savoring each thrust. Then as if he could sense she was close to climax, he sped up, pushing her over the brink. She cried his name, long and loud, and he grunted once, then shouted, his shaft pulsating inside her. Still quivering, he rested on top of her, his chest heaving and taking great gulps of air with a look of complete astonishment on his face.

Shaken by the intensity of the experience, Mea lay still beneath him. Never had bunking been like this and she had no words for what had happened between them. She tried to remember if any of her former lovers made her feel this way, but somehow just thinking about being with a man other than Kavath made her stomach queasy.

She didn't know why … but Kavath wasn't like anyone else.

Even so, there was something very familiar about the way he leaned up on his elbows and smiled at her, the smug smile of male satisfaction. Somehow, though, that smile didn't irritate the way it normally did. Kavath deserved to feel satisfied … she certainly did.

"That was amazing," she told him.

"Of course it was." He kissed her, not hard like before but softly, gently. It was a sweet kiss, a kiss that lingered on the lips and made her sigh when his mouth pulled away from hers. Abruptly he sat up and pulled her with him, holding her on his lap.

He nibbled the back of her neck. "You will see, my own. This is only the beginning. From now on, everything is going to be wonderful. I'll see to it."

She was too comfortable to argue with him. It had been too much for one day, what with nearly drowning and then finding herself in her Kavath's embrace after all this time. Leaning back into his chest, she let herself be cuddled as the sun settled closer the ocean and the light began to fade from the sky.

Finally Kavath sighed and released her, letting her slide onto the sand. "There is too much to do to sit like this. We should eat and those fish won't cook themselves."

He stood up and grabbed his shorts, pulling them on then his shirt, not bothering with any other clothes. Before he buttoned the shirt, he stopped. "Oh, I almost forgot." Grinning sheepishly he reached up and with one hand took off his necklace and to her surprise looped it around her neck, holding onto her shoulder as he did. As he released her he stroked her cheek with the back of his hand.

Mea fingered the pendant with the three stripes now dangling between her breasts. "I don't understand. What's this for?"

"For you, of course. Your marriage band--we don't have the materials to make another so I guess I'll have to wait for mine." He stopped to smile proudly at her. "Unless you want to use those amazingly inventive powers of yours to put something together for me. I wouldn't put anything past you."

With a light step he headed for the woods. "You rest while I get some sticks to roast the fish on." Just at the edge of the firelight he turned and flashed another happy grin at her. "I'll be right back--wife!" Still grinning Kavath headed to the forest.

Wife? Mea gaped after him, rolling the pendant between her fingers. Then she groaned. He'd said "If I make love to you, you will be mine." In the heat of her passion she'd thought he'd meant bunking, but of course he'd meant

more than that. He'd told her before what the price of
making love with him would be.

Oh, frack! She seemed to have married the Gaian after all.
Sure she'd enjoyed lying with him ... totally enjoyed
making love with him ... but marriage? She'd never have
agreed to that....

Or would she?

Dismay mixed with a secret pleasure as she watched his
gorgeous form enter the nearby trees. Still tingling from
their lovemaking Mea wondered if she hadn't known all
along what making love to him would mean and if she'd
maybe forgotten...on purpose.

Chapter Ten

Kavath had no words for his feelings at the moment. Happy seemed too mundane, pleased not nearly strong enough. He turned to stare at the scene behind him. The sun setting into the ocean was a bright red ball and it lit the sky with colors he couldn't imagine seeing anywhere else but on this beach. The sky's glory seemed a fitting backdrop for the woman he'd left sitting next to the fire.

His woman now in reality. His woman--his wife.

A great bubble of laughter threatened to overwhelm him. Jubilant--that was the word. He was jubilant over Mea. Having her as his wife and making love to her was the best thing that had ever happened to him. No wonder getting married was all the guys on his ship ever talked about.

He collected several long green sticks to use as spits from the nearby jungle. There was plenty of driftwood on the beach so he didn't need firewood, but freshly cut sticks wouldn't burn as fast and would be better to use for cooking the fish. Selecting several, he even tried to find some that had an aromatic bark to help flavor the meat.

Since they were here for the night, he'd roast some directly over the fire, enough for dinner and possibly breakfast, and then he'd let the flames die down and smoke the rest for longer storage. The coals would also keep their camping area cozy, good for their first night together. Their wedding night.

Kavath paused for another grin.

Maybe he'd even go out tomorrow morning and see if he could catch some more fish before they left, so they'd have some to take back to camp. He would work overtime to show Mea what a good provider he was.

He spied some clusters of fruit and snagged several, using a pair of leaves folded together as an impromptu basket. They looked like berries of some kind, a dull red in the dying light. As he grabbed them, several birds flew from the bush, which suggested they were edible. Still, he'd let Mea use her portable scanner to verify it.

Roasted fish and berries--not much for a wedding feast, but stuck on a planet the way they were, they couldn't be that choosy. Too bad they didn't have any pink-zinger to celebrate with. Even the heavily fermented beverage would be better than water tonight.

When he brought her home, then they'd have a proper party, with his parents and sisters. It was sad her brother wouldn't be there, but he had enough family for the both of them.

How his folks would take to having an Earthforce pilot in the family--that is, a *former* Earthforce pilot, there was no way she was going back to Earth's military after this-- remained to be seen. Of course their marriage was a little unorthodox already, not the least of it being that he hadn't given Mea his band before making love or gotten one from her in return.

He doubted that was the source of the look of shock on the bride's face as he'd left her with his band. But she'd agreed to become his wife, that much he was sure of, otherwise he'd never have actually consummated it. She'd said yes.

Of course they'd both been overcome with passion, too much to do much serious thinking. Most likely she was thinking very hard now about what she'd agreed to.

There was still the three day probationary period where she could change her mind and give his band back, but he'd see to it she didn't change her mind. Apparently she liked making love ... he'd keep her preoccupied with that.

Kavath smiled to himself. It would be a difficult job, to make love to his little lehen for three days solid, but he was up to the task.

Armed with berries and spits, he returned to the fire. Mea had dressed in her grey uniform, hiding her beautiful body and even her pink undergarments. He hoped it was because of the cooling breeze.

It was getting to the point that he detested the color grey. When he got her home, he'd make sure she never owned anything that color again. She'd look good in bright colors, reds, and orange, and of course, bright pink.

She looked great in pink.

As he came closer she glanced up at him, her hand fingering the wristband still looped on its chain. She hadn't yet unfastened it and put it on. Technically she should be wearing it around her wrist, but between her nearly drowning and then their fight where she'd claimed that he didn't care about her, the appropriate flow of events of a Gaian wedding had gotten away from him.

The wristband was only a symbol, anyway. The important thing was that she understood they were married. Kavath stopped to study the uncertainty on her face and a disturbing thought occurred to him. It was possible that she understood, but wasn't completely thrilled by their new relationship.

Kavath's eyes narrowed. He wasn't going to lose her now. He'd just have to work real hard to make her thrilled with being his wife.

Curbing his desire to grab and kiss her, he handed her the berries instead. "I found these. Could you check to see if we can eat them? Please?"

The pleasantry obviously took her by surprise and she blinked at him before accepting the leaf. From her pocket she pulled the portable scanner and verified that the birds hadn't been in error. "They're fine," she said, then nibbled one, chewing it carefully. "Tart, but nice and juicy. They'd probably be really good cooked with the fish. Maybe we can stuff a few inside."

"Good idea!" He went to work cleaning fish. She moved around him with one of her little pans and got some water from the stream, and a couple of large flat rocks. When he turned back he saw that she'd moved some hot coals to one side of the fire to lie between the rocks and was balancing the pot on top. She picked a couple of large seashells and cleaned them out, then put in each a couple of leaves from her pack.

He smiled to himself. That was Mea, even in the midst of turmoil, making tea for them. She was going to get along wonderfully with his mother.

Then she was kneeling next to him, her knife out. "Can I help?"

Surprised, he rocked back on his heels. "You sure you want to?"

"You caught so many. Let me try."

So much for sparing her blood and guts. But he'd just cut open the fish in his hand and while pale she didn't seem about to throw up. He liked it that she wanted to learn how to cope with preparing meat for cooking. It was more evidence she was willing to move past her upbringing.

Kavath handed her one of the fish and watched with approval as she followed his lead in removing the inedible parts. With two of them working, the pile was finished quickly and Kavath speared enough of them for a good dinner, stuffing several with berries. He reserved the rest for smoking over the dying coals of the fire.

After washing her hands in the stream, Mea sat on the sand while he suspended the spits of fish over the fire. Out of the corner of his eye he noticed how nervously she turned over in her hand the wristband still attached to the chain. She really was thinking about the situation. Thinking real hard which made him more than a little worried.

He should probably tell her everything that she needed to know about Gaian marriage, but he was reluctant to do so. No telling what she would do if she knew that the next three days were a trial period.

Even so he had to tell her eventually. Maybe he'd do it three days from now and only earlier if absolutely necessary. That way she couldn't end it sooner and he'd have the full time to convince her to stay with him. In the meantime he could enjoy not having to wear a respirator around her.

Actually there were a number of things he was enjoying, not the least of which was the idea that very soon he was going to be making love to her again. He now understood just exactly why she had been trying to seduce him all those weeks ago.

Sex was wonderful. It was everything great he could imagine, all holidays rolled into one, including Founder's day and the more recent Gaian Independence Day.

Most importantly it was *fun!* His first time had gone a bit too fast. He knew he would need to work on that and increase his staying power next time. Mea hadn't complained, but then she hadn't said much at all since he'd dropped his marriage band around her neck.

After taking a moment to prepare, Kavath cleared his throat. "I guess we should decide where we are going to live."

Mea quit fiddling with the marriage band, sat up straighter and stared at him.

"I mean, now that we're married, we'll want to spend more time together. Sleep together and such. We have two camps, would you rather live in yours or in mine?"

"Your place or mine?" she said, her voice sounding vaguely disbelieving. "Is that your question?"

He wasn't sure just why she was putting it that way. "Um, I guess. After all at this point we don't need two camps. At least we should be sleeping together, don't you think?"

Mea played with the wristband strung around her neck. He wished she would take it off the chain and put it where it belonged, around that pretty little wrist of hers. Maybe she didn't know how to properly size it. He was sure it was too big. In spite of having three sisters, he hadn't realized how small a woman's wrists really were when he'd made it. Who looks at their sister's wrists?

She nodded, slowly. "I guess you have a point. We should spend time together." She looked down at the band between her fingers. "I didn't really expect this, Kavath."

"I didn't expect to feel this way about you either, Mea. But I can't stop the way I feel now. We're bound together."

"I know that. I just … I don't know what to say."

She sounded so uncertain he couldn't help coming to her side and putting his arm around her. At first she stiffened at his touch then seemed to accept it and melt into his side. How could this woman feel so much like a part of him in so short a period of time?

He kissed her forehead. "I know that. I understand how strange this must be for you. But give it a chance, little lehen. Give *us* a chance." He emphasized the word hoping she'd understand. It wasn't that much to ask. After all they were practically together all the time anyway. Give their marriage time to feel real to her.

It was already very real to him.

He indulged himself, holding her close to his side while their dinner cooked and the ocean pounded the shoreline before them. For the moment she leaned into him and he allowed himself to believe that this was going to work out for them, that he'd keep her as his wife.

Gaia knew that he wanted to, more than anything else in the universe. It was more than just her being part of him. With her by his side all the rest of his life fell into place. His position in his family, for example. He wouldn't have to take a desk job, but could fulfill his dream of becoming a long-range pilot and travel with his wife ... and with his children when they arrived.

His future was assured and he wouldn't have to worry anymore about whether or not he'd attach at the next marriage meet. All that was done with. Kavath was set for life and with a woman he wanted and desired--a woman with unusual skills, a woman who could actually out-fly him. Sure she was from Earth, but so what? She was someone he cared about and respected.

Respect and more. *She was someone he loved.*

Kavath stiffened as he recognized the truth in that. He'd told Mea that a Gaian man always learned to love his wife, but that wasn't strictly true in his case. He'd already fallen in love with Mea, long before he'd given her his band. The band, their making love--that was only an acknowledgement of what was already between them. All the rest of it, even his desire to take over one of his family's trade routes, didn't mean half as much as just having the woman he loved with him.

He was in love with someone from the opposition and it didn't matter at all. She was his and he was hers and that's what was important.

Mea slipped out from under his arm and moved closer to the fire. For a moment he sat and wondered if now she'd tell him that she'd changed her mind and didn't want him anymore. He braced himself for that expected pain.

Picking up one of the unused wooden spits, she poked a fish suspended over the fire, releasing a small plume of steam. Turning, she gave him a tentative smile and Kavath felt his heart beat faster just from its effect.

"I think the fish might be done," she said.

Kavath smiled back. "Then we should eat," he told her. It was enough for now that she was willing to eat with him and sit with him. It was enough that for tonight she was his to love.

Tomorrow perhaps things wouldn't be so simple, but he'd deal with that then. After all, that would be another day. Sometimes the best you could do was to take things one day at a time.

He pulled the fish onto large palm fronds and laid them onto the sand in front of them. Mea poured the tea, her eyes still showing uncertainty as she handed him a seashell mug. Then she reached into her pack and pulled out a large folded leaf, opening it to show a handful of off-white crystals.

She offered it to him. "Salt--for the fish."

The item that had almost gotten her killed, but had sparked their finally coming together. Kavath let his smile show his appreciation as he took a pinch between his fingers and sprinkled it lightly over the cooling fish.

"Thank you, Mea."

"You're welcome, Kavath." She sat back down again and drank a little from her mug, then used her chopsticks to pull off a chunk of fish, blowing on it before putting it in her mouth. She smiled, her pleasure obvious. "It really is very good."

"Yes it is." He hadn't even tried his, but he knew already it would be wonderful.

She hesitated. "I was thinking … about what you said."

Kavath stiffened. Was she now going to demand release from their marriage? Was this the time he needed to explain about the trial period and ask for the three days? He schooled his expression into one that he hoped was non-committal.

"Your place or mine … maybe we better stay in my camp. My stove is already there and it's bigger...." Her voice trailed off as he broke into a relieved grin.

He leaned forward and collected his fish and a pair of eating sticks of his own. Wolfing down a piece of fish--it really was quite good--he gave her his warmest smile as if nothing else could have been on his mind. "Actually I was thinking the same thing. Your place it is."

Chapter Twelve

How had she gotten herself in this predicament? She couldn't be married and certainly she couldn't be married to a Gaian.

Kavath was a very attractive man. All right, so he was more than that, but how could she even consider treating this as if it was real?

Well, for one thing the fact that she was wearing that band of his, even if it was only around her neck instead of her wrist. She should have given it back to him already, and she would have but she found that she actually rather liked having it.

Plus the discussion of him moving to her camp had made her happier than she'd expected. In the past she'd thought about how nice it would be to have Kavath around all the time, and now it seemed it was actually going to happen.

For a moment Mea thought about lying with him in a tent at night. She got hot just thinking about sharing a blanket-- and more--with Kavath. Waking with him in her arms every morning. Loving him before she went to sleep at night.

Loving him. Only his presence kept her from groaning aloud. Okay, so she was more than a little infatuated with him. That wasn't necessarily love. Was it?

She looked up to see him staring at her, the look in his eyes as bright and hopeful as if he'd just been handed the best present ever. And that present was her!

And she felt the same way when she looked at him. Okay … that could be love.

Once they'd finished dinner, Kavath and Mea fell into a silence broken only by the low crackling of the fire. She couldn't decide if the quiet was due to discomfort over their new relationship or simply weariness over the long day. Maybe it was a little of both.

Kavath seemed content to not push her about how she felt over their marriage, consummated just a few hours before. Instead he devoted his attention to mundane tasks such as dealing with the bounty he'd collected that day from the sea. After suspending the extra fish over the fire-pit, he pulled coals under them, letting them cook slowly, turning the spits at the same time.

That reminded her of her collection of multi-legged shellfish. She dug it out of her collecting bag and handed it to Kavath. "I couldn't figure out what to do with them. Maybe we could make a soup?"

His eyes lit up at the creatures. "We could, but since they're so fresh, they'd be even better steamed. I wish you'd showed them to me earlier, we could have made them an appetizer."

"I had other things on my mind," she told him wryly.

He laughed and Mea wondered if she'd ever see him in a bad mood again.

"You have a point. An odd choice for dessert, but there's no point in letting them go to waste."

Bringing the water in her pot to a full boil, he suspended the leaf-wrapped package over it and let it sit for a while. The smell that emanated from the package was enticing. After cracking the shells with a rock, Kavath separated the small creatures from their legs and other non-edible bits, and after eating several he managed to persuade her to try one.

"They aren't that different in taste from pranas," he told her, holding the prepared morsel just in front of her mouth. "That's a delicacy on our ships. I wish we had some butter for them, but they're pretty good as they are."

Multi-legged shellfish a delicacy? With trepidation Mea nibbled it directly from his fingers and discovered to her surprise she liked the tender little item.

It was strange seeing him without the mask. She knew he had to be close to her age, early to mid-twenties in Earth years. But he seemed older than that sometimes. Most people like her drifted along, not having a plan for their lives, but not Kavath. She'd never known anyone like him, so intent on what he wanted--particularly since what he wanted was something she'd never known a man to desire.

Men in her experience didn't want the responsibility of a wife or a family. Even her own father hadn't hung around long after getting her mother pregnant. Their home had been a way station for him, a place to visit once in a while. With time he'd stopped coming around at all, leaving her mother to raise their offspring by herself.

If it hadn't been for Grandda and the rest of the tribe, they'd have been all alone. Fortunately her mam's knack with machinery had given them a place in the off-beat world of the asteroid belt, and she and her brother had grown up with most of the necessities of life.

Unlike her father, Kavath seemed like he couldn't wait until he had a family. In fact he was so impatient to have one, he'd taken her for his wife rather than wait until he was home. She didn't believe for a moment he'd have had trouble finding a wife, even if the women were blindfolded. All they had to do was breathe deep and catch some of that sexy smell of his. At that moment she did just that, and grew far more aware of him, her body heating in places where he'd touched her.

Kavath's smile grew and she knew he understood just what he was doing to her. She hadn't seen that smug a male expression in a while.

"Look, Kavath, maybe this isn't such a good idea." She held up the wrist band. "As you said just yesterday, we come from such different backgrounds. You don't know very much about me and I barely know you."

She expected him to protest but instead he just nodded like she'd said something very wise. "So let's talk. What do you want to know about me? Ask me any question you wish."

She wanted to ask him if he really wanted her as his wife, or was she simply convenient for his purposes.

Perhaps a safer topic could be found. "You seem so at home in the ocean. How did you learn to swim like that?"

"My family's land is on an island, water all around. I was practically born in the sea. I took my first steps on a beach and could swim before I could run." He leaned back, happy and relaxed. "My sisters and I are ... that is were ... all good swimmers." A shadow crossed his face for a moment, but when he looked at her again it was gone.

"I love being in the water almost as much as I do being in space. In some ways, when you go out into deep enough water it is like flying. You don't feel gravity like you do when you're on land. I'll show you how to float tomorrow."

"I'm not sure I want to learn, Kavath. I may have learned my lesson with the ocean."

"You'll be safe with me. There is nothing that will hurt you when I'm around, little lehen."

"What is that? What you keep calling me?"

"Lehen? It is a bird on Gaia. A magnificent bird that flies with all the grace of the eagles that no longer exist on Earth...." She perked up at the compliment only to see his teasing grin as he continued.

He moved to stroke her arms in her uniform shirt. "You remind me of it, Mea. A brilliant flyer--with dull grey feathers!"

"Oh, you!" She swatted his hands away, and he moved only to capture her hands and hold them close to his chest.

"You are my little lehen, my brilliant flyer, and when I can, I will give you dresses of equally brilliant color."

"Dresses?" The women of her tribe loved to dress up, but it had been a while since she'd worn anything but pants.

"Gaian women wear dresses, or skirts and blouses. But I can get you pants if you like." He stroked her cheek with the back of his hand. "I will give you anything you want, my wife."

Her freedom to roam the universe, would he give her that? Not with the possessive way he was watching her.

She didn't say anything but his eyes grew watchful. "I answered your question. Time for you to answer one of mine. Where did you learn how to fly?"

She might as well tell him. "You know how you said you were practically born in the ocean? Well, I was born in space. My family lived in the asteroid belt."

That caught Kavath's interest. "The one in Earth's solar system? They were miners?"

"Not exactly." She hesitated. "Have you ever heard of the Travelers?"

He broke into a grin. "You mean Vacuum Gypsies? Yeah, I heard of them. They were squatters on the old mining platforms." Mea stiffened in sudden anger and his grin faded as he recognized it.

"We don't call ourselves gypsies--we adopted the old Earth name of Traveler. Many of us had ancestors from that tribe. And we weren't squatters. The platforms had been abandoned for almost a century before we came. They were of no use to anyone. We made them useful and in turn we should have been given leave to stay."

He looked over at the pot she'd made, reworked from a gas canister. "You're one of them? I'd always heard they were good with their hands."

Her chin went up a hair. "That's why we were sometimes called tinkers. We left Earth years ago, twenty families crammed into a half-dozen ships with barely enough fuel to make it to the platforms. For the next fifty years it was our home. We called it Baile Na, our home in the old tongue. My mother was born there, and my brother and me. Sure, I know how to make things. I grew up where you made do with what you had. Traders would come with goods we could use, and we'd trade them ore, or the items we'd made. It's why I learned to sew and make things. Mam.... " Her voice trailed off and she looked down. He noticed and put his arms around her.

Mea brushed a tear from her eye.

"You think I'm good at making stuff? My mother was so much better." She laughed but the sound was brittle. "It was said she could make a tea set fit to serve a queen from a rusty boiler. And she was such a flyer--it was as if she had wings herself. She taught my brother and me.

"We had these little single-man space scooters. They were once used to haul mined ore around, but we made them into transports with five times the speed. Jack and I would race and have mock battles with the other kids on the platform."

"Jack was your brother?"

She nodded and hesitated. "I haven't seen him in a while."

"You said you had no family on Earth."

"None are on Earth, or in Earth's solar system any longer. The Travelers are gone from Baile Na."

Kavath stilled and his face turned sober, apparently recognizing the seriousness of what she was telling him. "What happened to them?"

"The platforms were just space junk, but they were on the books of some big corporation on Earth. No one had any interest in them for over a hundred years. But then we put the platforms back together and made them into a popular trading spot a few hours' flight away from Earth.

"The corporation suddenly saw value and decided they wanted the platforms back. We tried negotiating, but they decided to evict us. We said we wouldn't go and the government sent in troops to do the job."

She took a deep breath. "We fought, some of us died, the rest were arrested."

Kavath held her closer. "Who died, Mea?"

She broke down into tears and Kavath held her, his presence a comfort she hadn't expected. "Mam and Grandda. Their ship was clipped by an Earthforce fighter and both ships went into an asteroid. I saw it happen--it was an accident, it had to be. The Earthforce pilot died as well as my family. Jack and I were on our scooters. We were captured and put into prison with some of the other young Travelers who'd lost their families. The rest were deliberately scattered to the Outer Colonies to keep us from joining forces again."

"So how did you end up in Earthforce, particularly after they killed your family?"

She shrugged. "I wasn't given much of a choice. It was Earthforce or prison without any possibility of parole. I'd have died rather spend the rest of my life in a cage. Jack and I both joined and they let us fly again."

Kavath seemed outraged. "This is your prison sentence? To fly for Earthforce?"

"It hasn't been so bad. I've served almost four years and they will let me go once the war is over. Then I'll go to the Outer Colonies and find the others."

His arms tightened around her and she realized what she'd said. "You are my wife now, Mea."

She didn't like the trapped feeling that rose inside her. It was almost like being back in the Earth-side prison, with no options ahead of her.

"What about your father?"

Mea laughed. "He wasn't a Traveler, but he traveled through our home, stayed just long enough to father Jack and me. Jack's about two years older than I am. Mom loved my dad, I think, and he might have even loved her, but for him the chase was definitely the thing. He came around sometimes when we were young. Mom was always glad to see him and cried when he left."

"And so you worry that I won't be different from your father? Mea, I can't even begin to tell you how different I would be. I couldn't imagine behaving towards you the way your mother was treated. You are my woman, now and always, and I couldn't cheat on you even if I wanted to. But believe me, I could never want to."

He reached for the necklace she wore and twisted it to show the emblem it bore. "When you decide to accept me for all time, put this around your wrist. I will never ask for it back, and if you give it back I'll never offer it to anyone else. It's you I want, Mea, for all time."

His vehemence overwhelmed her. "I don't know if I can say yes, Kavath...."

He tilted her head up to look into her eyes. "Just don't say no, then. At least not right now." Then his lips descended onto hers and no way could she have said anything at all. She fell under his spell, loving the way he held her as if she were the most precious thing in his life.

Mea responded with her own lips and hands, the latter restlessly moving over his back, then under his shirt to find that tantalizing skin of his. She stroked him, enjoying his hard smoothness, the feel of his muscles rippling beneath her fingers as he pulled her closer, pressing her breasts into his chest. Her nipples hardened and ached and Mea moaned into his mouth.

Breaking their kiss, Kavath lifted her into his lap, his hands now exploring her, moving under her shirt to clutch her breast, kneading the softness there. "I've never felt anything like this before," he groaned into her ear. "They can tell you as much as they want but some things need to be experienced to be understood."

Mea looked up to see him smiling at her, the sheer joy in his eyes speaking to her louder than any words.

The right words didn't seem to be hard for him to find. "I want to love you again, my wife. But this time I want to take it slow and make it memorable. I want you to want me as much as I do you. Show me how to please you."

As if there was anything lacking with the last time they'd bunked … that is, made love. Somehow the Earthforce nickname didn't seem to do justice to the experience of sex, not when it was Kavath who held her.

Apparently stamina was the least of his problems. His heartbeat sounded triple-time against her chest, and he hadn't bothered to put on more than his outer shirt and shorts, so she easily felt his erection through the thin fabric.

As rapid as he'd stripped her before, now he took his time, undoing the fastenings of her shirt with deliberate slowness, letting his hands and eyes worship her as each inch was revealed. Since she'd dressed completely, it seemed to take forever before he was down to bare skin again, taking her now aching nipples into his mouth, one after the other, to suckle long and hard, teasing them into awareness.

He explored her body with hands, lips, and the heat of his gaze, as if setting into his mind the sight of her, and her feel, taste, and smell. Perhaps he was imprinting her in his mind as he made love to her.

On her back his fingers paused, carefully tracing her small tattoo, three interlocking rings colored blue-green, just below the top of her shoulder. "What's this? This mark?"

"My tribe tattoo. All Travelers have one, or something like it."

She looked up to see his possessive grin. "It's the same as your ship, isn't it, marking it as yours. Our people aren't so different in setting claims are they?"

He was right and to her surprise she found herself matching his grin. "It reminds me that's what's mine is mine and I won't lose it."

With the back of his hand he caressed her cheek. "You won't lose me, little lehen. I'm yours forever." He hesitated then set his jaw. "Nor will you lose your people now that I know what they mean to you. After the war, I'll help you find them."

It was as if he'd sucked the breath out of her. Could he mean it, that he'd go with her to the Outer Colonies to find her tribe? "You'd do that for me?" she asked breathlessly.

"Your kin are mine. Of course I will, if you'll let me."

Of course she realized his proposal depended on her staying in this marriage. Could she really bargain away her future so easily? But when he was holding her this way, and kissing her, a future with him seemed like a good thing. He turned his attention back to making love to her and the rest of her dismay faded under his sensual assault.

"Kavath!" She cried out as he fastened his mouth to her breasts, this time delving his hand into the juncture of her legs, seeking soft folds and her clit. With one hand he brought her to climax, not stopping as he had earlier when trying to convince her to accept what she now realized was his form of a marriage proposal.

As she came down to earth, shuddering from the aftermath of his attention, she wondered if he no longer felt the need to hold back now that he had what he'd wanted from her.

Mea tried to summon up some kind of indignation, only to discover that she just couldn't maintain it. Not when she was still feeling the effects of one of the fastest and most intense orgasms of her life.

The future was looking real promising at the moment.

In the meantime the present was pretty good as well. Kavath pulled off his shirt and shorts and, gloriously naked, stretched himself on top of Mea, pushing her nude form into the soft sand beneath. Mea's thighs opened of their own accord to him. Her body seemed to have no trouble recognizing him as lover, even if she might still have doubts.

She waited for him to take advantage of his position to enter her, but he didn't immediately. For a moment he simply smiled into her face and stroked her cheek.

"I know you aren't certain of us quite yet, Mea. Be certain of one thing, though. I have no doubts that we are meant to be together."

"Are we?"

His smile broadened. "Oh, yes." Stretched out across her he looked as comfortable as if he'd been there a hundred times before and not just once. Mea wondered at that. She knew he had been inexperienced the first time, but apparently Gaian men learned quickly.

The hand on her cheek trailed over to finger her hair, letting it curl around his finger. "I can't imagine anyone but you beneath me like this, little lehen, now or ever."

She couldn't help her sharp retort. "Beneath you? Why do I have to be on the bottom?"

A flash of laughter sped through his face and he had the nerve to grin. "You want to be on top this time?" He rolled suddenly, taking her with him, and then she was staring down at him, his arms firmly holding her in place. Against her backside, his erection pulsed.

Kavath grinned wickedly at her. "Does this meet with your approval?"

She couldn't say that it was her favorite position to bunk in, but at least sand wasn't filling the crack of her bottom. That was an improvement. Mea reached behind her and grasped his shaft, stroking it gently, watching as Kavath's face lost its grin and his eyes grew wide with appreciation.

"I approve, Kavath. Do you?"

"Anything you want, Mea. I'm all yours."

He was hers and there was so much of him to appreciate. His shaft was full and tight in her hands. She pulled it up to rest in the crevice of her backside and slid up and down against it. A low growling noise came from deep within Kavath's throat. "Keep that up and you won't have me to play with for very long."

"Oh, I think I have you just where I want you." Rising on her knees, she placed him at her opening and sank down onto him. The little growl he'd made before became a full-fledged roar as she impaled herself on his shaft.

Mission accomplished, Mea leaned over him. "Big, bad Gaian man. Now I really have what I want."

A wild grin spread over his face and he raised his hips, plunging himself deeper inside her. "And so do I."

Mea let out a small screech as he did, not because it hurt but because it felt so good. Even so, Kavath's eyes went wide with alarm. "I didn't hurt you, did I?"

She shook her head, too excited to answer him. He took that as permission to continue and this time she was ready for him, rising and falling with him in rhythm with each thrust. As they moved, he slowed, and she matched him and it became like a dance between them, the dance of making love.

Illuminated by the firelight, the heat between them grew hotter than the flames as they came together. Mea realized how different sex was with Kavath.

It wasn't bunking, not this. He might be right. Perhaps they were made for each other. The fit of him was so right and she couldn't help reacting to him. For weeks she'd watched him and wondered what making love to him would be like and that was after months of feeling nothing for the men around her.

Mea certainly felt something now. Kavath matched her cries with small noises of his own. "Don't stop, mine, I want to hear you with me." He sped up and the dance between them grew more frantic. She felt his stomach clench under her thighs and his shaft inside her seem to grow. His hands on her hips clutched her tighter and in the firelight his eyes seemed to glow.

"Now, Mea. Take your pleasure now!" And she did, unable to resist his call, erupting in a long cry of female satisfaction. Kavath slowed, milking the moment, then with a shout of his own finished. Inside her she felt his hardness pulse, filling her with his seed.

Later there was no sound, just the crackle of the fire and the steady drum of waves hitting the beach a few meters away. Mea rested on Kavath's chest with her head pillowed on his shoulder. Between them lay the pendant, the rolled up wristband he'd given her.

She thought about unfastening it and securing it to her wrist. In her post-coital mood, the insanity of their marriage no longer seemed quite so insane.

She looked up to see him watching her, the slightest hint of a smile on his face. Did he actually know her thoughts? His mouth opened as if to speak, then he closed it. Instead he cuddled her closer and kissed her forehead, then leaned back to stare at the sky above them. "One thing about the beach, there is nothing between us and the stars."

Mea slid to Kavath's side, turning onto her back to face the sky. He made room for her, tucking her under his arm in a move so natural, it was as if they'd lain like that many times before. Mea felt that strange sense of rightness at being with him.

Instead of focusing on that, she forced herself to look up at the stars. Myriad pinpoints of light dotted the still blackness above them. Mea tried to appreciate them for their beauty and not think about the war still raging above them. The entire universe should be in harmony tonight, the way she and Kavath were at this point, not opposing forces, but in concert together.

She hummed an old tune, one her mother had sung to her when she was a child.

"That's pretty," Kavath said. "What is it?"

"A love song."

"Are there lyrics?"

She sang the words that she could remember. It was in the old language and Kavath listened quietly, his hand stroking her waist.

"What does it mean?" he asked when she was done.

"It's about a boy and girl who want to marry, but their people are fighting and can't. They ask the moon to take them away so they can be together." She hadn't realized how appropriate the lyrics were to their situation, although in the song the young couple couldn't escape the powers that separated them.

At least they were out of reach of both of their people at the moment. The Gaians were more likely to find them than Earthforce.

She leaned up to stare into Kavath's face. "If your people come, what will happen to me?"

"If you are worried about being planted in a prison somewhere, that won't happen." He kissed her forehead gently. "Or at least it won't happen without me. We don't separate husbands and wives, Mea."

Lying back down she rested her head on his shoulder again. "I can't see myself living on a Gaian ship, Kavath. Not when they are fighting Earth."

She felt him sigh and his hand slid around her waist to cinch her tighter to him. "We'll deal with that when it comes down to it, my wife. Just know I won't let you go anywhere without me."

For a time he was quiet. "I used to watch the stars like this with my sisters. They would talk about their spouses and children and make plans." He glanced down at her. "They'd tease me that I'd never find a woman on Gaia to suit me. Funny that. I guess they were right."

"Are they married now?"

"Anda and Delia are. Kaleen...." his voice grew quiet. "She was younger than I was, and in school ... she was at Carras."

Something in the way he said it made her sit up to stare into his face. "She was where?"

"Carras...." his voice trailed off. "It doesn't matter now, Mea. We should sleep."

She knew it did matter, but if Kavath didn't want to talk about his sister, she wouldn't press him.

He pulled their clothes over them to make something resembling a blanket. With their bodies so close together and the wind partially blocked by the log behind them, she wasn't cold, in spite of the chill breezes coming off the sea. The fire had burned to embers but it still put out quite a bit of heat. Kavath put her between him and the fire so she benefited most from it.

As always he was looking out for her, just like the first time they'd slept together, when he'd protected her during the storm. A full stomach, near drowning, and two enthusiastic love-making sessions now combined to make her drowsy and she drifted off to sleep locked in his arms.

* * * *

Mea's breath evened out as she fell asleep and Kavath held her close. Her question about the future had opened up fresh concerns that had bothered him from the beginning. What would happen when they finally got back to his people, and he had to introduce his woman from the enemy camp to his family and shipmates? Not that anyone would question his decision for long. One look at her and they were bound to agree that she was perfect for him.

One advantage of attachment was that there was no question whether a woman was right or not. If you attached to her then that should be enough for anyone.

Even so, he knew better than to say that her fears weren't justified. Kaleen's death had devastated his parents and bringing into their home a woman from those responsible would not go over well. Perhaps after a couple of years of peace things would have been different. But that wasn't going to happen now.

His arm tightened around Mea. His family didn't have a couple of years to get used to it. She was his now and he'd die ... no, worse, he'd kill before he'd see her gone from his side. He didn't care what anyone said or thought--if anyone tried to separate them there would be hell to pay, and that included family and friends.

For the first time in his life Kavath had found someone more important to him than what others thought and he wasn't going to lose her.

Chapter Thirteen

Mea woke with the first sun's light streaming over the jungle before her. The fire was nothing but cold ashes, the sand gritty beneath her and their clothes had slipped off during the night, leaving gaps that the early morning sea breeze had no trouble exploiting.

Even so, she was comfortable. How could she get cold when she had a big, heat-generating man keeping a possessive hold on her? She turned towards him and he stirred a little in his sleep, one hand restlessly stroking her lower back until she settled into his side. Once she'd stopped moving, his hand curved around her bottom and came to rest.

Mea gazed into his face. His eyes were closed and his breath even. Fine blond hair stubbled his cheeks where his beard suppressor no longer functioned, a symptom of how long they'd been here.

They'd been here long enough for her hair to grow to finger length and his beard to come in. She took a moment to appreciate the way the thin growth lined his face. Unlike most men she knew, Kavath actually looked good with a little bit of a beard.

She tried to remain quiet, but it became difficult when she felt the large ridge of his morning erection pressing into her upper thigh. Immediately she thought of the first morning she'd awakened with him and what she'd found when looking under the blanket. In this case it was just his jacket, but the tenting was still impressive.

He hadn't much liked her touching him that way before, but maybe now that they were better introduced--and married--he wouldn't mind. Tentatively Mea slid her hand under the jacket until she found the blunt tip of his cock.

As her fingers closed around him, Kavath stirred and muttered, but the noise he made didn't sound like a complaint. She stroked him gently and what she'd assumed was a full erection suddenly became a lot more full and erect. A few moments of play resulted in a few pearls of fluid leaking into her hand.

Now Kavath stirred and his eyes blinked and he opened them to stare at her in confusion. Mea's hand stilled and she waited to see how he was going to react this time. When a smile played around his lips, she relaxed and squeezed the solid shaft in her hand.

He gave a deep chuckle that sent sensual shock waves rippling along her spine. "My, my. It seems I'm being attacked again."

"Do you mind?"

Kavath pursed his lips as if thinking about it, then he leaned back, putting his hands behind his head. "Not at all. Do your worst, woman."

Given permission, Mea continued her play. It was fun touching Kavath this way. Everything she did he responded so positively to that pleasuring was nearly as enjoyable for her as for him. In fact, she liked it so much that something else she didn't normally do struck her fancy. Feeling his gaze solidly on her, she sat up and carefully licked the tip of him.

His eyes widened and he grinned. "Oh, I've seen holo-vids of this."

She smiled and took him into her mouth. A few moments later, a deep groan erupted from him. "Oh, Mea--your worst is very good indeed," he gasped out. "But if you don't stop, I'm going to explode."

She sat back up, still holding him in her hand. "Are you sure you want me to stop?"

"What I'm sure of is this," he said and before Mea could react, she found herself on her back in the sand and her legs over her head. "I've always wanted to know what you tasted like down here."

With that Kavath's face disappeared between her thighs and Mea cried out as his tongue found her most sensitive spots. For someone just learning how to make love, the man was a very quick study. In moments Mea was writhing on the sand. She cried out and before she regained her senses Kavath was leaning over her, fitting himself to her once again.

Three times in less than half a day, Mea thought to herself. That was certainly a record for her.

Then he smiled at her so lovingly that the next thing she thought was that it was a good thing that Gaian men always learned to love their women--because she suspected she was already very much in love with her Gaian.

* * * *

After a morning spent making love, they cleaned up in the ocean and Kavath taught Mea the basics of floating in the water. He caught a few more fish, then they packed up and headed back to their camps.

Half way back from the beach they stopped to rest in the shade. Mea put down her pack and Kavath put down his string of fresh fish. He took her into his arms and nuzzled her ear. "You don't know what a miracle you are, do you? I can't wait to get you to camp and make love with you again, even if it is in a tent and a sleeping sack." He sighed. "Imagine what we could do in a real bed."

Mea could and she shivered in delicious anticipation. She even looked forward to sharing her tent with him and their combined bedding. The beach had been fun, but it had taken her nearly an hour to wash all the sand out of her crevices before they'd left the sea.

But Kavath was thinking of more than a tent and their sleep sacks. He was thinking of Gaia.

"A bed sounds wonderful and I'm looking forward to visiting your home." She smiled up at him. "But how will your family feel about you bringing an Earthforce officer home as a wife?"

Kavath went very still and Mea wondered what she'd said that was wrong.

After a moment he kissed her forehead and sighed. "I won't lie to you, Mea. That may take some time. Kaleen, my younger sister--she was at Carras and that will be hard for my family to cope with. But I don't care any more about where you are from, or that you've been serving in Earth's military. I was sure I'd never be able to have anyone, there were so few women my age."

That was the second time he'd mentioned Carras, and every time it was as if she should know the significance. "Carras? I don't know what Carras is."

Kavath's eyes narrowed and when he looked at her there was near shock in his face. "You've been in Earthforce since the beginning of the war. Surely you know about Earth's first great victory." His voice held such heavy ridicule it was all Mea could do to not pull away from him.

"Earth's great victory?" She thought back to the beginning of the war. "You mean the attack on Gaia when it took out the arms factory?"

"Arms factory?" Kavath looked outraged. "What are you talking about? We never had an arms factory. All we had was Carras. That's what Earth destroyed."

Surprised, Mea actually did step away. "But that's why there was a preemptive attack on it. Gaia was planning on making war against Earth so Earthforce came in and destroyed it." She stopped for a moment, suddenly concerned. "Did your sister work there?"

Kavath shook his head. "No, she didn't work there. My sister was sixteen and she was there because it was a girl's school! Destroying Carras was what Earth did to teach us our place."

Mea stared, now completely confused. "I don't know what you are talking about...."

"Of course you know," he said. "You're in Earthforce, you must know."

Desperation filled her and her voice. "I don't! Really, I don't."

Kavath stared for a moment. She saw some of the anger leave him and knew he believed her. "Maybe you don't know. Hard to believe, but a lot about Carras is hard to believe."

For a moment he kept his unseeing attention on the ground, not meeting her eyes. "It was at the start of the war. The Gaian government was still negotiating, trying to convince Earth we wouldn't be bullied anymore."

"Bullied?" she said. "What do you mean bullied?"

Kavath glanced up. "Haven't you ever wondered why our communit parts were so alike, Mea? Why so much of our technologies are the same?"

"Not really. Gaia was a colony of Earth's. They would buy Earth's technology wouldn't they?"

"Sure they did ... at first. But then we started building our own and it was better." He gave her a near humorous look.

"You saw both communits. Which would you have said was the more advanced? Yours or mine?"

Now that he mentioned it. "Yours, I guess. It seemed to be a little less bulky. I thought it was a newer model."

"It is newer. The most advanced design from Gaia, made to be smaller, use less power, and have a greater range," he added. "Some of the best technical minds in the universe are on Gaia and after a while we started improving on the Earth technology. Then we found out large Earth corporations who'd seen our designs were selling our improvements under Earth patents without any compensation. They even tried to make us pay for the use of our own technology. Court negotiations didn't go well and Earth's government refused to help so we declared sovereignty and independence from Earth assuming that would make them decide to work with us to resolve the problem."

Kavath shook his head. "Unfortunately they didn't think that would be necessary. As soon as the message about Gaian independence was delivered, Earth responded with an unexpected attack and by the time we mobilized, Earthforce ships were past our defenses and into one of our main cities. They hit some other targets, but saved their real firepower for Carras. Flattened it. Destroyed it completely and killed everyone there."

He took a deep ragged breath and Mea saw the pain in his face. "It was a girl's school, Mea, ages fourteen to twenty-one. Our biggest. A third of our young women went there." He faltered. "Kaleen, my sister, was there. She was only sixteen, still a girl."

Mea could barely stand to listen to the anguish in his voice. His story was hard to believe, but she believed his anger.

She knew for herself that the big corporations ran things on Earth and that the government was corrupt, but surely they wouldn't have done that. No Earthforce squad would have done such a thing, and she would have heard about it if they did. The military wasn't that good at keeping secrets.

Mea stiffened. Well, most of it wasn't. Mea blinked and took a deep breath. "The Death Angels," she said, just under her breath.

Even so Kavath had heard her. "What?"

She couldn't ignore him. "The Death Angels. It's special branch of Earthforce. Elite pilots, trained for special operations. That's who attacked Gaia the first time. I applied with them, once, when my commanding officer noticed my piloting skill and recommended me to them. I failed the tests."

He blinked at her. "Failed? Not a good enough pilot?"

Mea took a momentary pride in the disbelief in his voice, knowing it meant he truly appreciated her skill. "No, not piloting. Personality tests. I wasn't ruthless enough for them." She shook her head. "First time I've ever been pleased not to get a promotion. Trust me, if you'd been up against a Death Angel before we landed, you wouldn't be here now."

That was all true, but even so she couldn't believe it possible. "The Death Angels can be coldblooded, but they couldn't have known it was a girl's school," she said finally. "It had to have been a mistake."

Kavath stared at her, his face flushed. "You think that ten thousand young women died as a result of a mistake? Two dozen ships attacked that school and hit it with everything they had. When the girls took to the athletic fields they bombed those to finish the job."

He took a deep breath. "They knew our weakness--that we have to keep our young men and women separated to avoid attachments when they are too young. Because of this they could select one target and do the most damage."

"I don't understand. Why not just kill the men?"

Kavath glared as if it should be obvious. "Because our men need the women but the reverse isn't true. The women could take anyone for a husband, but for a man a woman must be someone he can attach to. That's why you are so important to me, Mea."

She fingered the band around her neck. "So, that's the way it is … because I somehow give off the right smell, I'm important. You want me to be your wife, even though you say my people were responsible for the death of your sister."

The rest of Kavath's anger slipped away and all she could see was a man who really loved her. In some way it broke her heart. Particularly with this new information she knew there was still something about her that he should know and she wasn't sure how she was going to tell him.

He reached for her. "You aren't responsible. As you say, you failed to become a Death Angel and they were the ones who attacked Carras. I was wrong to blame you in the first place ... it wasn't your responsibility. Besides, you're important to me because you are. I don't care who your people are."

All she could do was shake her head. "You should care, Kavath, and you probably will eventually."

Kavath touched her face and flinched when she avoided his hand. "I don't want to fight with you, Mea. These next two days I want to be perfect."

Mea caught his words and looked up. "Why the next two days?" she said sharply.

Kavath seemed to suppress a groan at her question and she knew the answer. "Our marriage isn't permanent, is it?" she said. "There's a probationary period."

She'd guessed the truth and she knew he hated to admit it to her. "Three days," he told her, "including yesterday, and I want all of them."

He took her by the shoulders and forced her to look at him. "I know that we aren't the most compatible couple ever created. I know that, yes, we're going to have problems. We can hardly eat a meal together sometimes without it becoming a battle, but there is a lot of good between us too. I want your promise to give me all three days before you take that off." He pointed to the wristband still strung around her neck. "If you still can't see how I can be your husband, then we'll break up, but until then I want you to be my wife."

"Why? Is the sex that great?" she challenged.

"It isn't just sex between us and you know it." Kavath moved toward her, and Mea wondered if he intended to fight with her...or make love.

Unfortunately he didn't get the chance to either fight or make love because just then a ship broke the atmosphere above them with a loud sonic boom. Both Kavath and Mea stared as a small black speck dove into sky and grew larger until it was a black shadow against the sun.

Still too high overhead to be identifiable, the ship hovered for a moment near the sea behind them then slowly moved in the direction of their camps.

Chapter Fourteen

"Mine or yours?" Mea asked, and for a moment Kavath was gratified that he couldn't tell which she would prefer.

He knew what he wanted. With his people they'd both be safe. He'd take her back to Gaia and keep her with him forever. It could be a Gaian ship looking for him, or it might be someone else. "I'm not sure yet," he told her. "Let's get closer to our camps. If they're following a homing device, they'll head for one of our ships."

They hurried along and were within half a kilo when the speck became a full-blown ship, and much as he'd wished otherwise, Kavath knew it wasn't one of Gaian design. It headed in the direction of Mea's camp.

"Yours, I guess," Kavath said finally, when it was close enough to see clearly.

"I guess," she said. Now he was certain she wasn't happy, and he took some comfort in that. Mea watched the ship as it passed, but then she seemed to come to attention and her eyes widened.

For a long moment she stared after the ship, then abruptly she turned to him. "You should go someplace and hide, Kavath."

Her change in attitude was so fast it bewildered him. "What are you talking about? I'm not going to hide, at least not without you." He held out his hand to her. "Come with me and we'll hide together."

Meagan shook her head. "I know who these people are …" She seemed about to say more, but closed her mouth firmly. "They are following the beacon to my ship and when they find it, they will know I'm here. Once they land they'll look for me and they won't quit until they find some sign of where I've gone. The chances are they won't know you are here and you'll be safe. Find a place away from your ship and wait there."

He couldn't help himself. In spite of wanting to let her make her own decision he grabbed her arm and pulled her closer. "And what about you? Do you intend to leave with them?"

Mea hesitated and didn't meet his gaze. "I ... have to." She pulled out of his grasp and turned to face him. "Kavath, I can't stay here on this planet, or with you. My people have come for me and I need to go with them. That's what we'd agreed on from the beginning."

"That was before you became my wife." He wouldn't let her go that easily. "You can't leave me now."

"I have to, Kavath. Even if I wanted to stay...."

"What do you mean, 'even if you wanted to'?" Kavath folded his arms and stared at her, investing his glare with all of the disappointment he felt. Did she really not want to be with him? "Why wouldn't you want to? You are my wife, we belong together."

"But we don't, don't you understand that?" She yanked the chain bearing his wristband off over her head, leaving her short curls even more disheveled than usual. He wanted to reach out and smooth them, but kept his hands to himself.

Mea tried to hand the wristband to him but he didn't take it. She stared at him. "I can't be your wife, Kavath. We're too different and we don't really know each other well enough, certainly not enough to be married."

"We know each other better than most Gaian couples, Mea."

"But I'm not Gaian. I'm from Earthforce." She stared at him, her face showing her frustration. "I took an oath to serve them and my people are here to take me back."

"You swore an oath to people who killed your family?"

Pain showed on her face, and for a moment he regretted baiting her. "It was an accident ... I told you that," she replied finally. "It is my duty to go with them."

"You don't think you have a duty to our marriage?" Kavath had nothing left to lose. He had to force her to recognize just how much they had together.

For a moment Mea held the chain in her hand and stared at the wristband it held. He could read the hesitation in her face and for a moment his hopes rose. If she came with him he was sure he could find a place the Earthforce soldiers wouldn't find them. Once he and his little lehen were in the woods they'd be impossible to locate.

He'd grab her and drag her off anyway, but trouble was he needed her cooperation to do it. All she had to do was scream and she'd probably bring them on to them. Besides, after all this time he didn't want to overpower her. He wanted her to agree to hide with him.

For a long moment he waited for her decision, hoping she'd choose him over the Earthforce officers waiting for her back at her camp.

But she shook her head and his hopes fell. "It isn't that easy, Kavath. I gave an oath. I can't abandon Earthforce this way. I have to go to them."

Her rejection hurt and he couldn't help his anger. Kavath gave into it and drew away as much mentally as physically. "I was willing to face my family and friends for you, Mea. If I don't mean as much to you, more than your military, then I guess you are right. You should go."

He was almost happy when she flinched. "Kavath...." she said, her voice breaking over his name, but he didn't want to hear it. He turned and started to walk away, but she caught his arm.

"Wait," she said, her voice softer than before. In her eyes he saw mirrored the same pain he felt. "You'll want this." She tried to hand him the chain with his wristband.

Again he refused to take it. So long as she kept it, he considered her his wife. "Keep it, Mea. Put it on if you change your mind, otherwise ... " His voice broke. "Otherwise use it to remember me."

After a moment's thought he thrust the string of fish he carried into her hand. "It would be best if you had some excuse for being gone from your camp. These will help."

Before she could say another word, Kavath headed into the jungle. He left her standing alone and looking forlornly after him, but he only went a little ways before doubling back.

When he arrived back at the clearing, she wasn't where he'd left her, and it took a few moments to find her trail.

Mea moved fast towards her camp and Kavath followed at a distance, careful not to let her see him. He wasn't sure what he intended to do, but he wasn't about to leave his woman alone with the Earthforce soldiers. As far as he was concerned she was still his wife and he was going to keep an eye on her. Following, he kept as quiet as he could and he didn't think she noticed him. When he reached the outskirts of her camp, he climbed the tree he'd used first to spy on her, settling onto the branch overlooking her camp.

Another ship had landed next to her clearing, smashing and burning the vegetation. Rather than find a clearing, they'd made their own and Kavath couldn't help feeling a little anger over the destruction. It was so typical of those from Earth.

Larger and heavier than Mea's sleek little Starbird, the dark sheen of the metallic covering of the craft gleamed like a black pearl in the sunlight. A set of three emblems decorated the tail, in addition to a larger one on the fuselage, a pair of wings on either side of a blue globe. The number of pilot marks on the tail indicated a three-man crew, but Kavath couldn't make out the designs from his perch in the tree.

From his studies of Earthforce ships, Kavath knew the make and model of their visitor. It was a Skyhawk, a fighter-transport that could also take passengers, and he knew it normally carried a complement of three.

Only two men were visible at the moment, exploring Mea's camp. Unlike Mea's grey uniform, they were clad all in black, down to the helmets they carried under their arms. Obviously this was a different branch of Earthforce.

One stood on the ladder to her ship, head inside the cockpit, probably accessing her logs. The other seemed intent on the symbol decorating the tail and stood next to it, running his hand along the bottom ring. His attitude reminded Kavath of something. Hadn't he seen Mea make exactly that gesture?

Suspicion rose. She'd said she knew who they were. Perhaps one of these men was someone she cared about?

Far below, Mea entered the clearing and stood completely still for a moment. Then she shouted something and dashed forward to throw her arms around the man standing next to the tail.

Kavath's heart sank as the newcomer returned her embrace and lifted her high in the air. Smiling and laughing, the stranger hugged her close.

So much for her having no other men in her life. Obviously there was at least one man who appealed to his little lehen. Kavath glared at the Earth man who seemed to be a rival for her attentions.

The man wasn't as tall as he was, nor did he look as strong, although he'd learned in the past that being bigger didn't always translate into better as far as fighting was concerned. Even so the man didn't look like he'd prove that much of a problem if it came to a fair fight.

Unfortunately it didn't look like fighting, fair or otherwise was going to be involved. Mea clung to his arm and showed more animation towards the stranger than he'd seen towards himself. Fighting the newcomer would probably be the wrong approach if Mea really cared about him.

"Hey, Tink!" The man on the ladder had descended to face the pair. "So who is your little friend?"

Kavath may not have liked the dark-haired man with his arm around Mea, but he most certainly didn't like the way his pale-haired companion was looking at her. At least the darker man appeared to regard Mea with simple affection.

There was nothing but lust in the other man's gaze, particularly as he fixed it not on her face, but on her body, which Kavath now realized was woefully under-dressed. Mea wore her grey uniform pants, but had left her shirt unbuttoned against the heat of the day. Only her pink undershirt stood between the men's eyes and her breasts.

The pale-haired man was staring at her pink top in a way that made Kavath want to charge into the camp and slap that stare off his face.

Fortunately, Tink, the darker man, also must have noticed the way his friend ogled the woman under his arm. He whispered something to Mea and she turned away and buttoned her shirt.

"I've been here alone so long," she told them cheerfully. "I've almost forgotten how to dress." She laughed, as did the blond man, but he didn't mean it the way she did, Kavath could tell. The darker haired man named Tink said nothing.

Mea had told Kavath to find a good place to hide, but that wasn't going to be possible now. She might think she was among friends, but he knew better. At the very least, the lighter haired man had evil thoughts and was no friend of his wife.

As for Tink ... Kavath suddenly had a suspicion. Could this be Mea's brother? With his dark hair and eyes, and the protective way he had his arm around the woman, that wasn't impossible. Perhaps Mea didn't want him to meet her brother for some reason.

Not that it mattered. Brother or not, Kavath wasn't going to let anyone else protect his lady from men who were clearly up to no good. Grimly he settled against the tree trunk behind him. No hiding in the woods for him. He was going to have to keep an eye on things.

* * * *

Mea couldn't believe her luck. Of all the people to find her on this little planet, her brother Jack was the last person she'd have expected. Her joy at seeing him was tempered only by concern over what Kavath was likely to do.

She didn't for a moment believe that he'd taken off to a place of safety. She'd told Kavath to hide, but she expected him to hide in the woods nearby as he had that first night. She could almost feel his eyes watching as she greeted her brother and his shipmates.

The last thing she needed was a headstrong Gaian running in to claim her as his wife in front of three Death Angels, particularly when one of them was her own brother. Of all the possible bad timing ... this was not an opportune time to introduce them.

Had he seen her hug Jack? What would he make of that? For a moment she regretted not telling him that one of the newcomers was her brother, but if she had, she would have had to explain everything. She'd already told him that the Death Angels had been those who'd attacked Gaia and knew Kavath held them responsible for killing his sister. What would he do if he knew that not only some of them were here on the planet but that her brother was one of them? As much as he hated them, he might decide to take revenge.

Mea remembered the hate in Kavath's eyes when he'd talked about Carras and the relief she'd seen when she told him she wasn't one of those involved in that attack.

If he were here she'd have to tell him that her brother was one of those he blamed for his sister's death. That might have been enough to kill what he felt for her. Even now Kavath might even know what a Dark Angel ship looked like or their emblems … he might attack them and kill her brother.

Or worse … Kavath might be killed.

Her heart ached at leaving Kavath, and more at losing his love, but she couldn't risk his life or that of her brother. She had to keep them apart, no matter what it took.

Even if it meant losing the man she believed she might love.

Another man appeared from the black ship and came towards them, standing next to the man who'd descended the ladder. Even with her shirt now buttoned, Mea felt distinctly underdressed beneath the pair's lascivious gaze.

Jake's arm pulled her tighter to him. "This is my sister, Lieutenant Meagan An Flena. She's a standard-force pilot," he said, indicating her ship. "These two are Captain Wilcox and Lieutenant Harris, my shipmates," he added to Mea.

Captain Wilcox was tall and blond, with a significant cleft to his chin. She would have found him handsome, once, before an even taller and blonder man had taken her fancy. Wilcox stared at her, his gaze raking across her body in a way that would have once given her goose bumps. Instead an incipient queasiness awoke in her.

Mea turned her attention to the other man, but looking at Harris wasn't much better. Short, with pale reddish hair and a sallow complexion, he didn't appeal to her at all. Unfortunately from the way they were staring at her, her disdain was one sided. After nearly two months on the planet, the limited diet had slimmed her down and she had the femme-fatale body she'd always wanted.

Funny thing. Once she would have been happy to see men like this desiring her, but now they did nothing for her. Not one of them, even her brother, could compare with her Gaian husband. Mea thought of the wristband she had secured in her pocket, and for a moment wondered if she hadn't made a mistake. It was possible that she should have hidden with him.

"Where were you, Mea?" Jack asked. "When we arrived you weren't anywhere around."

"At the shoreline. I was fishing." She held up the fish Kavath had given her, glad to have the excuse.

Harris stared at the fish in her hand and his expression grew greedier than it had when looking at her. "Those look great," he said enthusiastically. "It's been a long time since I've had fresh fish. How about cooking them for us?"

Carefully Mea put the fish down. Having the Death Angels hanging around her camp wasn't such a good idea. If Kavath was hiding nearby they might find him, or if they looked carefully around her camp they might discover evidence of him among her belongings.

"Maybe we should get going," Mea said. "It won't take me very long to get packed. If the convoy isn't far I can follow you in my ship. I have some fuel but if we have to go far I'll need to get some fuel cells from you."

"I'm afraid we don't have any extras," Wilcox said and he looked at her ship with what seemed to be genuine regret. "Much as I hate to, I suspect you'll have to abandon your Starbird for now, Lieutenant, and catch a ride with us."

He looked up at the trees and stretched his arms. "It sure feels good being on solid ground for a while and breathing fresh air. We've been in space for nearly a week. The convoy won't go very far in the next few hours."

He glanced meaningfully at the fish that Harris had also coveted. "We aren't in any real hurry. It sure would be nice to have a hot meal."

Uneasily Mea glanced at her brother, but he only nodded agreement with his shipmates. "Fresh food really does sound good, Mea. We've been on rations for what seems like forever."

There wasn't going to be any way to get them off the planet without putting up some kind of fuss and that would only attract unwanted attention. Mea resigned herself to making dinner.

Wilcox walked around her encampment, examining the stove she'd fashioned by stripping the metal plating out of the interior storage area of her Starbird. "You've made quite a little home here." He picked up the two plates, noted the two cups and two pairs of chopsticks. "Two of everything. Expecting company?"

"Company, here? This place is as deserted as it gets." She took the dishes from him. "I don't like to wash up after every meal."

"Hey, what's this?" The redhead, Harris had found her pitcher. He examined it carefully "What did you do, make it out of a gas canister?"

"It was empty and I needed a pot," she said.

"Once a tinker, always a tinker," Wilcox said. He nudged Jack in the ribs. "I guess your sister isn't that different from you."

Jack looked uncomfortable but didn't say anything.

"What's in it?" Harris pulled the lid off the pitcher and took a deep whiff of the contents. "This stuff sure smells good."

Mea started to tell him not to drink it, but before she could speak he took a deep swig directly from the pitcher. The redheaded man's eyes widened in appreciation. "This is fantastic. Try some." He offered it to Jack.

She found her voice. "You don't want to drink too much of that. It was a fruit juice but it's been fermenting for a couple of days. It has alcohol in it and is probably really strong by now. I was going to use it to clean things."

To her dismay, that information did nothing to stop the Death Angels. She might as well have told them the heavily fermented pink-zinger was the nectar of the gods. Even her brother's face lit up and the next thing she knew they were helping themselves. The men confiscated the pitcher and grabbed cups from their ship, settling around her fire as if they owned the place.

Wilcox took a gingerly sip, then another deeper one. "Mmm, good stuff."

With a sinking feeling, Mea watched the three men drink heartily and realized that the chances her guests were going to leave soon were growing worse all the time. "You really should be careful of that. It's stronger than it tastes and you don't want to get too drunk to fly tonight."

Wilcox shook his head. "No hurry. They aren't looking for us. We could even stay the night here and still catch up."

Mea didn't like the way he said stay the night at all. She looked over at her brother, but if he'd noticed his captain's emphasis, he wasn't saying anything. Mea sighed. That was Jack when given drink, too preoccupied to see what was going on in front of his face.

From the way Wilcox was staring at her, he was formulating plans she was sure involved her in a way she didn't like. She wished she had some kind of weapon other than her knife. She'd have to protect herself if things got ugly.

Glad that she'd spent time yesterday learning how to clean fish, Mea pulled her knife and prepared Kavath's catch while her brother hunted wood for the fire. His shipmates drank and didn't offer to help him with the task or her with preparing dinner.

Mea realized that even in the Dark Angels, being a Traveler made Jack a second-class citizen. At least in the rest of Earthforce, she'd rarely been singled out that way.

She sighed over that, but put her mind to putting dinner together. A half-hour later cleaned and filleted fish sizzled on the stove, sprinkled lightly with some of the aromatic herbs she'd found on the way back from the shore.

While the fish cooked, she found fresh fruit and a few potato balls from a bush that hadn't gotten completely crushed by the Death Angel's ship landing on it.

Her visitors were gathered about the fire-pit, well into their second cups of pink-zinger. She had to admit, they could really hold their liquor. They'd watched as she'd prepared the last few fish, mesmerized by her cooking skill.

Mea laughed a little at herself, remembering how watching Kavath clean his kill the first time had made her sick. The blood and guts didn't faze her visitors at all. They were Death Angels, after all.

The men pulled their uniform jackets off and the tattoo of the wings and globe stood out on their bare upper arms as they sat around the fire and drank.

Wilcox pulled himself to his feet. Lumbering over, he stood behind her, closer than she liked. He put his hands on her shoulders, leaned in to sniff at her hair. "Ah, the scent of a woman. Nothing much like it. You must've been pretty lonely here, all by yourself."

She took a step back, deliberately grinding her heel into his foot. He yelped and pulled away. Mea turned and kept the knife at waist level, pointed directly at his groin. "It hasn't been that bad. You'd be surprised how little I've missed having company."

Anger flickered in his eyes then he smiled. "Sorry I got in your way--Lieutenant."

"That's all right--Captain. I'm used to having this place to myself. I need elbow room." For a moment his smile turned into something else, something feral and ugly, but he took the hint and returned to his buddies, leaving Mea alone to cook.

While the fish sizzled, she collected her few belongings and stowed them in the lizard skin bag. Her heart sank at the thought of leaving her ship behind

Mea stood at the base of her ship and ran her hand over the bottom ring of her emblem and wondered if she'd ever see her sweet little Starbird again.

Leaving her ship was only part of the problem though. Even more she wondered if she'd ever see Kavath again, or was the man who claimed to be her husband going to be out of her life forever?

Chapter Fifteen

The Death Angel ship was intended for longer voyages and so carried dishes as well as eating utensils. Mea had Jack raid the ship's galley for both so that everyone could use a plate and fork.

She drank water instead of the pink-zinger, leaving the alcoholic contents of the pitcher to her companions. Somehow a clear head seemed like a great idea, particularly with the way Wilcox and Harris seemed to take turns staring at her.

"Very good," Jack said between mouthfuls of hot fish. "You've really learned to cook, little sister. You weren't half this good at home."

Mea shrugged. "Necessity is the mother of invention. The food here wasn't going to cook itself."

"Yeah, but you even seasoned it, and this is great." He held up a slice of potato ball. "Needs a little salt, but that's all."

Mea sighed. Salt had been the reason for her and Kavath's trip to the ocean, her near drowning and their subsequent marriage ... if marriage it really was. She fought her depression over that. It was real enough to her would-be husband. Would he give up on her or was he somewhere nearby, hoping she wouldn't really leave him?

She eyed the forest in the direction of the stream. That's where he'd hidden before, the first night they'd slept together.... Was there a flash of light off something high in that tree?

"So are there any dangerous animals around here?" Wilcox's voice interrupted her thoughts. Mea turned to him. The man sounded altogether too hopeful that there were predators, and she was glad to be able to tell him the truth. The last thing she wanted were half-drunk Death Angel pilots running through the woods with drawn weapons, particularly if Kavath was hiding in the trees.

"Nothing much larger than a lizard or bird. Even the snakes aren't venomous, although I wouldn't eat the insects because they do carry some kind of poison."

"Oh," the captain said, obviously disappointed. "I thought we might have a hunt of some kind."

"Sorry, nothing around here worth hunting." Nothing other than a handsome Gaian who'd better stay out of the way.

Harris poked a stick into the fire and set it ablaze. For some reason the red-haired man seemed to find the flames fascinating and couldn't resist playing with them. It had been all Mea could do to keep the fire small for cooking as he insisted on "helping" by feeding the fire. Now that the fish was done he was back to building it up again.

Again Mea sighed. She'd have to put the fire out completely before they could leave, and Harris' feeding it would only make that more difficult. It was another symptom that the men weren't really eager to leave.

She supposed she couldn't blame them. After being in a ship out in space for so long, of course this planet with its sweet air and natural surroundings would seem wonderful.

Abruptly Mea remembered her own first thoughts on landing, how the air had smelled bad and how the jungle had seemed overwhelming. Now the smells and sounds made the place feel like home. She laughed a little. Funny how a place could grow on you.

Particularly when the company had been so fine. Would she have grown so used to the planet without Kavath around? She doubted it. It was the Gaian who had made her feel so at home. He'd taught her to make a fire, cook and clean fish, and had given her the courage to live here on her own.

Mea buried her head on her arms and tried not to think about the chain and wristband in her pocket. She would miss him when she was gone.

"Too bad there's nothing to hunt," Wilcox said. "I'd really enjoy a good kill. The trouble with this war is that there isn't that much to it. The Gaians don't want to fight for real, just disable and capture." His voice was slurred, the result of too much pink-zinger.

"Yeah," Harris agreed, holding up his now burning stick, poking it at some dry leaves on the ground. Probably looking for something living to set on fire. "What we need is to get back on their planet. Maybe another attack like the first would make them fight for real. Get them riled up."

Jack stiffened and cast a nervous glance at Mea, then his shipmate. "Not supposed to talk about that, Harris," he said in a quiet voice.

Mea grew very still. She knew that Jack had been in the Death Angels when the war began, but she hadn't been sure he'd been in the first attack, or that he'd been sworn to secrecy over it. Suddenly Kavath's claim that the attack on Carras had been deliberate didn't seem so farfetched.

Harris was too drunk to care about secrets. "Hey, she's your sister, Tink. She probably already knows the truth."

Mea decided to take a chance. "About Carras? I heard something about it."

All three men stared at her. Jack paled a little while the other two laughed.

"So it has gotten out to the fleet," Wilcox said. "I was wondering how long it would take before that happened." He leaned closer than she liked and gave her a steady stare. "So just what did you hear?"

"That it wasn't an arms factory, but a girl's school." She stared at Jack who was suddenly very interested in the ground at his feet, not meeting her gaze at all. "I heard our forces deliberately destroyed it to make the Gaians give up independence."

For a long moment no one spoke, then Jack lifted his head. Mea saw the agony in his eyes and she knew the truth. Kavath was right. The slaughter of Gaian girls had not been a mistake.

Jack sat in troubled silence and Mea's last hope that he hadn't been involved disappeared. How could Kavath think to keep her as his wife with her own brother involved in such a terrible crime?

Wilcox broke in. "You know too much, Lieutenant, for your own good, and if you're smart you'll forget you ever heard of Carras. It wasn't a conventional military target, but it was the best way to strike at the Gaians and make them give up."

Mea took some comfort in the fact that Jack turned away in disgust at his captain's comment, and she knew in her heart that even if his captain defended the action, her brother hadn't wanted any part of the destruction of Carras.

Fury for those innocent deaths ripped through her. "Except they didn't surrender, did they?" Mea said. "It horrified and infuriated the Gaians and made them only more intent on gaining their freedom from Earth. Even worse, it made it hard for hundreds of their men to marry. That's who we are fighting, the men whose women died before they even had a chance to meet them. They fight so hard because they have no one to come home to and nothing to lose. They'd rather die than live alone."

She realized she'd used Kavath's exact words--that he would rather die than not have a wife. Reaching into her pocket she fingered the band he'd given her. She was the woman he'd chosen to be his wife and she'd left him. But he hadn't taken the band back and all of a sudden she was glad for that. Maybe there was still a chance for them.

She wished that she could have gone into hiding with him. She'd known that the Death Angels, particularly her brother who'd have known from her ship's emblem she was on the planet, would have torn the forest apart looking for her. Nothing would have remained hidden from them, even a wily Gaian. But that wasn't the only reason she'd gone to her camp.

When she'd seen the symbol on the tail of the ship and had known it was her brother, she had to see him. Kavath's accusations had made her want to talk to him, to have him deny that he'd been involved in Carras.

But now she knew that he had been, and her heart sank under that knowledge. Her brother tried to put an arm around her shoulder and Mea's felt queasy. She shrugged her brother's arm off and rose to collect the now empty plates.

As she took Wilcox's plate, he held onto to it and grabbed her wrist. His eyes narrowed into a predatory glare. "Sounds to me like you know a lot more than you should."

She tried to shrug nonchalantly. "I heard about Carras and figured the rest out for myself. It doesn't take a genius to realize that when you take away a man's reason for living it makes it hard for him to care about staying alive. We'll never get back to Gaia, because they will never permit it.

We're lucky the Gaians don't like to kill, otherwise we'd have been dead long ago."

"You sound like you admire them," Wilcox said through narrowed eyes.

"Maybe I do," she said evenly.

"I wonder who you've been talking to."

Jack said nothing, but Mea watched him stare down at the plate in his hand and the matching one in hers. His gaze wandered, took in the fire that she wouldn't have been able to build without help, and she knew he was wondering who'd given her lessons.

Mea hoped he wouldn't say anything, but she could tell Jack was suspicious that she hadn't been alone all this time.

Wilcox tugged her closer. "Maybe the Gaians do have one thing right. They'd rather make love than war ... perhaps we should emulate them."

The queasiness inside her grew stronger until Mea wondered if she was going to throw up. The sweet smell of pink-zinger was heavy on Wilcox's breath as she turned to face him. Lust dwelled in his dark eyes--and anger.

She knew what he was thinking. She'd been putting him off and hadn't immediately swooned into his manly Death Angel arms. Having been in Earthforce since she was eighteen, Mea had met his kind before. Those meetings hadn't generally gone well, but usually she gave in before she was forced.

She glanced over at the other two. Befuddled by pink-zinger, Harris just grinned at her, obviously thinking that he'd have a turn at her later. Jack looked pale and she wondered if he'd really come to her rescue against his shipmate. He might want to, but he'd had enough to drink to make him slow.

Still clutching her hand, Wilcox drew her closer, put one hand on her back. "You've been here a long time, forgotten how to make a man feel welcome. You need a lesson or two to remember your place. But don't worry--I've got just the training tool for the job."

Time to make her point official. "I don't want to bunk with you."

His laugh was ugly. "You will when we get to it, and even if you don't, I'll say you did. It will be my word against yours, and who do you think will win?"

She shouldn't fight. Fighting would be useless. He was much bigger and there were at least two of them--assuming Jack did nothing. If she fought, Wilcox would hurt her and force sex on her anyway.

Just relax, allow it to happen. It would be over soon.

Wilcox leaned forward and his lips slammed down on hers.

Nausea--raw, ugly, and overwhelming attacked her. The fish she'd eaten felt like it had come alive and wanted to leap from her stomach. Mea shuddered and let out a low moan.

Of course Wilcox grinned at her. "See, that's what you wanted."

The idiot actually thought she'd enjoyed his kiss! Mea wondered if he'd get the point if she threw up on him.

Jack staggered to his feet and grabbed Wilcox by the shoulder. He tried to pull the man off her. "That's my sister and she said no."

If anything Wilcox's laughter got uglier. "So, the tinker thinks his sister is too good for me?" He looked behind Jack. "Harris?"

Jack grabbed his stunner, but the redhead had already pulled his weapon. He fired and with a brief yelp, Jack went down, legs twitching convulsively from the stunner.

Obviously drunk, Harris grinned at them. "Okay, boss, got him. Wake me up when it's my turn." Apparently not bothered by the fact that he'd stunned his shipmate, he leaned back against a rock and seemed to pass out.

"Jack...." Mea tried to go to her brother, but Wilcox tugged her back into his arms.

She considered her chances. Harris seemed to have passed out so she all she had to do was deal with Wilcox. If she could get away from him, she might get to the woods.

Drunk as these two were, she should be able to elude them until she could find Kavath. The Gaian had a lot of tricks up his sleeve as well as a stunner of his own. If she could get to him, he'd protect her. The trick was getting away.

Wilcox dragged her closer, one hand grasping her rear end. "Okay, let's try this again." He leaned in for another kiss.

One chance at this. Mea stomped down on his foot, much harder than she had at the stove. Her boots were the same as his--steel bottoms but soft tops, easier on the feet during space travel. Under the heel of her boot, she felt the crack of his foot bones through the thin upper lining.

As Wilcox gasped in pain, Mea drove her clenched fists into his stomach and heard the satisfying whoosh as the air left his lungs. His grip on her loosened and she sprang away and took off for the far edge of the clearing.

At least Wilcox wouldn't be following too quickly. She might have actually broken the bastard's foot. The dense brush ahead beckoned--a few more steps, she'd be in the forest and beyond their reach. She ran as fast as she could.

An electric jolt struck her back and radiated outward. Pain followed as each overloaded synapse in her back announced itself before lapsing into silence. In agony, Mea collapsed to the ground. A bolt from a stunner had hit her, set on half-strength, just like her brother.

She turned her eyes to the fire pit to see the redheaded man sitting up with his weapon in hand. Apparently Harris hadn't been as asleep as he'd seemed to be.

Immobilized, she could only stare as Wilcox limped over to her, his face a mask of fury. "You little tinker bitch. How dare you do that?" He knelt beside her, then holding her face, he hit her hard, once, twice. She heard it, noted the pressure of his hand, the warmth at the point of impact, but felt no pain.

It would hurt later, she knew, when she could feel again. There was a metallic taste in her mouth, the taste of blood. Her blood.

She could hear, see, and feel warmth and pressure, but no pain. Nor could she move.

"I wanted to be nice, and this is the thanks I get. Very well, I'll still get what I want, only now there's nothing you can do about it." He pushed her onto her back, worked on stripping her pants away, then unfastened his.

Mea couldn't move or protest. He was going to take her, right now, in the middle of her camp and in front of his buddy and her brother, who was stunned but could still see and hear. She would feel nothing, but there was no way he was going to be gentle. If she lived through it, she'd be badly hurt.

If she lived. That suddenly seemed unlikely. Drunk as he was, Wilcox would probably kill her to hide what he was about to do. Even Earthforce frowned on the actual rape of a female officer.

Of course he'd have to kill her brother, too, to cover it up, but somehow she didn't think that would worry him any. Wilcox and Harris hadn't been worried about stunning Jack and that spoke volumes for their relationship.

Mea watched as Wilcox dragged his pants down, revealing an ugly erection, and through the maelstrom of thoughts and emotions flowing through her, one thought in particular stood out, encircled as if in a pool of bright light.

She'd never told Kavath what he meant to her. He didn't know--how could he when she hadn't even admitted it to herself? She'd never said the words. *She loved him--and she would for all time.*

Mea wanted to fetch the wristband from her pocket and fasten it where it belonged. She wanted to tell him she'd be his wife as long as he wanted … and she knew he wanted her forever.

Without warning her eyes filled. She closed them, felt a thin trail of warmth as her tears flowed down her cheek.

Wilcox crouched between her legs. She couldn't feel him, just the pressure and warmth of his body and his breath in her face. She kept her eyes closed, the better not to see, wished she could close her ears as well. Maybe it wouldn't take that long....

From the edge of the clearing came a thin buzz and the man on top of her gave a great groan and collapsed. His weight crushed and drove the last of her breath from her. She heard the buzz again and from the fire-pit came a matching groan.

Footsteps, then abruptly Wilcox's weight was dragged away. She opened her eyes just in time to see Kavath, his face furious, deliver a ferocious kick into the man's ribs. If she could have moved, she'd have winced at the sound. Wilcox was not going to be in great shape after this. That kick probably broke a couple of ribs and she knew she'd broken the man's foot.

Then Kavath was next to her, kneeling beside her. With one motion he gathered her into his arms and when she looked at him his face was anguished.

"I'm sorry, Mea, I'm so, so sorry I wasn't faster. I should never have let you go, never." His hoarse whisper was music in her ears. Green eyes, dark with concern, gazed sadly as he used his fingers to gingerly examine her face. "He hit you. I saw, I couldn't believe it."

Harris's stunner must have been low on juice after he used it on Jack. The paralysis she felt was beginning to wear off. "My brother?"

"That is who he was. I thought it might be." An almost relieved smile covered his face. "I heard them calling him Tink."

"Short for tinker … a slur."

"Got it. These guys don't seem to be the most politically astute men around. I'll check on him, but first I've got to see to the others." Reluctantly, he lowered her to the ground. "I'm going to tie them up."

"Can't … let them … see you...."

"They won't see me. I used the highest setting of my stunner and they'll be unconscious for at least an hour. I'll put them inside their transport once I have them secured."

He held a gentle hand on her cheek. She felt the pressure, the warmth. "I'll be back."

By the time he'd finished dragging the last man into the Skyhawk, she was able to move her arms and reach a sitting position. With an effort she pulled her pants back on and got a wet leaf to put on her face. It was starting to hurt.

Kavath sat on the ground next to her. "Mea--"

She interrupted him. It was still hard to speak and to control her tongue but she needed to. "Thank you. For coming. You must leave."

His posture stiffened. "Not without you."

She shook her head. "No. Can't take me. There's a convoy. They'll come, look for the men. Find us."

One hand stroked her damaged cheek. "Mea, my people will be here soon."

She stared at him. "What?"

"When you started cooking I figured you'd be safe for a while, so I went back to my camp. There was a message waiting. They'll be here in a couple days, maybe sooner."

Two days … it sounded like a short time, but it wasn't soon enough. If the Death Angels didn't report in, Earthforce would be here tomorrow. It was only serendipity that had kept them from finding Kavath's ship in the heavy underbrush. The better sensors of a command vessel wouldn't be fooled.

Plus there was her brother to think of. He'd tried to protect her against his shipmates and she couldn't leave him alone to face their wrath. She needed to go back to Earthforce with Jack, and Kavath needed to get away tonight and meet his people.

"Kavath, you need to go now and I can't go with you."

"I'm not going anywhere. My ship still isn't repaired, remember?"

"I remember." She glanced over at her Starbird. "You'll have to take mine."

Kavath threw a startled glance at her ship. "Take yours?"

"It isn't damaged and it has fuel. Add your fuel to mine and you'll be able to reach your people without waiting for them to arrive. I'm sure you can figure out how to fly it. You're a good pilot."

"Sure I can fly it, but I'm not going to. It won't take two."

"Kavath be reasonable. If these men don't come back, then Earthforce will be here tomorrow. You need to get away before then."

"What about you?"

"I have to go with the others. It's the only way we'll all be safe."

Kavath was outraged. "I can't leave you with them! They hurt you."

"I'll be safe enough now. By the time they wake up we'll be halfway to the fleet, and the authorities there will protect me."

"What makes you think they won't side with them?"

This time her laugh was real. "Against me refusing to be raped? Don't be concerned over that, I'll be fine. Wilcox was right. It's my word against his, but if I show up like this, battered and bruised, with those two still stinking drunk, my word will look pretty good. I'll say they got drunk and unruly … it's true enough and I'll have Jack's word on it as well."

"Assuming he will support you against his own shipmates."

Another male voice broke into their conversation. "Don't worry about that. I have no intention of letting those two get away with hurting Mea."

Jack had made it to a sitting position next to the fire. He and Kavath exchanged long looks, not entirely hostile but challenging.

Mea shook her head. "I know you don't think much of us, Kavath, but it is still not considered proper to molest an Earthforce officer, even one of lower rank. The worst that will happen to me is a reprimand for stunning them. They need pilots too badly to lose one over something like this."

"It's not the first time those two have gotten in trouble," Jack added. "I thought they'd behave themselves with Meagan since she's my sister, but I was wrong." He took a deep breath and looked directly at her. "I'm sorry, I shouldn't have been drinking. It made me slow to notice what was going on."

Kavath gave him a steady stare. "You'll protect her from them, flying with her in your ship?"

"With my life, Gaian."

They continued to glare at each other until Mea wanted to use the stunner on both of them. "This is getting us nowhere. Kavath, you need to go, and Jack and I need to fly back to the fleet."

He turned to her. "But you're my wife!"

Jack looked like he was about to have a heart attack. "Mea, you married a Gaian?"

In answer she pulled out the chain with the wristband. "Kind of. He gave me this."

"And you promised to give me three days to prove we should be together," Kavath said. "This is only the second day so I get one more."

"We can't stay here another day, Kavath, be reasonable."

He folded his arms and looked stubbornly at her. "I get another day, Mea."

Jack made his way to his feet and stumbled over to stand next to her. He faced Kavath, his expression impassive. For a moment both men stared, sizing each other up.

Jack broke the silence first. "You attached to my sister?"

Mea wondered how he knew about Gaian attachment, then realized that most likely the Death Angels knew a lot more about the Gaians than regular Earthforce. They would have had to know to understand how devastating it would be to destroy a girls' school.

"Several times. Last time I decided we were fated to be together." He took a deep breath. "Besides, I'm in love with her."

"I guess you'd have to be. She isn't exactly the easiest woman to get along with."

Mea elbowed her brother in the ribs. "That's not funny."

"Who's trying to be funny?" He almost looked like he was going to crack a smile, but it faltered and died. "I need to know something. Her past and her family. That's not going to be held against her by you or anyone else, is it?"

"I don't care about her being a Traveler or that you're one if that's what you mean."

"Good to hear, but not what I meant." Jack hesitated and took a deep breath then looked Kavath square in the eyes. "I'm talking about Carras."

Kavath stiffened and his jaw clenched. "My sister was at Carras."

Jack flinched, then nodded slowly. "I figured someone you cared for might have been. You see," he hesitated. "I was at Carras too."

With a roar Kavath lunged and threw a fist into Jack's face, knocking him to the ground before Mea could react. She jumped in front of the furious Gaian and grabbed his arm, keeping him from jumping onto her brother and pummeling him further.

Jack took the punch as if he'd expected it, possibly even welcomed it. Still weak from the stunning, he lay on the ground for a moment and then unsteadily regained his feet. Kavath resisted Mea's interference for a moment, but when Jack didn't raise a hand to fight back, he allowed himself to be held.

Rubbing his jaw, Jack eyed her enraged husband with a new respect. "Got a pretty good punch for a pacifist."

"Jack, you aren't helping matters," Mea said.

He held up his hands. "Look, you got the first one in, and I deserved it. I figured you better know about it now."

Kavath turned on Mea. "You said you didn't know about Carras," he said angrily.

"She didn't," Jack said. "No one outside of the Death Angels or the higher levels of government knows the truth."

Kavath swung back to face Jack. "You expect me to believe that?"

"Yes, I do. If you love Mea the way you say you do, you'd know she wouldn't lie to you." Jack shook his head. "Besides use your head, man. You think the Death Angels go around bragging about killing young women? We don't ever talk about Carras. If Mea hadn't mentioned it tonight, I'd have never told her. Carras is a secret and we don't talk about it. That's why the Death Angels were used in the first place and not regular Earthforce, because we know how to keep something quiet when it's needed. Harris is an arrogant bastard and Wilcox a moron, but even they know better than to talk."

He took a deep breath. "Everyone else was told it was a military target, a hidden arms factory, and they believe it. Holo-pics shown to the general public were altered to show just that. You expect that anyone on Earth would approve of the destruction of a girls' school?" His laugh was bitter. "I know our society doesn't seem as noble as yours, but even we have our limits."

"If that's true, then why did you do it? How could you justify it to yourselves?" Kavath said. Mea could have cried over the heartbreak in his voice.

Jack closed his eyes. "We weren't told up front what the target was. Only that it was militarily important and would help stop the war before it began. Only the captain of each ship knew. In our case that was Wilcox and he kept his silence. We did our first bombing run and cut away quickly, then a second...." his voice broke off. "It was only after the third run that we came in close enough to see the bodies."

Eyes bleak, Jack shook his head. "That isn't a sight I'll ever forget. For what it is worth, Harris got sick, and Wilcox didn't crack a smile all the way back home."

"What about you?"

Jack looked at his hands and then at Kavath. "I have to live with it, live with the memory of what I saw and what the weapons I fired did. I won't ever forget it and I'll die before I ever blindly follow orders again. But that's me."

He raised his chin and returned Kavath's stare. "I don't expect forgiveness from you or anyone else, but I don't want you ever to blame my sister for my actions."

For a long moment Kavath stared then shook his head. "She's my wife, and I'm Gaian. We love and protect our women above all things and I would never hold her responsible for another's crime."

He turned to her. "I love you, Mea, and I want you whatever the circumstances. I only have one question. Do you love me?"

"I … I think so. But that doesn't change the situation. We've got to split up."

He held her in his arms for a long time. Then he stroked her face with the back of his hand, the feel of it gentle after the slap Wilcox had given her.

"I suppose you're right. I don't want you to go, but if you love me, then you'll love me when I find you again. And I will find you, Mea. Then we'll finish out the third day."

"All right. Some time in the future we'll meet again. The war can't last forever and until then I'll keep this." She hung the chain around her neck again, under her shirt. "I only hope I'll see you again."

"Oh, you will. I'll arrange it," Kavath said firmly. "But until then, you are *my* wife. No bunking with other men."

Mea laughed. "No problem there. I nearly threw up on Wilcox."

"Threw up? You mean you felt sick?" Kavath stared at her in consternation.

"Yeah, why?"

"It's what our women do when they're with a man they aren't matched to. Strange."

So now she was behaving like a Gaian woman, just because she'd matched with him? That was too much for Mea to handle at the moment. She turned to leave. "We better go before the others wake up and realize you're here."

Before she took two steps he swept her into his arms. "You didn't think I was going to let you leave without this?" And then his lips captured hers in a soul-searing kiss that she felt clear to her toes. Mea's heart sped up until it matched the furious pounding of his. She felt no queasiness, just a mad desire to do as he'd asked, run away with him, hide, and let the rest of the universe go to frack.

He broke off the kiss and cuddled her close, nuzzling the top of her head. "Don't leave me, Mea."

He'd saved his best argument for last. Honor, duty, what was all that when you were in the arms of the man you loved? But Mea already knew--*part of what makes you who you are* ... that was the answering whisper.

They had no choice. Kavath's ship couldn't fly, and hers couldn't take two people. It would take the fuel from both to get one person away. They could take the Skyhawk, but she couldn't maroon her brother and the other Dark Angels on this planet when there was a possibility they might never be found.

Even if Jack hadn't been her brother, she and Kavath both respected life too much for that. Reluctantly she pushed him away.

"No. We can't. I can't."

In silent defeat Kavath watched as she walked away from him. Jack waited as she grabbed the bag with her belongings and then followed her to the Skyhawk. She turned one last time before entering. "Goodbye, Kavath."

He didn't say a word, just stared. Kavath was still staring after her from the clearing when Jack lifted off in the Skyhawk, careful this time not to catch the woods in the backwash from the engines. Mea watched from her seat in the cockpit as he dwindled in size, then disappeared from view.

Chapter Sixteen

With a scowl Dr. Jones finished running the scanner over Mea's belly. Grunting, he turned the machine off and gave her the same glare he'd been giving her for the past four months. "You know, I really should take you off flight duty."

For the moment ignoring the comment, Mea slid off the examining table and pulled her pants up. Rather than requisitioning a bigger size, she'd added a loop of string to the fastener to increase the width of the waistband, allowing it to fit over her expanded belly. After securing it, she pulled on her uniform top, leaving it untucked.

Not quite regulation and sure she looked a little sloppy-- but that was better than looking pregnant. Or at least too pregnant, since almost everyone had already caught on to her condition but were refusing to officially acknowledge it. They needed pilots too bad to ground her.

She turned to grin at the scowling M.D. "You can't take me off duty, Doc. I'm one of the best pilots we've got. A little acceleration isn't going to hurt me."

"Getting launched out of a battle ship and into a fight isn't just a 'little acceleration', Lieutenant, and you know it," the doc fumed. "You subject yourself to too much stress and you'll lose that child."

She laid her hand over his. "I'm healthy, the baby's healthy and I come from a long line of pilots. My mom used to do barrel rolls in a space scooter when she was eight-months pregnant with me."

"And that explains so much about you," the doc said sarcastically and waved his hands at her. "So go ahead and scramble your baby's brains. See if I care."

He looked at the info on his chart and pointed to the big open space on the form. "I don't suppose you are ready to volunteer the father's name yet. He should know what chances you're taking with his child." He gave her a suspicious look. "What about the men you brought back? Was one of them responsible?"

It was six months since her return to Earthforce with her brother and two bound, angry, and still very drunk Death Angel officers. On her way to the convoy she'd come up with a description of the effects of heavily fermented pink-zinger that included temporary insanity. She told the authorities that after drinking it the men had become dangerous and she'd had to immobilize them.

Jack had supported her story and rather than being reprimanded, she was commended for keeping her cool under such terrible circumstances. It didn't hurt that she'd managed to survive by herself on an unknown planet for so long.

Between the pink-zinger hangover and the aftereffects of stunning, Harris couldn't remember enough of what happened to dispute her version of the story. What he could remember was her feeding them, and warning them not to drink too much. Wilcox had drunk far less, and probably remembered that someone other than her must have stunned him, but knew better than to argue. He'd probably rationalized that somehow Jack had recovered enough to rescue his sister. With Mea's face showing evidence of someone's abuse, her explanation kept him from taking blame for his actions.

Shortly afterward Jack obtained a transfer to another ship away from his "buddies" and so the matter had been dropped.

Not everyone bought the official version. Several Earthforce women made a point of dropping by and complimenting her method of dealing with Wilcox. It seemed she wasn't the only one who'd been subjected to his forceful brand of wooing in the past and bringing him in with a broken foot and two cracked ribs had made her a local hero.

She could have stayed drunk for a week on the free drinks offered. Fortunately she'd declined, even before she'd known about the baby.

Mea paused in the middle of sealing her jacket. "As far as Earthforce knows, there is no father and that's the way it is going to stay."

A speculative look crossed the doc's face. "You were on that planet about the time of conception. Were there natives there?"

Mea laughed. "That's it, Doc. The father was a jungle man I met."

She'd meant it as a joke, but the doctor's face lit up as if she'd confessed to something. Fortunately, before the conversation could hit any closer to home Mea was saved by the bell.

Overhead the emergency lights began flashing and the familiar recording of "battlestations" started. "Sorry, doc. Love to talk more, but it's time to earn my living," she said and headed to the door before the he could say another word.

A fine sweat broke out across her back as she joined the rest of her squadron in route to their ships. The doc was getting a little too perceptive. He'd come way too close this time to guessing the truth.

Mea ran her hand over the swell of her belly, enjoying the feel of the life within her. She was still amazed that she'd gotten pregnant. She'd been up to date on her anti-conception shots until she'd spent nearly two months on a planet without them. Then she and Kavath had only done it over those two days. Just her luck that they'd managed to hit a window when she was fertile.

Before climbing into her new Starbird, she patted the freshly painted lower ring of her pilot's mark. Never hurt to have a little luck on your side.

She tensed in her ship as the launch catapult snagged each ship in line and sped it on its way, then felt the exhilaration as her ship sped through the tunnel and out into space.

Around her, the rest of the squadron held formation, on guard against the Gaian enemy. It was her first time back in combat--and she regretted it already. It had been easier to fight the Gaians before she'd met one and before she knew what they fought for. All they wanted was freedom, the chance to be their own people. Knowing about Carras only made it worse.

Knowing that Kavath might be out there made it virtually impossible.

A soft whistle came through her communit. "Enemy spotted. Four minutes until contact."

Tension filled her. What was she going to do? Could she really fire on them? She moved a trembling hand over the phase gun controls and swallowed. She was an Earthforce officer and it was her duty to fight. She'd do what she had to do ... even if her heart wasn't in it.

It didn't take four minutes. Her chrono still showed two minutes to spare when suddenly Gaian fighters were all around them, moving faster than any ships she'd seen before. Mea groaned as the tiny ships ducked and weaved around her, nearly impossible to hit.

They must have made another improvement in their technology. There were at least two-dozen of them, half again as many as in her squad.

Trying for room to maneuver, Mea pulled back on her controls and headed for open space. Her rear viewer showed one of the fighters take off after her. Something about it seemed strange, but she didn't have time to process what that was as it accelerated in her direction.

She waited until it came almost within shooting distance and pulled back on her control, pulling the ship into a three-sixty turn that would leave her behind her adversary.

Well, that was the plan, anyway. Instead as she reached the top of her turn, she realized the fighter had turned with her, as if anticipating such a trick. She aborted the maneuver, pulled the stick the other way, into a right hand turn that spiraled back towards him. It fooled the other pilot for a moment, but he recovered, and by the time both ships were flying straight again, the Gaian was still on her tail and she was within range of his weapons. She gripped the controls, ready to pull another turn, hoping he'd give her time before firing at her.

Abruptly the steady background noise of her engine silenced and she drifted instead of accelerating. She pulled on the controls and nothing happened. The lights on her display flickered and died.

Dismay filled her and she stared at her incapacitated ship. The Gaian's paralyzing ray, somehow she must have run into it. Desperately she flicked the controls for the communit, then tried engaging her emergency back-up power. Nothing. The only thing that seemed operational was life support.

Helpless, she waited as her small ship drifted along its last trajectory. How long would it be before she was picked up? Would her Gaian pursuer inform them where she was?

Speaking of which, where had that fighter gone? Without her screens, all she could see was the view through her canopy--she could see nothing of the battle left behind.

Her wrist chrono showed about thirty-five minutes had passed before she felt a tug on her ship, as if a giant hand had grabbed it. The hand pulled until she was turned about to face the opposite direction. At a distance a Gaian fighter lay, too far to see more than its outline. At least she thought it was Gaian … the shape wasn't quite right. With a smooth movement, the enemy fighter headed to where the other ships gathered and like a toy boat on a string, her Starbird followed, towed by a tractor beam.

Well, at least she hadn't had to make any decisions about killing anyone. She'd been captured before she had a chance. Mea tried to be philosophical. Knowing the Gaians, their prisoner of war camps were probably pretty nice. The food had to be pretty good and since she was pregnant they'd most likely take special care of her. She might even get a chance to send Kavath a message and tell him about their child.

At that last thought her spirits rose and the last of Mea's dismay faded away. Her Gaian husband might even come and rescue her from a POW planet … assuming he still wanted her.

As she got close, she saw the others of her squadron dragged or pushed into the open docking bay of the captured Resolute, the ship she'd called home for the past four months. Resigned, Mea leaned back, waited for her turn.

But the fighter dragging her didn't deliver her to her ship but pushed on, moving directly for the Gaian battlecruiser that floated on the edge of the battle area. At the same time, the beam holding her strengthened, tugging her closer to the ship in front. They grew closer and then suddenly Mea sat straight up, her jaw dropping as she realized two things about the ship in front of her.

The first was that it wasn't a standard Gaian fighter before her, but an Earthforce Starbird. That's why the shape had seemed so odd when she'd tried to out fly it.

The second was that the tail held two sets of marks ... one a familiar set of interlocking blue-green rings, the other a set of three green stripes.

Her old ship--with Kavath's mark on it and the man himself at the controls?

Astonishment warred with joy as her fighter was dragged closer. By the time they'd entered the Gaian docking bay, her ship was less than six feet from the rear of his. As soon as they passed into the hold her ship returned to life, allowing her to lower the landing gear but as soon as that was done, the power cut out again.

As she watched, the canopy opened on the ship in front, and a familiar form pulled himself out, jumping to the floor below, not even bothering with the ladder. Several men congregated around him, smiling and laughing, one slapping him on the back, others shaking his hand. He accepted their congratulations, pulled off his helmet, and tossed it to one of them.

It *was* Kavath. Pilot Kavath Terrell, in the flesh and looking better than any man had a right to look. He was laughing when he turned to face her ship--and noticed that she hadn't opened her canopy. The laughter died and his face turned apprehensive.

Mea narrowed her eyes. *Good.* What was he thinking, dragging her back to his ship like some sort of prize? She was no primitive woman to be pulled by her hair into a cave. Despite her joy at seeing him, alive and well, and obviously still wanting her, a wave of indignity filled her. She crossed her arms over her belly and glared back at him.

He ran a hand over his still finger-length hair, said something to the other men. Grinning, they scattered, leaving him alone. Carefully Kavath approached her ship, and when she didn't lower the ladder, he grabbed a portable set of steps and rolled it over to her.

Climbing up, Kavath stood at the top and stared at her through her canopy. The pleasure in his face at seeing her almost made her want to rush into his arms. But she was still annoyed at how he'd snatched her from the sky without so much as a by your leave, so instead she stared impassively at him through the transparent shield.

He smiled at her. She didn't return it, and his smile died.

"Mea? Would you please come out of there?" His voice sounded distant through the heavy plastisteel of the canopy.

"Why? So you can show everyone your captive Earth woman?" She let her indignation show in her face.

"No, don't be silly. So I can have everyone meet my wife."

She was not going to make this easy for him. "What makes you think I'm your wife?"

"Of course you are!" Now he looked annoyed. "For at least one more day, according to your promise. You still have my band, right?"

She sighed. "Yes, I still have it."

"Mea...." He lowered his voice. "I don't know why you're acting like this but I promise it will be all right. Remember how good it is with us. You do, don't you? If you don't I'll remind you."

He leaned over the canopy and his hands caressed the clear material. A little thrill swept through Mea, seeing those talented hands and remembering how they'd touched her.

His voice turned seductive. "I remember you in my arms, Mea, and kissing me like you loved me the way I love you. I remember our bodies joined and how glorious it was even on a bed of sand. I promised you a real bed next time and I have one waiting just for us. I've planned for our meeting for a long time now--open the canopy and I'll show you."

She remembered what making love with him had been like, too. She also remembered that making love had consequences and she wasn't sure just how Kavath was going to take the consequences of the last time they'd been together. Apprehension swept through her. He was expecting a lover to emerge from her ship, not someone carrying his child. Did he even want children so soon?

When she didn't move he raked his hands through his hair and growled. "Sweet Gaia, why are you being so difficult?"

The answer was going to be obvious as soon as she got out of the ship, but she couldn't stay inside forever. She might wonder how Kavath was going to react to having an instant family, but she wasn't going get any less pregnant sitting here.

"Okay," she told him. "I'll open it. But you need to get back."

"Back?" he responded eagerly.

"Get down so I can climb out."

Kavath jumped off the ladder and waited for her at its base. Cautiously she opened the canopy and removed her helmet, then pulled herself out of the cockpit. She climbed down the steps, happy to have them. Mea would never have told anyone in Earthforce for fear of being grounded, but her ship's built-in ladder had become hard to negotiate in recent weeks.

As soon as she was down he started toward her but she waved him back, keeping her arm folded across her belly. "No, not yet. You don't think straight when you're around me. "

Kavath laughed. "Mea, where you're concerned, I haven't been thinking straight for a long time. It took me months to get assigned to a ship that would be intersecting with the one you would be on. I've missed you so much."

He'd planned that much? "How could you find out where I'd be posted?"

A big grin was her answer. "We have our ways. I told you I intended to arrange for us to meet again."

As always, he was being impossible. Mea put her hands on her hips to glare at him and as she did, it tightened her shirt across her belly. Audible gasps from the other Gaian men still occupying the hanger deck told her that her secret was out.

Kavath stared at her pregnant belly, open mouthed and uncharacteristically silent. After a few moments of quiet gaping he pointed to it. "Mea ... are you ... is that ... I mean.... Is that mine?"

Stupid question. "Given that other men tend to make me throw up ... yeah, it's yours."

"How? I mean your people bunk ... I mean have sex all the time. You must do something to prevent ... I mean, how could you get pregnant?"

"Well, most of the time we don't go six weeks without our monthly anti-conception pills," she said dryly. "That improves the chances. Plus I guess we're both unusually fertile."

He started to preen but that ended quickly when she pulled the chain around her neck up out of her shirt and off her neck.

"Here," she said with a bit of a grin. "This is yours too."

She tried to place it in his hand but with a look of horror Kavath moved back so she couldn't reach him. Mea glared at him. "What's wrong now?"

He put his hand his face loaded with righteous indignation. "I'm not taking back my band, Mea. In the entire history of Gaia, there has never been an unwed father and I'll be damned if I'm going to be the first." He pointed at her and her pregnant belly. "You are my wife, that is my child, and that's all there is to say about it!"

So, he did want the child after all. Hiding her sudden feelings of joy, Mea folded her arms again and pretended to glare at him. "So that's what this means to you? You don't want to be the first unwed Gaian father? Does it matter at all what I want?"

"Of course it matters."

"Then why don't I have a choice?"

"You do." Kavath paused and in his expression Mea saw all the love and acceptance she would want from him. His voice became quieter, seductive. "Of course you have a choice. I just wish … I wish you'd choose me. I wanted you before, and I want you still. That you're pregnant only enhances the situation. I want both of you."

He took a deep breath. "I know that you don't think that you need me. Your mother raised you without a father and you think you can do the same. I'm not going to argue that you can't. I believe you can do anything, Mea."

His voice turned pleading. "But I want to be with you and I want to be a father to this child and any others that follow. Stay with me, and be my wife, Mea, and give me that chance."

From across the hanger someone dropped a tool and it rang in the sudden quiet of the room. Mea glanced around and realized that just about everyone present was watching and listening. In fact it appeared that several additional people had entered the landing bay since her arrival. For one thing there were several women present now, all of them watching her with interest.

It seemed the entire Gaian ship was waiting for her answer. Well, they'd all have it, but first she'd make a point. It was wrong for a man to simply grab a woman and declare her to be his wife. No Earth woman was going to become a Gaian spouse without some kind of proper protocol.

She returned her attention to the now anxious Gaian man before her. "If you want me to be your wife, I think you should ask me."

He came to attention and hope blossomed in his eyes. "Mea, will you be my wife?"

Mea crossed her arms and tapped one foot impatiently. "Not like that. Ask me properly and use my full name. Also, on Earth it is customary for a man to go down on one knee."

"You want me to kneel?" Kavath asked in disbelief.

Mea simply stared at him until Kavath sighed and with a great show of exasperation, knelt on the hanger floor. "Meagan An Flena, I'm asking you on bended knee to be my wife."

"And here is my answer." Mea stepped to him and dropped the chain with its rolled up wristband around his neck.

Disbelief, hurt, and pain sped across Kavath's face as he jerked to his feet. He held up the band. "After all that, you're rejecting me and giving it back?"

No longer even trying to hide her amusement, Mea shook her head. "Don't you think you should look at it-- husband?"

For a moment Kavath stared at her. "Husband?" he said in a disbelieving voice.

With a tug he pulled the band from the chain and uncoiled until it lay flat in his hand. It was bigger than the one she'd been given and when he looked at the flat panel with the engraved emblem it was different--three interlocking rings, the same as on her ship.

His gaze shot back to her and with a grin she pulled up the long sleeve of her uniform shirt, revealing that she wore his wristband on her arm.

"I put it on before we even left the planet's atmosphere, Kavath," she told him softly. "I realized as soon as I was gone I belonged with you and that I needed you as much as you needed me."

She pointed to the band in his hand. "I had to improvise a little to make it. I hope you don't mind that it's made of Earth-based materials instead of Gaian."

"Mind?" Kavath gasped out. In one move he fastened it around his wrist and then he was lifting her high off the deck before she had a chance to take a breath, burying his head in her neck.

"Why should I mind? You're made of Earth-based materials too." He kissed her long and hard. "You are the most infuriating woman I've ever known and life with you will no doubt be challenging--but I wouldn't have it any other way."

Through her overwhelming joy at finally being back in Kavath's arms Mea heard cheering and for a moment she thought it was for her and Kavath. But then she heard what people in the landing bay were shouting, and she and Kavath broke off kissing to pay attention.

"The war is over! Earth surrendered! We won!" Those words were coming from a hundred throats, most of them male, but here and there Mea heard a woman's cry as well. Astounded, Mea and Kavath stood with arms around each other and stared as the hanger broke into jubilation.

All of a sudden everything seemed just right. She leaned her head on his shoulder. "Well, I guess it's a good thing I've already surrendered to you, Kavath."

He kissed the top of her head. "Oh, no. I was your prisoner long before you were ever mine."

They kissed and held each other until all Mea could think about was getting alone with her husband. "You know, Kavath, you promised me a bed the next time we made love."

He smiled at her with all the love she knew he had for her in his heart--which was just about the same as hers. "Ah, and my little lehen, I have one in mind for just that purpose."

Chapter Seventeen

Kavath watched his beautiful wife stretch out across the master cabin's bed and wondered at his luck. Who would have guessed that six years ago he'd have found the woman he'd wanted all his life, not in a traditional Gaian marriage meet, but on a battlefield in deep space?

He adjusted the narrow band on his wrist with its triple ring emblem on it, the symbol that showed he belonged to her, then slid onto the soft surface next to her and rubbed his hand lightly over the slight swelling of her abdomen. "How are you tonight, my wife?"

"Happy to see you," Mea replied, returning his caress, although much lower. Kavath grinned as she found his hardness and closed her hand around it, not letting his pants get in the way. "And you are happy to see me, as well."

"I'm always happy around you, Mea. You know that."

She leaned back, exhibiting her belly to him. "And that's why I have this again," she said ruefully, rubbing it gently. "For the third time. Not that I'm complaining."

He crawled on top of her. "I'm glad to hear that. I'd hate it if all my hard work wasn't appreciated."

"Hard work?" Mea laughed. "Your part in making a baby is easy. I have to do all the heavy lifting for the last few months as well as the delivery. Why do you think they call it labor?"

He kissed her lightly. "Enough for now. I'm not looking for a battle with you, my wife."

Mea's smile turned sensual. "So what are you looking for?"

"This," he said and closed his lips over hers, letting her mouth seduce him even as he seduced her. Mmmm--six years of marriage and he still couldn't get enough of her taste, the honey sweetness of her mouth.

Even after all this time, his hands nearly shook in their eagerness as he pulled her soft green blouse open to unveil the weighty softness of her breasts, heavier now that she was with child.

Since becoming his wife Mea had thoroughly taken to Gaian clothes and their bright colors, his little lehen shedding her grey plumage with all the enthusiasm he could have hoped for. On their wedding night she'd practically torn off her Earthforce uniform and had never donned it again. Not that they'd worn many clothes at all for the first few days of their marriage.

Actually, they'd barely left his quarters at all.

Now he spread wide the blouse that she'd embroidered, to reveal the bright pink undergarments she still favored. Kavath smiled as he saw them. Some things never changed and he hoped never would. He ran his hand over the silky fabric and enjoyed the low moans she made. He nuzzled her neck and fondled her breasts, teasing the nipples through her supportive top. As always they were bigger and more sensitive with her pregnancy.

He couldn't help his self-satisfied grin. Mea might complain about being pregnant, but there were some aspects of her gravid body that he simply loved. The memory of the first time he'd seen his child nursing from her perfect breasts still gave him a thrill like no other. Not sexual exactly, but masculine and very satisfying.

His woman, his child, his family. Nothing else in the universe was as sweet as knowing he had them to love and hold and protect. A primal need since the time of the caveman, to take a woman, embrace her and with her build a family. To make her the center of his life and to become part of hers

Even his family had accepted her as one of their own. It had taken a little time, but they'd come to value Mea and welcome her with open arms, as much for her sake as his. She had a way of making others appreciate her.

He hadn't told anyone about Jack's involvement in Carras, and since their marriage they'd only seen her brother a couple of times, once shortly after he'd been released from Earthforce, then again after their son's birth. The relationship between the two men had been strained, but for Mea's sake they'd kept it cordial.

The last thing he'd heard, Jack had gone to the Outer Colonies to search for the other Traveler families. That was the same mission they were on, in the guise of setting up trade routes for his family's trading company. After five years he'd finally gotten a ship to fulfill the promise he'd made his wife back on the little planet where they'd been stranded. For the past month they had been looking for the scattered remnants of Baile Na.

Kavath couldn't be happier. He had his entire family around him and nothing was as sweet as that. Well, nothing except for Mea's lips. He kissed her again and pulled her top up to fondle her nipples. Mea moaned and squirmed until her crotch was against his and she was rubbing herself against him.

She always had the most direct way of getting his attention. He'd planned to take his time with her, but Mea was clearly impatient. He let her help him out of his pants, and then roll him over onto his back.

With unerring aim she buried him deep within her. Hands on her hips, Kavath eased her up and down on his shaft and within moments both of them were near their peak. Mea cried out first, but Kavath didn't last much longer.

As always they tried to keep their voices down, but it was a struggle to be quiet when it felt so good. Sometimes a man just needed to shout his joy in spite of the crowded quarters of the ship.

As they lay in the warm aftermath of love making, Kavath swore to himself that after the baby came and could be left for a week or so, he'd find a little deserted planet for just Mea and him where they could make all the noise they wanted and wouldn't be disturbed....

"Mom, Dad!" Through the closed door to the passage came the excited voice of their oldest child, Morgan. "You better come! We got a message on the communit and Ana can't read it!"

With a groan Kavath disengaged himself from his wife's embrace and pulled on his clothes, very much aware of her doing the same, all the while casting amused glances at him. She knew how much he hated being disturbed when in post-coital bliss.

The control room of their small trading ship, Traveler's Choice, was crowded between the two excited children, Morgan and their three-year-old daughter Kavy, as well as their co-pilot, Ana. A Gaian widow whose husband had died during the war, she'd been happy to take the position of third-shift pilot, giving Mea and Kavath a chance to spend time alone as well as with their children instead of having to devote themselves full time to running the ship.

They were grateful to have her. Not only was she an excellent pilot, but the children loved her and she often took charge of them and even acted as a tutor on occasion. Most likely the three had been on the bridge doing some sort of educational activity when the communication had come in.

Ana looked at them ruefully, probably suspecting what they'd been up to even if they had tried not to make much noise. Meagan had never been able to keep very quiet when they were making love ... not that Kavath was about to complain about it. Her responsiveness had always been something he loved.

Kavath cleared his throat. "So what have we found, Ana?"

"There's a message I can't make any sense of, but it was sealed with a very familiar emblem." She pointed to the screen and he and Mea were startled to see the set of three interlocking rings acting as an ID.

Absently Kavath ran his hand along his band that held that same emblem as Meagan burst into delighted laughter. "It's them! A Traveler family." She sat at the console and keyed open the message. "And it's written in the old tongue. I can read it, I think." A moment later she turned to him, and he was moved to see tears in her eyes.

"It's the An Gavans, Kavath, a family that was close to mine. They're on the fifth planet from this sun." She pointed to the place on the star chart fixed to the nearby wall. "They say there are several families with them, gathered from the other colonies. Someone else has been searching and has helped to gather them together to re-form the tribe."

A tear of joy slid down her cheek. "It's a new Baile Na."

Something inside him froze at that tear. He'd rarely seen Mea cry and it showed just how much she'd looked forward to this moment. This was what Mea had been in search of for so long. She'd mourned the destruction of her home and scattering of her people and had always wished to find them again.

It awakened a secret fear he held for so long. Would she leave him now that she'd found her people? He nodded and tried to keep his fear of losing her from being obvious. "A new home for all of the Travelers then. A place for all of you to belong--I'm glad we found it."

He'd never been that good at hiding his emotions and Mea had known him for far too long. She smiled and shook her head and went to put her arm around his waist. "No, my husband," she whispered in his ear. "A new home for them."

She looked around the control room of their ship, with their children excitedly talking to Ana about the message. "My home is here, Kavath, with you and our children. On this ship, on a primitive planet, or on Gaia--wherever you are, that's where I belong."

He closed his arms around her, letting her reassurance wash over him and end his doubts. A long time ago they'd started a relationship in opposition to each other but that was over. He nuzzled her hair and stroked her cheek with the back of his hand.

"And I belong with you, Mea, wherever in the universe that is."

The End

Printed in the United States
66450LVS00004B/227

9 781586 087388